W9-CMP-710

Fashion Victim

Fashion Victim

Sue Swift

FIVE STAR
A part of Gale, Cengage Learning

Detroit • New York • San Francisco • New Haven, Conn • Waterville, Maine • London

Set in 11 pt. Plantin.

LIBRARY OF CONGRESS CATALOGING-IN-PUBLICATION DATA

Swift, Sue, 1955–
Fashion victim / by Sue Swift. — 1st ed.
p. cm.
ISBN-13: 978-1-59414-930-6 (hardcover)
ISBN-10: 1-59414-930-5 (hardcover)
1. Women fashion designers—Fiction. 2. Manhattan (New York, N.Y.)—Fiction. I. Title.
PS3619.W546F37 2011
813'.6—dc22 2010041138

Published in 2011 in conjunction with Tekno Books.

Printed in Mexico
3 4 5 6 7 15 4 13 12 11

ACKNOWLEDGMENTS

This book was written with the help of The Lethal Ladies, the online critique group of the Kiss of Death, the Romance Writers of America's Mystery/Suspense Chapter. The advice of staffers at Parsons School of Design and the input of New York attorney Allen Bromberger were also invaluable.

Caroline Cummings, Jackie Hamilton, Cheryl Norman, Janet Shirah and Stephanie Wilson-Flaherty stood by me during the entire process. Thank you.

Chapter One

"Youch!" Sucking on a now-bloody finger—the one I'd stabbed with a pin—I raised my head and glared at my daughter. "Nat, hold still!"

"This isn't very exciting." Natalie tugged at the vest I'd been fitting around her thin, twelve-year-old frame. "Modeling's supposed to be glamorous."

I huffed. "Models work hard and aren't popular for very long. Hit thirty and you're all washed up."

Natalie's giggle lightened my heart, but only a little. Long story, but when her crazed multimillionaire father dumped her on my doorstep, Nat had fallen apart. Though I was ecstatic to get my daughter back (frankly, I'd never wanted to give her up), she hadn't been able to adjust to the Manhattan lifestyle after living in Berserk-eley with her sandal-wearing, pot-smoking, extremely dysfunctional dad.

Then my assistant, Maggie Andersen, decided to put Nat and her new schoolmates in my April show as models. I'd never before thought of Maggie as insightful, but now I did. Her brainstorm made Nat a part of something bigger than herself, a fun activity she could share with her new friends. Today, seamstresses fitted active, squirming children into bright leather vests and shorts, a new line of teen gear I'd designed especially for Nat and her buds. My usually quiet workshop was jammed with chattering, giggling girls, all jazzed because they were going to model in a real couture show in just a few weeks.

Shouts from the main workshop below cut through the kids' jive. Straightening, I headed toward the rail of my atelier's upper loft to peer over the edge. Okay, so maybe it was crowded down there. Maybe it was in a crappy part of Manhattan. And yeah, I was in hock up to my eyeballs. But it was my workshop, and it was crowded with my employees, my designs and my models. Mine. All mine. My dream come true, my ambition since childhood.

I leaned over the railing and saw a skinny guy in skintight black bike shorts and a yellow vest. He was tussling with Maggie. And, despite her tight red pencil skirt and Jimmy Choo heels, Maggie was winning the battle. She had the guy in a headlock.

I called, "Hey, Maggie! What's going on?"

Maggie loosened her hold on the cyclist, and he tossed up a sheaf of rubber-banded papers. It whacked me on the arm. "Cara Fletcher, you are hereby served with process!" the messenger shouted as the hefty bundle thudded to the floor.

I picked it up and pawed through the papers, reading, "District Court, Southern District of New York . . . Fletcher Tool and Gear, Inc., and Fletcher Wolf versus Cara Fletcher Couture and Cara Linda Fletcher . . . Request for a Preliminary Injunction and for Monetary Damages . . . YOU AND EACH OF YOU ARE HEREBY ORDERED TO SHOW CAUSE . . ."

My panicked gaze caught sight of the date. March 17.

March 17. March 17? March 17! March 17 was a mere two weeks away. In only two weeks, I was supposed to go to court. And . . . show cause? What did that mean? Show cause about what?

I'm being sued.

My breath came short, and my heart started to pound. My palms got sweaty. No, I told myself sternly. You will not freak out again. You will not. Nevertheless, my stomach clenched and churned.

I took deep breaths. My doctor had told me to take deep breaths whenever I got a panic attack. He'd also prescribed some tranqs. Sometimes I took them, sometimes I didn't. This morning I'd felt okay, so I hadn't dosed myself. Oops.

I told myself to take a mental chill pill instead. When the faintness and the nausea diminished, I scrabbled through the papers, seeking some clue to the mystery. What on earth had I done? What could he—whoever he was—want? A section labeled, in big capital letters, "PRAYER FOR RELIEF," jumped out at me. Then I read, *"Damages in the amount of fifty million dollars."*

Oh my God, oh my God, oh my God.

A gentle hand touched my shoulder. Swaying a little, I turned. Maggie was staring at me with blue eyes magnified by her oblong black glasses.

"What is it?"

Realization struck. "That man," I whispered. "That crazy-ass man. Remember the weirdo who phoned me after the Fletcher's Gear commercials started to air?"

"Yeah. What was his name? Fox?"

"Fletcher Wolf, and maybe he's not crazy." I shoved the papers at Maggie.

As she read, her brow furrowed despite her recent Botox treatment. "Damn. I thought he was just a stalker, like Kenney."

Merely hearing my ex's name brought a wince to my face. "I don't know, but this is trouble. Major trouble." I crammed the papers into my satchel before Natalie could see them, making a mental note to fax them to my attorney.

I barely slept that night. Along with the lawsuit and the panic attacks—something which only Maggie knew about—I'd been getting hang-up calls and wrong numbers. I was afraid I was being harassed by Nat's father, which made me even more edgy.

Fun stuff, huh?

Though I really didn't believe I had become a complete paranoid, I was engaged in a high-wire act keeping everything from Natalie. Nat was a hassle and a half who'd been allowed to run wild while in the care of her father and whichever arm-candy he had around that week. Kenney was a drug-dealing millionaire who'd lost his big bucks in the last economic crash and sent Nat back to me as—get this—a cost-cutting measure.

I believed that the real story was that when Nat became a hormonal, sharp-tongued preteen, he couldn't deal with her anymore. So back to Mommy she went. That he'd rejected Nat didn't stop him from phoning at all hours, even though she generally refused to talk to him. I didn't blame her. Kenney was the kind of guy who'd leave the toilet seat up and laugh when your butt fell into the bowl at one A.M. I must have been in an altered state during the few short weeks we'd been together.

But I loved Nat, even though I didn't know how to talk to her. With Kenney's millions, he'd been able to get custody from me shortly after Nat was born. I'd been a student at the time, and so had little contact with my daughter during her crucial early years.

A brainiac, and snarky to boot, Nat's sharp hazel eyes missed little. With long, fluffy red hair she typically wore in a braid, she often showed flashes of the fabled redheaded temper. Despite her father, she was the coolest kid in the world. I wouldn't freak her out by hyper-parenting, but I had to protect her.

I wanted to forward all our calls to my cell and keep it turned off, but I worried about missing phone calls from my parents, who live upstate, near Ithaca. My father has MS, so I can't risk missing calls.

So I spent a sleepless night punctuated by hang-up calls,

fights with Kenney, and wrong numbers. By the time dawn rolled around, my nerves were tighter than the cables supporting the Brooklyn Bridge.

Later that morning, I blew off work and went to meet my attorney and BFF, AnnMarie Slye of Swift, Slye, Jonas and Crebbs. With conventioneers overrunning lower Manhattan, I couldn't make it to her office, so we met at a Starbucks roughly between our workplaces.

I'd known her for over fifteen years, since I'd arrived in the big city, a scared seventeen-year-old from upstate with a scholarship to Parsons School of Design. Another student's older sister, Ann and I had met at a party and hit it off. I admired her more than anyone else in the world. Sharp as a box of tacks, she'd warned me about Kenney, but I'd ignored her. Unfortunately, she hadn't finished law school when he got custody of Natalie. But she'd set up my business at a nominal fee and helped me negotiate the loans that had made Cara Fletcher Couture possible.

Still slim and gorgeous at forty, AnnMarie sat tall at a table and radiated legal-eagle attitude. She wore one of my business suits, a stunning creation (even if I do say so myself) emphasizing vertical seaming and a narrow line. In silver-gray gabardine almost the same shade as her short platinum hair, the outfit made AnnMarie look like an unsheathed knife.

I liked that image. AnnMarie was my sleek, sharp weapon, a stiletto I'd plunge into the heart of this Wolfman who threatened to destroy everything I'd built. *Fifty million dollars, fifty million dollars, fifty million dollars* . . . The insane amount of money Wolf demanded in his complaint droned through my mind like the refrain of a hated though catchy song.

After I picked up my latte (low fat, no caffeine to interact with my morning tranqs, but with extra vanilla) I joined AnnMarie. "I want to know more about Fletcher Wolf and his operation," I said. "Who is this man, and why is he trying to screw up my life?"

"I don't know if I can answer those questions, but I have a dossier on him. Here's a copy for you." Reaching into her gray croc briefcase, she pulled out a manila envelope and gave it to me.

The heavy file sagged in my hand. "Whoa. When did you have the opportunity to put this together?"

She shrugged. "The Internet is both a blessing and a curse. It deprives all of us of privacy, but the flip side of the coin is the availability of information."

"Why don't you give me the CliffsNotes version for now?" I tried to relax into the straight-backed wooden chair.

"Fletcher Wolf is a Virginia native. Graduated from the University of Virginia. He runs Fletcher Tool and Gear, which is headquartered in Delaware. He's been the CEO since he was twenty-two years old, and he's nearly forty now."

I narrowed my eyes. "That's a lot of power for a relatively young man."

"Some people might say that about you."

I shrugged. "We both know I owe everything to the First National Bank of Manhattan." Tired of working as a wage slave for other designers while they garnered all the money and fame, I'd taken out massive loans to open my own couture company. I looked forward to when the risk would pay off.

"Then let's make sure you don't lose your shirt." AnnMarie leaned forward. "What you need to understand about Fletcher Wolf is that he'll chew you up and spit you out like bad fish. A little operation like Cara Fletcher Couture is nothing to a corporate raider like Wolf."

My belly twisted, harbinger of another anxiety attack. Maybe more positive affirmations would banish the shakes. I told myself that I was safe.

"What's more, he writes his own rules for his own game. Nobody knows what he's doing until after he does it."

Though my throat was tight, I forced out words. "You sound as though you admire him. What's he done that's so special?"

"He inherited a small regional company and brought it into the new millennium. Fletcher Tool and Gear has become a nationally dominating concern in several specialized areas, such as marine transmissions and precision tools used in laser surgeries. Wolf knows how to spot a niche and fill it before anyone else has even perceived a potential market. Usually he does that by corporate acquisitions."

"Boat transmissions and laser surgeries? What do they have to do with sportswear?"

She spread her hands wide. "Obviously the products have nothing to do with Cara Fletcher Couture or even Fletcher's Gear. But the transmissions include gearshifts in a patented design called the Fletcher Gear."

I sagged into my chair, heart racing like a thoroughbred going down the stretch.

"That's apparently why Wolf became so upset about Fletcher's Gear, your menswear line," she said, sipping her cappuccino.

"Oh, please. What kind of fool would mix up transmissions and T-shirts?"

"Wolf and his attorneys think there are plenty of fools in the public who will confuse the two products. He's alleging, first, that you have no right to use the name."

I was dumbfounded. "You told me when we set up the company that I could always use my own name."

"Yes, that's true. You can use your own name, unless it's for a fraudulent purpose. I believe that the first cause of action in his complaint will fail, so he won't get a preliminary injunction. I think he'll lose the first round, but if he wins anything else, he'll win this case."

I went cold, clenching my hands together, sure they'd tremble like small, scared birds if released. So much for banishing the shakes. "You said he's got a lot of high-powered legal talent. Please be honest with me. Do I need to hire specialists for this?"

AnnMarie leaned back in her chair. "We *are* a specialty firm. We're corporate and business experts, which includes intellectual property litigation. C'mon, honey, you know I'll never let you down."

"What about your fees?" *Fifty million dollars* sang through my head.

For the first time, she looked uncomfortable. "I don't like to talk money with you."

"I can't take charity, especially if the litigation is going to be expensive. How could you explain it to your partners?"

Nevertheless, she continued to hesitate, then said, "There's no way I can predict outcomes, but I'd advise any other client to amass a war chest of at least a hundred grand."

"A hundred thousand dollars?" My voice came out in a horrified squeak.

"That's just to begin. The longer the case goes on, the more expensive it will become. But that's true for both sides."

"You said he's a major player. If he's wealthy, he won't care about a measly hundred grand. But I do. I have to." I was going to explode into little pieces all over the fashionably dressed patrons of the midtown Starbucks. I wrapped cold hands around my latte. "This could ruin me. I spent a lot of money on the ad campaign. Borrowed money. A lawsuit will break me. I don't have a hundred thousand dollars."

"Cara, you know I don't care about the money. I care about you. If you can carry the expenses—filing fees and so forth—don't worry about the rest."

My eyes filled. “Thanks,” I whispered. “I don’t want to take so much from you, but I have to.”

“Fuggedaboudid.” She let her Brooklyn accent show as she patted my hand.

I cleared my throat, pulling myself together. I didn’t want to draw attention by bursting into tears in public. “Umm, this seems to be happening awfully fast. Don’t legal cases take years? Is there any way to get this delayed?”

“That was my first thought, but opposing counsel turned down my request for a continuance. Wolf thinks that the longer the situation goes on, the more damage there is to his interests.”

“Damn.”

“His lawyer said that Wolf called you after the football playoff commercial aired. Is that true?” Ann fixed me with a steely gaze.

I raked a shaky hand through my hair. “Yeah, I guess so. I thought it was a crank call. I’ve been getting a lot of them lately.”

She winced. “That mistake could cost you.”

“Well, if this jerk wants a fight, let’s give him one. I don’t know where I’ll get it, but I’ll get some money to you somehow.” *Probably from more loans.* I gritted my teeth at the prospect, shoving panic into a nice, tight box in the back of my mind and encasing it with mental duct tape. I wasn’t going to let this creep trash my entire life. “File a response pronto, okay? Let’s get into that court and kick a little legal ass, and make him pay. If this request for a preliminary injunction is garbage, we should get fees for this hearing, huh?”

“Yes, I believe there are grounds for the award of attorney’s fees and costs. If we prevail. There are no guarantees, you understand?”

“Let’s go for it. Listen, my April show is costing a fortune. And even with the department stores helping, those TV commercials . . .” I grimaced. “I’m deeply in debt, and one more straw is gonna break the bank. I need this mess to go away quickly. Very, very quickly."

"You know we'll do our best. Like I said, his initial salvo is weak. If we beat them on this first issue, we'll be in a strong position to get fees or to settle out of court."

"That sounds like what I want." Taking a deep breath, I forced myself into a semblance of calm. "I'm sorry to have gotten upset, but I need to deal with this right away." I stared out the window, watching pedestrians scurry past like frantic ants. I didn't feel much different.

"Don't worry about it," she said. "What the hell are friends for?"

We hugged as I left, with Ann squeezing me extra hard. "How is Natalie taking all this?" she asked.

"She doesn't know."

Ann eyed me. "O-kay."

"She's another reason this has to go away fast. She's just starting to adjust. The last thing we need is more stress now."

In a taxi going uptown to my shop, my mind whirled as though I was stuck in the spin cycle of a washing machine. Fletcher Wolf could trash everything I'd worked for all my life! If I had to declare bankruptcy, I'd be toast. Without good credit, I'd never be able to put on another runway show again.

I had to fight. I had no choice. I couldn't afford to recall all of Fletcher's Gear and have new labels sewn in. Besides, why should I? Fletcher was my name too, and I had every right to use it.

Unbearably tense, I pulled out a sketchbook from my satchel and started to draw, sure that it would relax me, but what came out was a dominatrix with silver hair whipping a chained wolf.

I could only hope that Ann looked good in leather and knew how to use a bullwhip.

Chapter Two

With the survival of my business at stake, I obsessed about the court appearance. Along with a paralegal, Ann and I slaved over the papers we filed against the Wolfman's attack. Because I wanted to impress the court as an earnest businesswoman, I tinted my chin-length bob a serious shade of ash brown. The morning of the hearing, I bunched my hair into a tiny bun at the nape. After inserting brown contact lenses, I popped a pair of heavy tortoise-shell glasses onto my nose. I donned a serious suit and heels.

I scheduled a taxi for an hour before the hearing and waited in the entry of my townhouse, feeling as though my belly housed ten thousand writhing snakes.

"Don't worry." Natalie tried to reassure me. It had proven impossible to keep the lawsuit completely from Natalie, but I hoped that I'd minimized its threatening nature. Maybe not, if my child wanted to comfort me.

To hide my concern, I straightened her Peter Pan collar. She sighed, allowing me to fiddle with her clothes, even though we both knew she hated fussing. "We're early," she said, twitching slightly. She wore an adorable, knee-length pleated plaid skirt and a navy sweater that allowed her white cuffs and collar to peek out. You think I'd send my child to a school with an ugly uniform? No way.

"Who's 'we'? You're not coming." I turned my attention to her French braid.

"Aw, jeez. You know I'll learn a lot more from going to court than I will at school today."

"You won't learn algebra or French."

The phone rang. I reached for it, but Natalie grabbed it first. "No one there," she said. "Hey, haven't we been getting a lot of these calls lately?"

I faked ignorance. "Well, your father calls a lot."

"I don't mean him." Nat dismissed Kenney with a wave of her hand. "I mean the hang-up calls. When you pick up the phone and there's nobody there, or there's a dial tone. It's almost like some creep keeps calling our number."

Paranoid, I thought it very likely. Maybe it was Kenney pushing my buttons. Or did the zipperhead suing me have anything to do with it? But I wasn't going to talk to Nat about any of that. Instead I said, "Of course not. With so many people in Manhattan, there's bound to be some phone line mix-ups. Don't worry about it, okay?"

The door buzzer sounded. "Get your pack, Nat, and let's go." I herded Nat downstairs to the taxi, hoping I radiated comforting Mom's-in-control vibes.

I stared at the forbidding courthouse, repressing an unnerved shudder. The four-inch stiletto heels had been a big mistake. I'd worn them to add some height, since five-four isn't exactly impressive. Better, the gorgeous periwinkle suede matched my suit. But, given the slippery-looking stone stairs outside the building, as well as my morning tranquilizer, I had to struggle, picking my way to avoid falling on my butt. I told myself it was okay, since I still had twenty minutes before the nine o'clock hearing.

Even so, I clung to the rail with a death grip. Once inside, I passed through security and then found the correct floor. Ann-Marie had said we'd meet outside the courtroom, but I didn't see her, so I headed toward the nearest women's room for a last, nervous pee and primp.

A trio of males outside one of the courtrooms grabbed my attention. One of them raised his head to give me the eye, and even took a step away from his group. Despite the seriousness of the situation, I couldn't help responding.

First I checked out what he was wearing, a well-tailored Hugo Boss that retailed for a cool three thousand. That suit hadn't come off the rack, not on that bod . . . whoa.

Hot wasn't a hot enough word to describe this guy.

Unfashionably longish hair with silver streaks. A maverick. He wasn't afraid to buck the trend toward brush cuts and no doubt would never dye his hair to look younger. But despite the hair and body—big, solid, and buffed—it was his eyes that grabbed me in the gut and wouldn't let go. They were an unusual shade of hazel. Golden, really, feral and predatory, like a wolf. Or maybe one of the great cats. A lion or a cougar.

His face was all bold planes, with high cheekbones, a strong jaw, narrow but sensual lips. And a small scar by the side of his mouth . . . how had he gotten that? A knife fight? A beer bottle in a bar brawl?

I silently laughed at myself. He probably fell off his bike when he was six. But still, he was hot. Very hot. Beyond hot. Not in a metrosexual sort of way, though. This macho male would never bother to check himself out in a store window, like some men I knew. He oozed masculine assurance.

His gaze caught mine, and my temperature went from ninety-eight-point-six to at least one-oh-two inside of a second.

A set of nearby double doors banged open, and I blinked, jolted. A redheaded woman in chic brown tweed burst into the hall, followed by a phalanx of attorneys, bees swarming their queen.

"I didn't pay you thieves a grand an hour to get screwed!"

she screamed, her stride an angry clatter on the stony floor. Buzzing with temper, the group rushed by. I stayed upright until the last attorney in the swarm plowed into me.

The jerk didn't stop, though my feet slipped on the marble. I fell, mentally damning my shortness, my vanity, the four-inch heels, and the entire legal profession.

At my side in an instant, the mysterious, amber-eyed stranger grabbed me before I hit the floor. He lifted me onto my feet with a gentleness at odds with his size, his strength, and the uncivilized gleam in his eyes.

Vision blurry, I blinked some more, eyeing the stranger, the retreating horde crowding onto the elevators, and AnnMarie, who approached but didn't interrupt. Appreciating Ann's tact, I decided that she would not be struck down by the general curse I cast on all other lawyers.

"Are you all right?"

The stranger's pleasant bass had a slight, sexy southern accent, which turned me on even more. What was it about a southern accent? Something about it called up all my Rhett Butler fantasies. I was a sucker for a southern accent.

He straightened my lapels without brushing my breasts, which tingled anyway. Embarrassed, I tugged at my jacket as he again gave me the once-over.

"You look fine," he said, emphasizing fine, "but I'm afraid you've torn your stockings."

I looked down. He wasn't lying. One of the knees of my pantyhose had ripped. I sighed. "What else can go wrong today?"

He laughed. "It's not so bad. Look at it this way. You aren't paying someone a thousand dollars an hour to get screwed, are you?"

We shared a chuckle. "You're right," I said. Then I staggered a few steps away toward the women's room before recalling my manners. "Umm, thank you for your help. I hate to seem rude, but I have a very important court appearance, and I can't have a run in my hose."

I hurried down the hall as fast as I could without risking another fall while digging in my satchel for the spare pair of pantyhose I hoped I had in there. As I moved along, I passed AnnMarie, who wore a broad smile. Why? She couldn't be happy that I'd made a dork out of myself, could she?

"I'll just be a minute, Ann." Smacking the door of the women's room with an outstretched palm, I skidded inside, hoping I hadn't looked too much like all three stooges.

When I emerged, the hall was empty. Sweat broke out all over my body as I sprinted for the courtroom door. I scurried in as a bailiff was calling, "All rise!"

I found my seat next to AnnMarie as the judge, an older balding fellow, entered with a flutter of black robes. He thumped his gavel to begin the hearing as I looked down the long wooden counsel table.

Then I saw *him*. At the opposite end of the table. Oh, shit. Was the hottest of the hot my opponent? My opponent's attorney?

I met his glance then looked away, scrabbling for my glasses. I put them on, hoping to shore up the image of a serious businesswoman.

Yeah, that was me, all right. A serious businesswoman. I tried to look cool, calm, collected and in control, but the reality was that I was ruining my favorite blue suit with sweat rings because everything—*everything*—was on the line.

The bailiff announced the case, and a man sitting next to the hottie stood, buttoning the jacket of his navy pinstriped three-piece suit. "Michael Muckenmyer of Muckenmyer, Radcliffe and Soames, representing the plaintiffs, Fletcher Tool and Gear, Inc., and Fletcher Wolf, who is present."

Fletcher Wolf. I should have known. I had the bad luck to have fallen instantly in lust with my enemy, a man who could tear apart my life and destroy every one of my dreams.

Brilliant. Absolutely brilliant. I recalled what I'd said to Wolf outside the courtroom. *What else can go wrong today?* Now I knew.

AnnMarie rose, bringing me back to the very unpleasant present. "AnnMarie Slye of Swift, Slye, Jonas and Crebbs for the defendants, Cara Fletcher Couture and its subsidiary, Fletcher's Gear, and its owner, Cara Linda Fletcher, who is also here in court today, Your Honor."

When our respective mouthpieces sat, the judge said, "Well! Obviously this is a very important hearing to you both. We rarely have the principals of business entities present in court."

Wolf stood. "Excuse me, Your Honor—"

"Fletch! What the hell are you doing?" his attorney snarled, his voice low. "Sit down and shut up. You're not supposed to say anything."

I shared the lawyer's surprise. Ann had told me not to say or do anything, just show up to impress the court with the significance of the hearing. Otherwise, she'd explained, the judge might blow it off with an off-the-cuff, incorrect ruling.

"She's not Cara Fletcher," Wolf said.

I picked my jaw up off the counsel table. It had dropped open an improbable degree. He's a nutcase, I thought. A certifiable nutcase with money to burn.

I was dead meat, unless AnnMarie could protect me. She said, "This is as absurd as the rest of the plaintiff's case. This is most certainly Cara Fletcher."

"I'm sorry, Your Honor." Wolf sounded sure of himself, so sure that if I hadn't a firm grasp on my identity, I would have believed him. "But Cara Fletcher bears no resemblance at all to this young woman."

"What?" I squawked. Ann shushed me, and I glared at her.

She murmured, "This is perfect. Let him hang himself."

I calmed down.

Wolf continued, "Cara Fletcher has green eyes and her hair is . . . her hair is—" He stopped stuttering, and I grinned. Whatever he had on his mind, he sure was having trouble spitting it out.

"I have an, uh, what's it called? An exhibit." He waved a magazine in the air. "Cara Fletcher is somewhat, er, colorful. She has green eyes, and her hair is black on one side and red on the other. Quite unusual, unforgettable in fact. This lady has brown hair and brown eyes. She's not Cara Fletcher."

I lost it, and laughter burbled out of my mouth. I tried to shut myself up by burying my face in my hands and hoped I hadn't screwed my case by losing my decorum in front of the judge. At least not as badly as Wolf had just screwed his.

"Red and black hair, Mr. Wolf?" The judge's voice was frosty, but at least he wasn't holding me in contempt for laughing in court.

"Yes, Your Honor," Wolf said.

"Like that Cruella de Vil in the dalmatian movie my granddaughter likes?" the judge asked.

"Exactly, sir."

"Except black and red?"

"Yes." Wolf sounded satisfied, and I looked at him to see his smirk. He obviously thought he'd won a point. I heard him mutter to his attorney, "We're a shoo-in."

His attorney, however, didn't look too pleased, while I could sense that Ann, still seated beside me, could barely contain her joy.

"This occasion when you saw the defendant, was it a cocktail party, perhaps? Had you imbibed a bit of the fruit of the vine, or perhaps some other tipple?" the judge asked.

Wolf's jaw clenched and he lost his smugness. "Absolutely not. I assure you Cara Fletcher wears her hair in a very unusual style. This isn't Cara Fletcher."

"I'm not impressed by your statement, Mr. Wolf, but I will ask the defendant to produce identification. If this is not Ms. Fletcher, she will be asked to sit behind rather than in front of the bar."

"Your Honor, I would also request the court to consider the deception on the court as character evidence relating to the defendant in this proceeding." Though visibly rattled, Wolf's attorney jumped in with his two cents.

"This is ridiculous." AnnMarie slapped the table in a phony show of righteous anger. "I've never been so insulted in my life!"

I didn't want Ann going over the top, so I put my hand on hers to quiet her down before opening my satchel. It was jammed, as usual, and I had to dump a bunch of stuff onto the table in front of me.

I'll admit I carry an assortment of interesting goods, but who knows when they could come in handy? Hankies to wipe drippy noses and to catch spills. I like them much more than paper tissues.

Condoms (flavored) and candles (scented). Though I hadn't gotten laid since Natalie came to live with me, hope sprang eternal, and who knew when I'd want to create a little atmosphere?

A collapsible umbrella. A compass, for when we went hiking upstate. A Swiss Army knife, a really good one with screwdrivers, scissors, a corkscrew and a toothpick. For when we got lost while hiking.

String. I'm like Sam in *The Lord of the Rings*—the books, not the movie. He had an obsession with rope. Mine is with string. One can never tell when it will come in handy.

Pens and pencils, various colors, of course, for sketching. A tape measure and a drawing pad. Fabric swatches. Obviously important.

Feathered fishing lures stuck in a cork. Yes, odd, but last summer my father had given them to me for inspiration, and I had designed several outfits with feather trim. I couldn't bear to throw out a special gift from my dad. Okay, I'm sentimental. So sue me.

On second thought, don't. It's already gotten me into enough trouble.

Finally I found my purple eel-skin wallet and waved it in the air while telling Ann, "Knew I had it somewhere."

I opened it and took out my driver's license, which I handed to the bailiff. "My driver's license, sir." I kept my voice low and demure. Showing triumph might piss off the judge. My instincts told me that demure was better.

The bailiff compared the photograph to me and said, "This is Cara Fletcher, all right." He gave the license back. I hoped I didn't smirk as I put it away, but keeping a straight face was tough.

I couldn't help checking out the Wolf, who looked like Wile E. Coyote after an anvil had dropped onto his head. He took out a handkerchief and mopped his forehead.

"Can we get on with this?" Ann asked. "Your Honor, the defendant has already asked for attorney's fees and costs, and I request the court take this incident into account when making a determination in that regard."

"I'm inclined to do just that." The judge glared at Wolf. "I've read the pleadings submitted by the parties in this matter. Does either side have anything new to offer?"

Wolf's attorney played it safe. "Submitted, Your Honor."

"Submitted," Ann said.

"Very well. I'm going to deny the request for a preliminary

injunction. Ms. Fletcher has the right to use her own name. I'm reserving a ruling on the more difficult issue of confusion by the public due to the use of similar product names, and direct the parties to investigate and brief the issue. I will award attorney's fees and costs to the defendant for this hearing and preparation. Ms. Slye, submit a fee and cost bill within seven days to the court and to opposing counsel."

"Woo-hoo!" I high-fived Ann.

"One more thing. Ms. Fletcher!"

Oops. The fat lady hadn't sung. I wiped the grin off my face and sat at attention.

The judge told me, "Just because you have won this round does not mean you will win the war. This kind of litigation is expensive and lengthy and generally benefits no one but the lawyers. I urge the parties to meet and confer with a view toward settlement. In fact, I order the parties to reappear in thirty days in this court. Between now and then, you shall exchange all relevant documents and meet for settlement on at least one occasion. Sanctions will be levied for disobedience.

"Prevailing party to prepare the order after hearing. Court adjourned!" Whacking the gavel down hard, the judge stepped off the bench.

In a more thoughtful mood, I stayed in my seat to repack my satchel, while Fletcher Wolf and his attorney left. I avoided grinning at Wolf. If the judge and Ann were right, my adversary was still formidable. Shaming him with a victory dance wouldn't help me in the long run.

"What now?" I asked AnnMarie.

"We have two choices. We wait for a settlement offer or their next salvo of litigation. Or, we plan a pre-emptive strike."

"That sounds expensive," I said. "I don't want to put you to the trouble. Can't we try to settle?"

"But we didn't start this. The ball is really in their court, so to speak."

"Okay, so we wait." I jammed my umbrella back into the satchel and stood. "Let's go."

When I left the courtroom, there he was, with his strange topaz eyes glinting in the dimly lit hallway.

"So, Ms. Fletcher, we meet again."

"Umm." Rendered inarticulate by those eyes, I felt like a possum in the headlights of an oncoming Mack truck. I mentally shook myself, resolving to stay aware. Letting Fletcher Wolf know he could get to me would be suicidal.

"We have been ordered to meet and confer regarding settlement," Wolf continued. "I suggest dinner between the principals."

My traitorous heart bounced like a kid's rubber ball, while my celibate body flushed with pleasure. At my side, AnnMarie stiffened. Muckenmyer, who accompanied his client, also looked tense.

"I don't think that's a very good idea," AnnMarie said.

"Why not? Are you afraid I'll give away the farm?" I eyed Wolf, whose mouth twitched in a small, ironic smile. I wanted to know what that smile meant. "Dinner will be fine. Where and when?"

Wolf whipped out a business card. "I expect to be in New York again next Tuesday. Have your secretary call mine with your address. I'll pick you up at seven on the dot." He turned and strode down the hall.

His attorney remained. "Ann, I'll phone you after I've had an opportunity to confer with Mr. Wolf. Later, Ms. Fletcher." With a nod in my direction, he hurried after his client.

As if by magic, an elevator opened for Wolf as he approached it. He and his attorney disappeared from view when the doors slid closed with a soft snick.

My breath whooshed out. I hadn't realized I'd been holding it.

AnnMarie swung around to face me. "Why did you agree to dinner with him? Don't you remember what I told you? Fletcher Wolf is a major player. He'll have you and your little-bitty company for supper if you don't watch out."

"Oh, come on, Ann, it's only a dinner date. He's just a man, and a very fallible one."

"What was he babbling about with the hair?"

"I'm not sure, but I wore my hair bi-colored for a photo spread in *Bazaar.* He was waving around a copy. Obviously they've done some investigating, just as we have."

"He was staring at you in the hall before the hearing," she said. "After you walked off."

"He was?"

"He couldn't take his eyes off your legs."

"Really?" I grinned. Though clumsy, the four-inch heels had done the trick. "Don't worry about dinner. I'll flirt a little, use the opportunity to pick his brains and find out what he wants."

"All right, then." AnnMarie sounded unconvinced. "But don't say I didn't warn you. Mark my words, there's an ulterior motive behind this dinner invitation."

Chapter Three

At 6:45 P.M. on Tuesday, I was as jumpy as a barefoot kid on summer asphalt. Standing in front of my dresser, I struggled to put together the right look for this dinner. My morning tranqs had worn off, but I didn't want to risk another. I had to stay sharp for my encounter with Wolf.

Footsteps thumped up the stairs toward my loft bedroom. "You spend more time in front of a mirror than anyone else I know." Natalie trotted into the room. A born athlete, Nat never walked if she could trot, stride, jump or dance. At least, when she was in a good mood.

"I'm a fashionista, baby." I preened, fluffing my hair, newly bleached and tinted. "It comes with the territory."

"You're wearing that outfit? I don't like it."

"What's wrong with it?" Made from the same silk Indian women used for their saris, my hot-pink Anna Sui was trimmed with gorgeous gold embroidery.

"It's too short. He's gonna think you want to shag him."

"Where do you get ideas like that? Minis are very stylish. Besides, longer skirts make me look like a dwarf." Using a brush, I smoothed the ends of my hair.

"Are you wearing these shoes tonight?" High-heeled gold sandals dangled from Natalie's fingers by the back straps. I created them while at Parsons when I'd considered going into shoe design, and loved them with a passion that sillier women devote to men.

"What's wrong with them?"

"Kathy's mom calls them shag-me sandals." Nat dropped them on the floor beside my bed.

"Natalie!" I flung my hairbrush onto the dresser with a clatter.

"I'm sorry, but that was what she said. What's with this date? You're acting funny."

"It's not a date, and I'm not acting funny." If Natalie noticed my nervousness, what would Fletcher Wolf think? Acting like a scared child in front of Wolf would be fatal. He'd be sure to take advantage of any weakness. "This is a business dinner."

"You're going to a business dinner in a mini-dress and, and, those shoes?" Natalie picked up a lipstick from the dresser.

I gritted my teeth. "My legs and my feet will be underneath the table, Nat. He won't see them." A total lie, or so I hoped. Wolf was clever and would notice everything. I was counting on that. I planned to dazzle him, though I knew Wolf wouldn't dazzle easily. Ann's dossier had told me that he had more tricks than David Copperfield and more facets than the Hope diamond.

"And what's with the bleached blonde hair? You look like a ho." Natalie flicked at my blonde bob.

What was it about twelve-year-olds? Had I been so difficult to satisfy? I batted Nat's hand away. "Blonde is just a color. Besides, the blue and amber bars in the front make all the difference. The pink silk is so bright that if my hair were boring, the dress would wear me and not the other way around."

Natalie continued to examine me with critical preteen eyes. "Yeah, you're right. What lens color are you gonna choose?"

"I'm not sure."

"How about turquoise or purple? Blonde looks good with turquoise or purple. Hey, you could have one eye in purple and the other in turquoise. That would be way cool."

"No, the man I'm eating dinner with is very conservative. I want him to be interested, not shocked. Ah." I grinned as I plucked amber lenses from their case and wet them with saline solution. Tonight, the wolf would gaze into mirrors of his soul.

"Amber? Why amber?"

A demanding knock rattled the front door. "Get that for me, Nat, while I put these in."

I finished primping and slipped over to the landing to spy on Natalie and the Wolf. He looked great, as though he'd also taken a flattering amount of time to get ready for our dinner. In a freshly pressed suit, he fitted into my upscale loft as though he'd been born to wealth and privilege, as indeed he had.

I swallowed. I wanted to blow Fletcher Wolf away, but exactly the opposite was happening.

"I'm Fletcher Wolf." He extended his hand to Nat with a truly charming smile.

I melted.

"I'm Natalie Fletcher-Madden." Nat glanced at his hand with a frown. I guessed she didn't know how to respond, and I figured I'd have to teach her about shaking hands.

"That's quite a mouthful for a little girl," Wolf said.

I winced. Nat was petite and slim, but hated to be labeled "little." The expressions on Nat's and the Wolf's faces told me that they both knew he'd blown it. Nat especially; she looked as though she wanted to throw him off a bridge.

She edged away from the door. Evidently taking her move as an invitation, Wolf walked in and checked out my place. He looked impressed, and why not? I'd spent a lot of thought, time and money on my home. My work was mega-stressful, so my home was my refuge.

Its floors and trim were yellow pine, polished to a high gloss. The door was also pine. I'd sanded and varnished it myself. The walls remained stark white, decorated only with a few abstract paintings that I or my friends had created. I don't like a lot of clutter in my home. The workshop's cluttered enough.

A huge, sculpted rug with rose tones lay in the high-ceilinged living room, adding a little warmth and color. A bank of houseplants grew beneath a skylight, with Nat's gray and red lovebirds in a cage suspended over the plants. She now poked at her birds with a stick, which sounds cruel, but they actually enjoy the stimulation. They like to hop on and off the stick.

Wolf walked over, blatantly curious. "What are the birds' names?"

"Hillary and Chelsea." Nat allowed him a tiny smile.

Hmm, I thought. If Nat liked him, maybe he's okay. Nat didn't take to many people.

Wolf chuckled. "So, you're interested in politics."

"Nope."

"I don't understand."

I guessed he didn't get that Natalie had named her birds after a mother and daughter with a tight relationship, but I understood. My child and I had been deprived of that special love. I rubbed my hand over my chest as though I could massage away the ache in my heart.

"You don't need to." Nat sounded snappish, so intervention seemed wise.

"Natalie!" I came down the stairs, walking carefully in my heels. "Go get your backpack."

Nat cooperated, and I extended my hand. "Mr. Wolf, please forgive Natalie. She's going through a difficult phase." I didn't say anything more. My daughter wasn't his business.

Wolf took my hand, but was staring downward, at my legs. I smirked. Ann had been right. Wolf was a leg man. Lucky for me, since I don't have much up top.

He mumbled, "Think nothing of it," giving my fingers a brief squeeze-and-release.

"Would you like a drink? I have some very nice California chardonnay." I smiled, hoping I could get him drunk and chatty.

"No, thanks. We have reservations, and I don't wish to be late."

I nodded and adjusted the strap of my gold evening bag over my shoulder. "Natalie!"

Nat reappeared, eyeing Wolf with obvious distaste. But I didn't have time to wonder what she thought and why.

"Nat, go next door and do your homework with Wendy. Hurry up, Ellie and Tom are expecting you." I opened the front door.

"See ya." She lifted her face for a kiss, and I melted again. She might be a cranky preadolescent stuck in hormonal hell, but I loved her, especially when she dropped her oh-so-cool pose. I wanted to give her a big smacky one, but that would embarrass her, so I settled for a peck on the cheek. She headed down the hallway and banged on Wendy's door. Tom opened it and let her in, waving at me.

I waved back, then turned to Wolf and said, "Well, I'm a free woman until ten o'clock."

"Good." Wolf took my arm, and in a rush of feeling I was fifteen again and on my first date, breathless and tense. Good God. Was I sweating? Would I ruin another outfit tonight?

Maybe Ann had been right and this dinner date was a big mistake. Why had I accepted Wolf's invitation? The reasons I had given Ann had been nothing but rationalizations and excuses. Despite the situation, I wanted to shag him silly.

I don't eat meat, so ordinarily I'd never stick even a toe of my pedicured feet into a steakhouse, especially one that stank as though it had a cigar-smoker's club attached. But I wanted Wolf to be happy and relaxed, so he'd picked where we'd eat. And he slid into this restaurant's masculine, cigar-scented ambience like a sword into its scabbard, settling into a leather-backed banquette with a happy sigh.

"Long day?" I ignored the queasiness in my belly from the traces of cigar smoke in the place.

"Actually, yes," he said in his resonant bass, smiling at me.

I again fell in love with his voice. That Virginia accent was like whipped cream and cherries on top of a banana split, making the entire package even more appetizing.

He continued, "As you may know, I live and work in Wilmington. Visits to Manhattan are a necessary evil and are tiring."

"Even with the driver?" I hoped my jealousy wasn't too blatant. I spent a small fortune on smelly, rattletrap taxis because I hated to drive in Manhattan. A limo and a driver would be heaven.

"Yes, even so. I work while Sam drives," he said. "Plus, I try to make the day here pay off by packing it full of meetings. By mid-afternoon, my head's spinning. Though I maintain an apartment where I can wind down, it's nice to have a quiet dinner with a beautiful lady." He gave me his heartthrob smile again.

I smiled back. So far, so good. "Aren't we supposed to be settling the case?"

"I don't know if it can be settled at this point. My attorney is doing some investigating to see how badly your use of the name damages my interests. Until we know the facts, we can't settle."

"If you didn't know the facts, why did you sue me?" I tried to keep my voice flirty and sweet, but it was tough. What kind of a moron would spend thousands to file a lawsuit if he wasn't sure there was a problem?

The moron sitting across from me, that was who. Just my luck. The hottest dude I'd come across in years, someone who actually seemed to be interested, and he was a wacko. He could even be the jerk making the hang-up calls morning, noon and night. Just because he ran a big corporation didn't mean he wasn't crazy, I reasoned. The stress could have caused him to break.

If Wolf sensed my annoyance, he didn't show it on his face or in his voice, which remained smooth. "Muckenmyer tells me that this situation is one which requires immediate action. Apparently, the law doesn't help those who sleep on their rights. In lay terms, you snooze, you lose."

He glanced at the wine list as a server arrived at their table. "Perrier-Jouët fleur, please, and two glasses. You do like champagne, don't you?" he asked me.

"Who doesn't? Champagne will be fine." I sipped from my water glass, remembering something Ann had said: *Fletcher Wolf is a major player. He'll have you and your company for supper.*

My pulse sped up. Was Cara Fletcher Couture the target of a corporate takeover? Why? All I had were debts.

The champagne, in its famous hand-painted bottle, arrived and the server poured for Wolf, who sniffed, sipped and nodded.

I watched the bubbles in my flute and tried to plan. How could I dazzle someone who'd obviously been with the best? He'd probably bested them. I decided to meet the situation head on. "How, exactly, does your attorney hope to show my use of my name affects your interests?"

Wolf gazed at me over the rim of his wineglass, his expression unreadable. "Very clever commentary, amber contacts," he murmured. "Quite intriguing, in fact."

"Thank you." I met his eyes, wondering what he really thought, but he revealed nothing. "The case?"

He smiled. "And a very beautiful dress. Is it your design?"

"No, it's by Anna Sui."

"Anna Sui," he repeated ruminatively. "I believe I've heard the name before."

"I used to work for Anna. She's very talented. I learned a lot from her."

"What did you learn from Ms. Sui?"

I considered for a moment, then said, "Cut and color."

"Cut and color." Those amazing eyes widened as he raised his brows. I saw darker flecks in his golden irises, like dappled sunlight. Damn, he was hot. That was at least half of the problem. I didn't want to fight. I wanted to find the nearest hotel room and mess up the sheets with him for, say, a weekend. A long weekend. No, a week. Maybe two.

"It occurs to me that part of our difficulties may be due to our differences. I have never in my life concerned myself with cut and color."

"Someone must have. That Armani you're wearing is a masterpiece."

"A masterpiece?" He laughed. "Ms. Fletcher, a da Vinci is a masterpiece. This is a suit, nothing more."

"So why don't you shop at a flea market?"

"Castoffs don't come in my size."

A server rolled up a cart covered with pieces of dead cow, red, bloody, and wrapped in plastic. My saliva suddenly tasted of bile. Stomach roiling, I pressed a napkin to my mouth and told myself not to retch. *Deep breaths, Cara. Deep breaths.*

Wolf ordered a porterhouse, rare. A suitable choice for a ravenous wolf. My tummy did a back flip worthy of an Olympic gymnast. The champagne, acidic and bubbly, churned.

I looked away. Breathed. Gulped. "Could you just give me some fish?" I asked the server.

"May I suggest lobster?"

Would I have to select my prey from a tank? "How about a salad?"

"Are you all right, Ms. Fletcher?" Wolf asked.

"Yeah. I'll be fine." I dredged up a smile. "I'll, er, have the crab salad, with bleu cheese dressing on the side."

He lifted his glass and smiled back. Did he enjoy my discomfort? I hoped my fate was not in the hands of a sadist, but he probably didn't know what I felt. How could he? I'd spent hours in front of a mirror preparing my façade.

"Your hair."

"What about it?" Grateful for the distraction, I ran my hand through my hair. Its short ends tickled my nape.

"You seem to change hair colors like others change clothes."

"Why not?"

He seemed startled. "Why not, indeed?" He sipped. "I suppose it strikes me as frivolous."

I sighed, with no patience for closed-minded zipperheads who mocked me and my work. "Decorating the body is one of the oldest human art forms."

"Is that so?"

"Yes. This tendency crosses cultural barriers and, incidentally, is the basis of my livelihood. If people didn't want to change the way they look, they'd wear the same clothes every day and I wouldn't have a job." Damn, but I sounded like a college professor. A college professor of clothes. How absurd.

"So you practice what you preach, albeit in a very extreme manner?"

"Albeit?" What a pompous jerk.

"Doesn't the bleaching and coloring damage your hair?"

"That's why I keep it short." Judgmental, too, based on his tone of voice.

His eyebrows drew together. "I really don't understand why. Aren't you all right just the way you are, au naturel, as it were?"

I chuckled. "Quite frankly, I can't even remember what my natural hair color is, and I don't care."

A predatory smile spread over his face. "I guess there's only one sure way for me to find out."

I gasped. "Just what are you saying?"

"Oh, I think you know what I'm talking about." That wolfish grin again.

"Excuse me, please." I got up and strode to the women's restroom before I did or said anything I'd regret later. Was Wolf actually implying that he wanted to get me naked? That was the weirdest proposition I'd ever received, and in the Manhattan dating scene I'd thought that I'd heard everything. Apparently not.

After I flushed and started to adjust my dress, loud voices attracted my attention. Two women had come in, and judging by the sound of running water, they were talking at the sinks.

"I knew he'd show up," one voice said, apparently gloating over some triumph.

About to leave, I shot back the door bolt of my stall.

"How did you know Fletcher Wolf would come here?" another voice asked.

I stopped.

"Wolf always comes to this restaurant. He has a taste for red meat. He's a real man and rich as Trump," the first woman replied.

Though the Wolf was successful, I doubted that he was worth upwards of a half-billion dollars, as was the legendary dealmaker Donald Trump. The dossier Ann had provided estimated his holdings at twenty million, corporate shares and other assets included. Though that was fairly decent, even in Manhattan.

"If he's anything like Trump, he'll be damn hard to get to," came the dubious reply.

"Just as long as he's hard when I get there," Woman Number One joked. I rolled my eyes at the bad pun.

"If he's rich and smart, there's no way you'll get anything

from him." The second woman wasn't convinced.

"That's true," Number One acknowledged. "I heard that his prenup is over thirty pages long. But marriage would be worth it. What a stud! And if I can get one roll in the hay, I can file a paternity suit."

I didn't know which place made me sicker, the smelly restaurant with its resident Wolf, or the conniving witches in the powder room. As I opened the stall door, the number one witch said, "I just have to figure out a way to get rid of the bleached blonde ho he's with."

Hmm. Maybe Natalie had been right. Taking a deep breath, I walked out of the stall. "Excuse me, but the ho would like to use the sink." They edged aside so I could wash my hands.

I left the washroom with visions of frying pans and fires dancing through my head. Because of Nat, I'd given up on men, at least for a while. Though I dated, celibacy was the rule of the house. I had to set an example. Though I missed sex, I had to admit that I wasn't into a serious relationship. I had enough going on.

After this evening, Fletcher Wolf was off my hot prospects list. Only a paranoid would demand a thirty-page prenup.

"I'm sorry, Ms. Fletcher. I didn't mean to offend you." Wolf's voice was smooth as I returned to the table. He didn't sound contrite, but I had to accept his apology. Otherwise, I'd be just as boorish.

"If you're really sorry, you'll quit looking at me in that weird way."

"What do you mean?" he asked as our meals arrived. I was about to answer when he cut me off with a wave of his hand, and told the waiter, "Please bring me a glass of the Rombauer merlot, 2002." He turned back to me. "Well?"

I was speechless. But if women all over the eastern seaboard threw themselves at him, he had no reason to be considerate. I sucked in another deep, calming breath. If I wasn't careful I'd hyperventilate.

"I'm not prey for the Big Bad Wolf," I said.

Smiling, he picked up his cutlery. "Is that how you think of me, as the Big Bad Wolf? I'm flattered."

"Don't be. It's not a compliment. Hasn't it occurred to you that neither your business associates nor your dinner companions want to feel as though they're on the menu?"

"But you aren't a business associate," he said in a very soft voice. "You are, in fact, prey."

Leaning forward, I decided to nail him, if I could. "I hate to trash your plans, but you've lost the first round and you have no facts to support your case. Why don't you drop the suit?"

"My attorneys and my experience tell me that it's early days yet in this lawsuit. No doubt the poll I've commissioned will reveal that there is a substantial likelihood that the public will be confused and misled by the similarity in the names."

"Meaning what?"

"Meaning I win and you lose."

"Only an idiot would mix up clothes with tools!"

His eyes brooded, the dappled sunlight growing shadowed. "The public is composed of idiots, Ms. Fletcher." He cut into his steak and took a bite.

As red juices flowed all over his plate, a geyser of bile erupted into my throat. Pressing a napkin over my mouth, I darted out of the restaurant before I ralphed all over the tablecloth.

Once safely outside, I managed to shove through the evening crowds flowing along the sidewalk and found a convenient streetlamp. I leaned against its pole, dragging in deep drafts of air. Just when I'd attained some sort of equilibrium, an arm snaked around my shoulders.

It was Fletcher Wolf. I stiffened.

"Tell me what's wrong. You've been upset ever since we

walked into the restaurant." His voice was surprisingly gentle.

I tried not to choke, instead pressing my lips together until the nausea passed. Thank heaven I hadn't disintegrated into a full-blown panic attack. It had been close, though. I said, "Oh, nothing's wrong. I just love going to dinner with someone who's deliberately intimidating and rude." I fumbled in my shoulder bag until I found a hanky. I dabbed my nose and mouth, then crushed the cloth in my fist, wishing I could crush my problems as easily.

He exhaled. "I'm sorry. I'm sorry. You're right. I've been a jerk all evening. Can we start over?" Giving me a winning smile, he extended a hand. "I'm Fletcher Wolf."

I paused, then took it with my free hand. "I'm Cara Fletcher."

"I'm pleased to meet you, Cara Fletcher. How strange that we have the same name."

I forced a grin. "Yes, isn't it? I hope it doesn't cause problems between us."

"That was very smooth," he said. "You're a sharp cookie. But only time will tell, Ms. Fletcher. Shall we have dinner?"

My body twitched involuntarily. "I'm sorry, but I'm not going back in there."

"I don't understand."

"I don't really want to talk about it."

He huffed. "Now who's rude?"

"Sweet of you to say so, but I guess you're right. I, uh, just don't do well around red meat since, umm, I, I . . ."

"What, honey? Let me understand." His voice had remained gentle, sweet.

Cajoling. Was he trying to manipulate me?

If so, he was doing a good job. "Some people got into a traffic accident right in front of me. Their car, like, crunched against a lamp-post. I had to try to get them out. It wasn't pretty. Their bodies were . . . their bodies were . . ." I clamped a hand over my mouth to keep from throwing up.

"Oh, God, Cara." His voice changed completely, becoming husky, rough . . . honest. He put one arm around me, but let go right away, as though he was afraid I'd push him away.

I didn't. The comfort felt too good. I looked up at him. His amazing eyes gleamed, luminous in the streetlight. "Were you hurt?" he asked.

"Not physically. I was lucky. Sort of."

"Oh, I'm so sorry. Believe me, I understand how you feel."

I doubted that. "How?" I asked.

He evaded, instead saying, "I'm an idiot. I should have asked you where you wanted to eat dinner. I'm very sorry. For what I said about your hair, about everything. I don't know why I'm being such an a-hole tonight." Grabbing my hand, he guided me to the curb. With one wave, a taxi emerged from the flow of traffic.

Opening the door, he urged me into the backseat. He handed the driver a folded bill, then bent down and said, "I'm sorry about this evening. I'll call you tomorrow."

He brushed his lips against my cheek. Shocked, I jerked away, but he didn't move, his gaze still pinned to mine.

He stood. "Take the lady wherever she wants to go," he said to the cabbie. "Good night, Cara."

I leaned back into the seat of the taxi with a sigh of relief. "Take me to, um, Battery Park, please. But don't go past Ground Zero."

I had to think, reason my way out of the hole I was in. I couldn't remember a more disastrous evening. Neither impressed nor intimidated, Fletcher Wolf had instead been blatantly contemptuous of my work, scared the bejeezus out of me, and then had the gall to touch me as though he empathized with me. Worse, he'd turned me inside out while remaining utterly calm and so damn sexy.

That viper in the restroom had been right about Fletcher Wolf. He was all male. His act had everything to do with mastery and nothing to do with real sympathy. I'd been weak this evening and told him things about myself I shouldn't have revealed. I couldn't appear weak to this predator. He'd bring me down like a wolf pack takes a fawn.

Ann had been right.

I hadn't smoked in years, but tonight I bummed a ciggie from a kid who was also hanging around the park, staring at the flat, dark water as though it would, like a scryer's crystal ball, reveal answers to the questions that had troubled him all his short life.

I didn't have those comforting illusions, not one. I gazed across the harbor to the Statue of Liberty, lit like a beacon in the night. The water between was no deeper than the crises bedeviling me.

I was in way over my head. Despair rose in my throat and prickled behind my eyes. I couldn't play with the big boys. My dreams and ambitions had led me into uncharted territory, like the blank parts of old maps where cartographers used to write *here be dragons.* And I'd just met with a real live beast.

People like Fletcher Wolf were as far beyond me as the stars. I'd never understand him and really didn't want to. All I needed was to make beautiful clothes and raise a healthy child. Natalie deserved everything I could give.

I wouldn't let anything or anyone threaten Nat's precious sense of safety, which had been so lacking when she'd lived with her father. If Wolf defeated me and took my company, everything would change. I'd lose my job, maybe even my home. Stability was best for Nat. Too much change risked her happiness.

I clenched my teeth, fought off a panic attack, and tried not to consider the possibility of losing. I'd win. I had to win, for my dreams and for Natalie.

But what about the consequences of winning? Sure, we'd come out of the starting gate looking good, even getting attorney's fees. But the judge's warnings rang in my mind like the tolling of funeral bells.

Worse, we could lose. Wolf was too smart to misstep again.

For the first time, I understood the impulse that led a trapped rabbit to gnaw off its foot to escape.

Chapter Four

He came to me out of the mists of dream. Tall and powerful, radiating masculine potency, his irresistible body could drive me insane with unslaked lust. His savage, streaked hair was long, feral, like a wild animal's, and his eyes gleamed with predatory intent.

He was a teenaged girl's wickedest wet dream, a woman's fall from grace, and my nemesis.

He flirted, taunted and teased, then moved in close, hemming me in. He'd have me, for I was his thrall. At his vivid touch, sensations bloomed, flowerlike. He palmed my breasts, sending my body into bliss and my mind into glorious oblivion.

Out of the mists of dream, he came, but why?

I loathed Fletcher Wolf. That conservative, uptight, judgmental, pompous boor threatened to trash my world like a twister roaring through a trailer park. So why did this dream feel so good?

The awful, the appalling, the inescapable truth goaded me into full consciousness, and I jerked upright in bed.

Despite that disastrous dinner, I still wanted him.

Damn!

Not only did I want him, I wanted him badly, in the worst possible way, crazier than my first teenage crush on Tom Cruise or my puppy love for the coolest dude in high school. I wanted to make love with Fletcher Wolf, to undress each perfect inch of his body, to uncover the glories beneath his formal, fitted suit, to do it, do it, do it . . . and then do it some more, with his glinting, golden, wolf eyes glowing into mine every time we came together.

With a bizarre sense of horrified, clinical detachment, I watched my nipples rise, silvery in the moonlight filtering though the gauze curtains. They lifted to taut little points even though all I was doing was thinking about Fletcher Wolf. I wasn't playing with myself or using a vibrator. I was just thinking about touching Fletcher Wolf, nothing more, but I was hot, I was wet, and I wanted him.

Damn. I'd thought I wanted him last night in the restaurant, when I'd been thinking about getting him into a hotel room. But now I was dreaming about banging him, explicit dreams that meant I was seriously in lust with Fletcher Wolf. This was real. This was bad.

But maybe I could persuade myself that it was just a crush. Just an infatuation and it would pass.

Yeah, right.

I flopped back against the pillow with a gusty sigh, staring at the ceiling. A shadow fell across my skylight. The blood froze in my veins as the shadow resolved itself into a silhouette of a person's hand and arm. A scratching sound filled my loft bedroom.

I screamed, my voice ripping raw from my throat. The dim shape disappeared, and footsteps thumped across the flat roof. I jumped out of bed and sprinted to the window. Pushing the gauze aside, I craned my neck to see the burglar leave. Was he on the fire escape?

A cry was followed by more thumps as Natalie, apparently roused, ran up the stairs, yelling, "Mom! What's wrong?" She skidded into the room, wearing a knee-length Raiders T-shirt.

"Nat, oh God, Nat, there was someone on the roof." I grabbed my daughter and hugged her hard to stop my shakes.

Natalie's thin body, warm from her bed, felt solid and comforting.

Nat hugged back. "Jeez, Mom, you're shaking. Get back into bed. You're not wearing any clothes."

"No, no. I want to see if I can see him leaving. The fire escape is out here—" I hauled and banged at the sticky latch securing the window.

"Stop it. Even if you open the window, the guy's probably gone. But call the police anyway."

"You're right." I grabbed my robe, which I always tossed at the foot of my bed. Thrusting my arms through the familiar chenille sleeves—another comforting feeling—I tied its sash at my waist as Natalie used the portable on my bedside table to call 9-1-1.

Natalie and I spent the rest of the night together huddled in bed, waiting for the police. Two officers finally arrived early in the morning, looking exhausted. They'd probably been up all night, too, and because of my sleeplessness, I had a lot of empathy for them.

"How can we assist you, ma'am?" The younger of the two cops asked. Seated at the kitchen table, he cradled a mug of coffee in his substantial palms.

It was six-thirty. I'd given up on sleeping an hour earlier, choosing instead to shower, dress, and brew some coffee. Both patrolmen had gratefully accepted a cup.

"Too late now to do anything about it, but at about four in the morning, someone tried to break into the upstairs bedroom."

"There was a lot of activity last night, with the full moon," the officer said. "Dispatch prioritizes the calls, and injury calls come first."

"Makes sense," I said. "Let's hope I never come first."

The older officer rose, putting down his mug. "Which is your room, Ms. Fletcher?" He clearly didn't want to waste time on chit-chat.

"I'll show you." I took my mug with me, heading toward the living room stairs. "Please pardon the mess . . ."

I led them up into the loft. Unsettling, the sight of uniformed officers in my bedroom, which otherwise contained only a few pieces of pine furniture and a fluffy white rug. And, of course, my messy bed, partially covered with a white cutwork duvet.

Burying my embarrassment, I pointed upward. "I was in bed. I, umm, was awake and heard scrabbling at the skylight. The moon was very bright last night, and I'm sure I saw someone trying to unscrew the bolts on the skylight."

The older officer grunted. "Wouldn't be the first time. Any way we can get up onto the roof?" He glanced at his partner.

Nat and I waited anxiously while they pried open the window and used the fire escape to check out the roof. After about five minutes, the officers climbed back inside.

"You're right," the older one said. "There are scratches around one of the bolts. They look like fresh marks made by a screwdriver or maybe a knife. But I doubt there's anything anyone can do about it."

I was appalled. "What? Why not? Isn't attempted burglary a crime?"

"Yes, it is, ma'am," the other officer said. "And we're very sorry, but the city doesn't have the resources to send someone out to test for fingerprints on a case like this. See, no one was hurt. He didn't even get in."

"Don't worry about it, ma'am," his partner rumbled. "He probably won't be back. Do you have an alarm system?"

"Yeah, and the skylight's wired. If it takes hours for you to respond, what's to prevent someone from getting in here and murdering us in our beds?" I probably sounded shrill and hysterical, but staying up all night waiting for Ted Bundy to drop in did that to a person.

The policemen looked uncomfortable. "I'm sorry, ma'am, but we feel we've done all we can," said the older cop firmly.

"Will you at least file a report?"

"We'll do that. There'll be a record if there's any other incidents."

I hesitated. I didn't want to seem like a nut, but if there was a connection, I wanted to explore it. "It's just, well, it's just that I'm getting an awful lot of hang-up calls lately."

"Are you concerned about a pattern of harassment?" the junior officer asked.

"I don't want to seem paranoid, but yeah, I am."

The older officer seemed unconvinced. "It's doubtful that this incident is related. Pranksters who use the telephone to harass generally stick to that tactic and don't show up at the victim's home. If you continue to get these calls, contact the phone company and put a trap on your line."

"A trap?"

"A modified trace. It'll show from which phone the calls originate. If the prankster is stupid enough to be calling from his own phone, we can find out."

"We'll be sure to write that report, Ms. Fletcher," the younger cop said.

"Are you sure there's no way to get the skylight tested for prints?"

"I'll put in the request, but don't expect immediate action. Don't let anyone touch the area until we get to it, okay?"

And with that, I had to be content. But I wasn't, not by a long shot. My troubles seemed to be piling on top of each other into an insurmountable heap.

However, what else could I do? I did my best to forget about it and go about my day, praying for an uneventful one.

The first couple of hours at work were wonderfully quiet and productive. My team of seamstresses and designers was as excited and motivated about my upcoming show as I was. The air hummed with creative energy.

Unhappily, at about eleven o'clock, we were blessed by a visitation from one-half of the infamous Covarrubia twins.

Supermodels both, nasty rumors had started to cloud Adam and Andrea's reputations when they'd been photographed by paparazzi in a seedy bar known for smack deals and smack-downs. I decided then that if I had to hire them occasionally, I would, but neither twin would be assigned to a really important shoot or show, a decision Maggie Andersen vehemently opposed. She said that their international reputation would lend cachet to Cara Fletcher Couture. I stood firm, though, and now Adam had arrived to plead his case with Maggie while I hid behind my drafting table in the upper loft of my workshop.

Curled up in my favorite old armchair—a relic of my student days—Adam and his nasal, Jersey-inflected whine scraped my last remaining nerve. With Adam clad in his usual Goth-black garb, his silhouette against the armchair's cracked teal leather reminded me of a nesting moray eel.

"See, Maggie, things have really dried up, and I really need this—"

Adam's pitch was interrupted by the clomp-clomp-clomp of heavy footsteps on the metal spiral staircase leading to my loft.

Peeking out, I saw Fletcher Wolf emerge from the stairwell, looking better than ever. I bobbed back behind my drafting table, breathing heavily, and told myself to calm down. But what the hell was Wolf doing here, in my sanctum? I didn't want him here. No way, no how. The man was trouble.

Adam said, "And whadda we have here? Armani, very nice."

"May I see Cara Fletcher?" That dark, smooth, southern-laced bass caressed my ears. I sighed and tried to push the memories of my wet dreams out of my mind. Fat chance, with the star of the porn show standing about four feet away from me.

Maggie asked, "Who wants her?" She sounded unfriendly, which was good. I didn't want Wolf to feel welcome in my atelier.

"I'm Fletcher Wolf."

I decided not to delay the inevitable and came out from behind my drafting table, still holding a piece of charcoal. I hoped to send the message that I was busy. "Mr. Wolf. What are you doing here?"

He was holding several anthurium flowers in his hand, delicate pink ones with two-inch-long spikes emerging from the centers of their fleshy, heart-shaped petals.

I flushed. He'd brought me flowers. And not just any flowers. Flowers were sex organs anyhow, and these pink anthuriums sent a blatant message.

Don't flip out, I admonished myself. It's just some flowers. He's still suing us for a gazillion dollars!

Did he feel the same way I did? I hoped not. I wanted him, and if he wanted me, surely we'd end up in the sack. An affair with someone who was suing me was impossible. How could I tell if he was sincere about his feelings? Maybe he was just after pillow talk.

On the other hand, maybe I could find out something from Fletcher Wolf in bed. I wasn't into learning new sexual techniques, but if I could discover his secrets, something that would help me win the case—

"Good morning to you too, Ms. Fletcher. I came to see how you were feeling."

I rubbed my cheek as he surveyed me, aware that I was a mess compared to our dinner date and the courtroom confrontation. I hadn't done much with my hair that morning, just put it up with a clip so it wouldn't get in my way. I wore blue contacts and a striped knit top. I had on old, bell-bottomed jeans and my fave pair of silver Converse high-tops.

He glanced at the flowers, then back at me. Of course he looked perfect. The Armani that Adam Covarrubia noted was beautifully cut. The charcoal gray complemented Wolf's unusual hair and eyes without taking anything away from his startling good looks.

Mr. Debonair made me feel sloppy, messy and scattered.

"Feeling? Feeling! I feel fine. Why shouldn't I?" Oops. I sounded defensive, which was bad. Wolf didn't need to know how much he got to me.

He raised his brows, all smooth self-assurance. "You were unwell at dinner last night." He fiddled with the stems, then thrust the flowers at me. "Here."

I took them. "You work fast."

"I would have been here earlier, but I wanted the right gift. Roses would have been too mundane for you."

I couldn't help smiling. "It was nice of you to come by. Would you like a cup of coffee and the grand tour?"

"Yes, I would." Looking into my eyes, he smiled, and my heart did a little bounce. Stop it, I told myself. He's off limits.

I cleared my throat. "This is Maggie Andersen, my business manager and personal assistant." Maggie gave Fletcher a smile that really was no more than a tiny stretch of her thin, glossed lips. I couldn't blame her. I'd been frantic since he'd had me served, and Maggie was a very loyal person.

Wolf extended his hand. "Ms. Andersen."

She grudgingly shook his hand, then turned back to the spreadsheet on her computer monitor. Before he could peer at my private business, I took his arm and steered him away. "This is Adam Covarrubia, one of our top models."

Adam uncoiled himself from the armchair like a snake preparing to exit its lair, then stood to give Fletcher's hand a limp shake.

"Let's get you your coffee now." I led Wolf to the north side of the loft past my bookshelves. He paused to admire my collection, which included thick, colorful volumes of art and fashion photography, decks of tarot cards and other memorabilia. I can't call myself a collector, but I do enjoy oddities.

Like anthurium flowers.

"You have some terrific books here." Wolf pulled out a thick volume on the history of costume, idly flipping through the pages.

"Thank you. I look through them when I need insight." I walked toward a bank of windows set into the brick wall. Below it, a long table contained a motley assortment of mugs, as well as three coffee machines, one of which held steamy hot water. "Unleaded or regular?"

"Caffeinated is fine." Fletch sniffed. "Irish crème?"

Was that contempt I heard in his voice? Why? "We take turns bringing coffees. This week Maggie brought flavored. I can live with it, though I usually stick to plain French roast. Want anything in it?"

He shook his head. In the background, I heard Adam renewing his pitch to Maggie. I shut them out of my mind.

"Let's start the tour here. This is my loft. Maggie and I work up here, but my set-up really doesn't differ much from any of the other designers, except for some of the computer equipment."

"Why does a fashion designer need a computer?"

"A lot of them don't use one. But after I create a design, I input it into the computers using a scanner. Any one of the designers can access it to make a floor sample, which they'll then use to draw a pattern. After sewing a couple of test outfits, the patterns go to a factory to make the ready-to-wear clothes."

He looked confused, so I said, "The off-the-rack stuff. The clothes that go to Macy's or wherever. As opposed to couture."

"What happens if someone wants a unique dress, something that you make personally and that no one else owns?"

"That's couture. Funny, Mr. Wolf, but I could have sworn last night that you had no interest whatsoever in couture."

"Ms. Fletcher. Cara." He reached for my hand, and I let him take it. Not necessarily a smart move. His touch affected me as powerfully as the dreams last night. I didn't feel the mythical electric zing that one finds in romance novels, but I did get a thrill. A definite thrill.

I removed my hand.

He continued, "For what I hope is the last time, I'm very, very sorry about last night, and I'm doing my best to make amends. We've really gotten off on the wrong foot."

I raised my brows. "Yes, Mr. Wolf. I would say that suing someone qualifies as getting off on the wrong foot."

"Look, I'm trying to do what we were ordered to do, which was find a way to settle this mess."

"You told me last night you didn't think that was possible."

"I said a lot of stupid things last night. Can't you just drop it?"

He was gritting his teeth. That was bad, even though he was saying all the right words. Okay, so he was making an effort. If he could, so could I, but only because it might help the case, not because I liked or trusted him.

I took a deep breath. "I'll try. I'm sorry, but I'm really not at my best this morning. Shall we continue?"

Wolf appeared to relax a bit. "Please. Would you be offended if I asked you why your workshop is in such an unusual neighborhood? I thought designers clustered around Seventh Avenue."

I grimaced. My workshop was located in a renovated brick warehouse at the Bowery's edge, a neighborhood through which no one should venture after darkness fell. Hell, you could run into problems during daytime, for that matter. I kept my atelier immaculate inside and out, never allowing graffiti to mar its walls. Instead, "Cara Fletcher Couture" was painted outside in ten-foot-high letters. A security system protected all the equipment, fabrics and clothes inside.

"I'm not at all offended," I said. "My workshop is here because it saves money. I rent a small showroom in the garment center on Seventh along with other couturiers, but the work gets done here." I gestured toward the lower floor, and noticed that Maggie was leaving with Adam, way before her regular lunchtime.

I was dismayed. I might need her as a buffer between me and the Wolf. "Hey, Maggie. Where are you going?"

Maggie turned and looked up at me. Her expression hardened as her gaze passed to Fletcher Wolf. Whoa. She really had taken a dislike to the guy. "Adam and I are eating lunch early today."

Given her attitude, I said, "Okay, fine. Let's review the press list again when you return." Smiling at Fletch, I waved a hand at the staircase. "Shall we?"

"Press list?" he asked.

"Yeah. My April show is in just a few weeks."

"Aha. May I attend? And my mother would love it."

"Really?" I paused at the top of the stairs.

"Yes, she's a fan of the Seventh Avenue crowd. She told me that suing you would be a big mistake. I still don't dare tell her that I actually filed."

"I'm with your mom. You are making a big mistake. Both of us know I have every right to use my own name."

He sighed. "The issue isn't Fletcher. The issue is Fletcher's Gear. Unless your attorney is blatantly incompetent—and she's not—you must know about our gearshifts."

"I've told you that only an idiot could mix up clothes and

tools." I trotted down the stairs. "Why are we even discussing this? We get along so well if we ignore the horrible reason we met."

"That's true."

Score one for the good guys, I thought. Maybe being nice to the Wolf will get him off my back.

On the floor below, I stopped at a dressmaker's dummy draped with canary yellow silk. The seamstress seated next to the mannequin set small, perfect stitches in the fabric's fluttery edges, embroidering a leaf-and-vine pattern in turquoise, violet, and emerald, following a drawing on her table.

"This is Esme. She's from Pakistan." I smiled at her as her tiny, gnarled hands moved with a sureness and speed at odds with her aged appearance. Esme lifted her head from her work and smiled back. I turned to Fletcher. "Esme is my ace in the hole. No one can embroider like she can. Craftsmanship like hers doesn't exist any more. This is part of the value of couture, Mr. Wolf. Arts like Esme's would die out because there are very few people who can afford handmade clothing like the dresses we make. Couture keeps this craft alive."

"Who drew this pattern?" He gestured at the paper on Esme's table. "It's fantastic."

I tried not to preen. "I did. These are all my designs." I moved along to another worker.

He followed me over to another dummy, where Santo seemed to be having some issues with the fabric I'd picked. He had potential, but he needed more grounding in the basics. Like how to handle different materials.

"What's this?" Fletcher asked.

"Santo is creating a prototype of one of the jackets in your favorite line of clothing, Fletcher's Gear. How's it going, dude?"

"Not so good," Santo replied. "I can't get this wool to drape properly."

"This looks like an expensive fabric, Cara," Fletcher said.

"Oh, it is. A good gabardine can cost thirty dollars per yard, or more, if manufactured to designer specifications." I twitched the fabric so it lay smoothly across the dummy's "chest."

"Why are you using something so costly for a prototype?"

"It's true that other designers use muslin for samples," I said. "But I believe that's a false economy. Muslin drapes differently than any other fabric. I want a prototype to tell me if an outfit's gonna work. If it isn't in the right fabric, how can I assess appearance and performance?"

The wolf was in the fold, and I tried my best to be cordial while limiting my statements and hiding my nerves. Plus, I was terrified that I'd lapse into a panic attack. Why had Maggie deserted me? I needed her. After last night, I was exhausted and mentally limp. My brain felt like lettuce left too long in the crisper.

Worse, the man could charm Little Red Riding Hood right into Grandma's bed. After less than a half hour, Fletcher Wolf had seen every corner of my atelier, chatted with the staff, snagged two tickets to the show and had gotten everyone to fall in love with him. The women, and some of the men, looked at him as though they wanted to eat him up for dinner.

Including me. As Fletcher left, he took my hand and gazed into my eyes with those unfathomable orbs. My body started to melt, and I hoped my hand didn't tremble in his. Every time I looked at him, dammit, I remembered the seductive brush of his lips over my cheek, that almost-kiss, to say nothing of the vivid dreams that had lit up my night.

"I'll instruct my attorney to get a continuance, Cara. No need to rush to judgment, is there?"

"Oh, no," I said gratefully, glad I'd been friendly to the Wolf. The longer I could put off the litigation, the more chance I'd have to pay off my debts and gather a war chest to pay Ann-

Marie's costs for the upcoming legal battle. I didn't want to take advantage of our friendship, but even with discounts, the case would inevitably get expensive.

"Come to Wilmington and see my corporate headquarters sometime." He smiled. "I'd like to show you my . . . tools."

"Did you say tool or tools?" I raised my eyebrows, then gave him a wink and a grin. This case might not gut my business after all. "I'd be happy to."

Chapter Five

The Cloisters, New York Metropolitan Museum of Art

"People, listen up!" Windmilling my arms, I tried to calm the tumult in the Cuxa Cloister. The normally placid garden, surrounded by medieval colonnades, was a maelstrom of color, light, and movement caused by gesticulating figures dressed in elaborate couture. Racks of clothing competed for space with makeup artists, hair stylists, dressers, and fancifully attired models in silk and sequins. And everyone chattered at once.

I climbed up onto the central fountain's wide rim, teetering on the stiletto heels of my killer thigh-high leather boots. In keeping with the setting and the eclectic themes of the show, I also wore tights and a parti-colored leather tabard that just skimmed my butt. I'd dyed my hair black and red, the striking style that had first caught Fletcher Wolf's attention. "Hello!" I called to the models.

The crowd noise didn't diminish a hair. I clapped several times, cupping my palms to increase the decibel level. A score of well-coiffed heads finally turned toward me as the horde quieted.

"Thank you in advance for your work today," I said. Aware that models, unless they were stars, were often handled like meat, I always made a point of treating them with extra courtesy. "Our guests will arrive soon for the show. Please be quiet and respect the surroundings. This is a museum, and we're lucky to be here."

"We pulled every string to get even two rooms," Maggie told everyone. "Usually the Met only rents to its own corporate members for business events."

"So look hot, be good, and let's have a great show!" I jumped off the fountain.

"How'd you get the space, Cara?" The question came from the male model I'd hired for the Fletcher's Gear print and TV ads.

"My loan officer at First National helped. I told him if the show was a washout, I couldn't repay the loan." I grinned, cheeky on the outside, scared within.

"Yeah, and it's not far from the truth," Maggie muttered into my ear.

"Thanks for reminding me." My smile twisted into a grimace. The seven-figure loan, borrowed to finance my foray into ready-to-wear, had radically overextended Cara Fletcher Couture. My fall collection had to be a hit. This show cost a bundle, and if the orders didn't come in, my financial house of cards would crash and burn. Plus, the Fletcher Wolf situation made everything worse. Knowing he was in the audience today made my stress level shoot to the stratosphere.

I flexed my taut muscles. Boulders in my shoulders yet again? A veteran of six couture shows since I'd opened my atelier, I ought to be used to the pressure. Instead, I was impossibly tense. When would I learn to handle this anxiety? Maybe I needed to pop another pill.

"Is everyone here?" I asked Maggie.

She flipped through a clipboard fat with notes. "Um, the Covarrubias are late."

I ground my teeth. "You know, sometimes those two are more trouble than they're worth. Did you hear about the stunt they pulled last week?"

"No. What now?" Maggie's expression was guarded.

"Andrea shot up some bad smack and had to go to the hospital. She claimed later it was something she ate."

"It's still early. Maybe they're sleeping in."

"Oh, please. At two in the afternoon?"

"Face it, hon. They're the hottest models in the world, and right now you need them."

That's what irritated me so much. Despite the rumors swirling around them, the Covarrubia twins, at the ripe old age of twenty, were the current spoiled darlings of the smart set, at least in the narrow world of high fashion. Alienating top models and their agent wasn't a recipe for success, so I'd hired Adam and Andrea for the runway show against my better judgment.

A burst of giggles erupted from the swarm of children dressed in Cara's Kidstuff. They surrounded Natalie and a classmate, who practiced their handsprings and cartwheels up and down the graveled walkways. I sucked in a tense breath as the kids barely missed bashing their brains out on the stonework. Outflung arms and legs whirled close—too close—to the expensive clothes sported by the chic, sleek models.

I grabbed Natalie by the arm. "Hey, remember our deal. No cartwheels in the Cloisters."

"Mom, don't be a jerk!" She wrenched away.

"What did you just call me?"

"Aw, jeez." Her voice rose to a whine. "You're embarrassing me in front of my friends."

I laughed to myself, hugged her, then leaned in close to give her a big smacky one.

"Mo-om!"

"Come with me, sweetheart. You can be my little helper."

"Your 'little helper'? What am I, one of Santa's elves?" Nat rolled her eyes but followed to watch the final check of clothes and hair.

Chuckling, I stopped by a rack of outfits in the west arcade to say hello to Ella Langer, a plus-size model with plus-size blonde hair and a plus-size Texas twang.

"Cara, this suit is a masterpiece. Every size eighteen businesswoman in Manhattan is gonna want one." She fingered the lapels of the surplice jacket she wore.

"Have you tried the evening outfit?" I asked.

"The one with the palazzo pants?"

"Yep. The layered silk georgette."

"Makes me feel nekkid and sexy. I want it!"

I smiled. "I hope everyone wants one, sweetie." Eyeing Ella's hair, I whipped out a rat-tail comb from my leather satchel and poked the long plastic end through her bangs, lifting them a tad. "You're glorious, darling, an asset to this show."

She grinned. "We'll make you proud, babe."

I continued down the disordered maze of clothing racks and personnel, checking each model's hair, makeup and outfit. Nat wandered behind watching and, I hoped, absorbing. I didn't particularly want my daughter to become obsessed by the rag trade, but she needed to develop interests which would take her mind off her father's betrayal. She was doing well, but every little bit helped. All females love clothes . . . it doesn't matter how old or young they are! I thought, watching Nat stroke a satin evening gown.

As I adjusted the fit of a model's gabardine coat-dress, someone tugged at my leather tabard.

"Hey there, Cara baby," a male voice with a thick Jersey accent crooned.

"Don't look now, but it's Adam and Evil," Natalie murmured into my ear.

I beetled my brows at Nat before confronting Adam Covarrubia and his sister Andrea. Both models looked even more disreputable than usual. Identical bird's-nests of midnight hair surmounted chalky skin. Enormous waif-like eyes, dark and rimmed with smudged kohl, peered blearily at me, the Cloisters, and the other models, as though they'd just dropped in from outer space and didn't know quite where they were or what they were doing. Taking yesteryear's Goth look to an extreme, both Covarrubias wore unrelenting black: leather motorcycle jackets, jeans, and boots. I inhaled the miasma of stale cigarette smoke surrounding them, and wrinkled my nose. Never again, I thought. I don't care what Maggie wants. Never again.

"Just where have you been?" I asked. "We're ready to go."

Adam pouted. "You told my agent that I got the wrong look for Fletcher's Gear," he said, his Jersey accent taking on a resentful whine. "I didn't think you needed us until later."

"You were supposed to be here at two. I'm paying you for your time as of right now, not forty minutes ago. Please get cleaned up and dressed. The rest of the men are in that corner, behind the tapestry." I pointed. "Get that garbage off your face, comb your hair and get into a tux, pronto. Andrea, come with me."

I led the model to a rack loaded with business suits and evening dresses. I eyed my child, who still tagged along. "Natalie, please ask your friends to line up with the models in front of that door. I'll be right over to do a last check."

"Okay." Natalie bounced away, her French braid bobbing.

I heaved a sigh and focused on dealing with the female half of the Covarrubia problem. "Andrea, are you feeling all right?"

"I'm fine." Andrea had the same nasal accent that characterized her brother's dubious diction. "I'm just tired."

Lifting Andrea's chin, I peered into her eyes. They were so dark a brown that it was impossible to distinguish her pupils from her irises, so a casual eye exam couldn't tell me if Andrea had been toking, snorting or shooting up. I helped her remove her leather jacket and took the opportunity to check her arms.

Noting no fresh track marks, I said, "All right. You have a few minutes, so clean up and get into a business suit. We're starting with Comfort Zone, Kidstuff and Fletcher's Gear, so we won't need you until three-twenty or so. You have a half hour to transform yourself into a chic, sharp businesswoman."

She giggled, a husky, sweet sound at odds with her tough girl appearance.

I smiled. "I know you can do it, sweetie. You're the best, and everyone knows it."

She ducked her head and grinned at the pavement.

I hung up her jacket, thinking: Andrea's almost likable when she's relaxed . . . you can see the little girl she used to be. How on earth did she turn into a twelve-step failure?

"What the hell is this place, anyways? It's really weird and spooky, like a vampire's castle. What is all this crap?" She pointed at priceless medieval stonework.

"This is The Cloisters," I said. "It's the Met's medieval art museum. You've lived in Jersey and New York all your life. Haven't you ever been here?"

She shook her head. "Never heard of the place. Had one hell of a time finding it." She laughed coarsely. "You better hope that *Vogue* and Bloomie's are smarter than me."

"That's why God made taxis, Andrea."

Never again, I thought as I stalked away.

People who aren't involved in the industry, like Fletcher Wolf, think that putting on a fashion show is easy. It's not. Producing imaginative, wearable, well-made clothes takes talent and drive. I studied for years at the Parsons School of Design, where I was lucky enough to win the Gold Thimble Award, which brought me the attention I needed to get my first job. After I had earned a reputation for hard work and creativity, I went into hock big-time and opened my atelier. For the first couple of years I went cheap, handling both the designing as well as the business-related chores, which included putting on two runway shows annually.

Then I got smart and hired Maggie Andersen to deal with the busywork, freeing me to do what I do best. As well as managing my day-to-day finances, she takes care of finding a suitable venue for my shows, one that's in keeping with the themes and ideas that the couture garments reflect. Fashionistas thrive on gossip, and the more unusual a design or a show, the better. Maggie also finds the right models, no small task since everyone wants the same famous faces and bodies on the runway at the same time. Fashion Week is wild, and I usually delay my shows to get the models I want. It's fine with me. Anything to stand out from the herd.

Even with numerous crises and stresses, the attempted break-in, Nat's father Kenney on my ass, and the Fletcher Wolf hassle, I was proud of my latest collection. It was fanciful and wearable at the same time, and the Cloisters was the perfect setting.

With satisfaction, I watched my models strut past me through a curtain and onto a runway set up in the Cloisters' Romanesque Hall. First we showed Comfort Zone, my line of women's work and casual wear. Then Kidstuff, my debut into children's wear, was followed by Fletcher's Gear. Showing the children's clothing and then the menswear allowed the women to change into the dramatic evening gowns that are, in my opinion, what I do best.

Fashion shows traditionally end with a wedding dress, and this time, I'd put Adam and Andrea Covarrubia into cream silk Renaissance-inspired garb which perfectly set off their dark, slightly wicked good looks.

The applause for each outfit was hearty, and as the show continued, I relaxed more and more. Even before the show ended, Maggie popped open a bottle of Dommy, and I risked mixing a little champagne with my tranqs.

Horns blared, signaling the end of the show. Excitement pulsed through my veins and danced along my skin. The models returned to the runway, looking like a fantastic and bizarre tribe dressed in exotic finery—my beautiful designs.

It was a gorgeous collection, even if I do say so myself. Flowing satin robes trimmed with velvet, lace and feathers worn over the jewel-toned, fluttery silks that I love so much. The kids followed, still in the leather children's sportswear, and through the curtain I could see everyone forming a double line along the sides of the runway.

I checked my look in a nearby mirror and blinked to moisten my leaf-green contacts. I quickly freshened my lipstick, crimson to match the trim on my tabard and the diamond-shaped insets on my boots. I drew a deep breath, threw back my shoulders and straightened to my full height, such as it is.

This was my moment.

The room erupted in applause as I stepped through the curtain. I smiled through a few happy tears, then heard a voice murmur, "That must be the bitch goddess herself."

Startled, I looked down to see Fletcher Wolf, leaning back in his chair. He grinned at me, so I guessed that he hadn't spoken. But the man sitting next to him had an expression on his face that reminded me of a great white shark devouring a helpless seal pup.

Screw him, I thought, and gave the Wolf's companion a little bump and grind.

Fletch winked at me as I stalked down the runway past him.

"Holy mackerel!"

I turned to see Fletch's buddy jumping to his feet, staring at my hair. Laughing, I gave him a little wave of the hand and continued down the runway. When I reached the end of the catwalk, I spread my arms wide and bowed. The applause crescendoed.

It's not modest, but I have to admit that I love the acclaim, the camera flashes going off in my face, the excitement, knowing that tomorrow I'll read rave reviews of my work. Creation is its own reward, but a little encouragement never hurts.

Natalie turned handsprings up the runway and reached my side. I grabbed her hand. "We did it, baby! We did it!" I hugged her close as the audience roared.

Everyone was on their feet, except Fletcher Wolf, the jerk. Why couldn't he and his snotty friend get into the groove?

Oh well. I already knew that he didn't respect my work or understand couture. He didn't matter.

After the show, the reporters, no doubt facing a deadline, headed out the door, clutching their teeny-tiny notebook computers and fancy cameras. The buyers remained, clustering around me, and I began to pitch them.

This was a crucial part of what I do, and I found myself using my daughter as a prop. "Leather! People don't want to make kids' clothes out of leather because it's expensive. But anything else is a false economy. Look how sturdy this is." I tugged at Nat's tabard, ignoring her annoyed expression. If she wanted to go to her chi-chi private school and continue gymnastics lessons, Mommy had to sell some clothes. Or, rather, a lot of them.

I continued, "This will never wear out. It's unisex, can be passed from child to child. Wipes clean with a damp cloth. The Kidstuff leather line—"

"Is marvelous. So is the designer." Fletcher Wolf shoved past a woman and seized my hand, lifting it. "Congratulations on a great show."

He caressed the back of my hand with his lips, and I could feel myself getting red. With anger. Flashbulbs popped, adding to my embarrassment.

"Oh, man! You gross me out." Pulling away, Natalie beat it.

I jerked my hand from his. "Stop it!" I snarled. "I'm trying to sell clothes. These people are buyers!"

"Oh, all right." He turned to the women, who watched avidly. He smiled, clearly getting a kick out of putting me off my stride. "Buy her clothes. That gal over there can take your orders." He pointed at Maggie Andersen.

The buyers left in a rush. Hands on my hips, I glared, tapping a toe against the stone pavement. I was about to give him a very large and mean piece of my mind, but then I noticed someone I loathed even more than the Wolf.

Shit. Trent Whiting. A louse from my Parsons days. He looked even more outlandish than ever, in a fringed leather jacket and a Stetson. These days he had shaggy blond hair and a string tie around his skinny throat. I winced at his affectations. Did the twerp think he was home on the range? What was he trying to pull? Everyone knew that he hailed from South Trenton, not Southfork.

"Trent Whiting." I crossed my arms over my torso. "A dubious pleasure, to be sure."

"It's Trent Nevada now."

Why would a supposedly sane adult take a name that would make a third-grader roll her eyes? I guffawed. "You think you're like Claude Montana? You've gotta be putting me on."

"Cara," he murmured huskily, "I see you haven't forgotten me."

"I haven't forgotten my root canal, either," I snapped.

Fletcher laughed. "Doesn't look like the lady wants your company, er, Trent."

"I've known Cara since Parsons." Trent still sounded like an arrogant SOB. "She'll talk to me."

"We have nothing to discuss." I turned and left, preferring the company of anyone else.

I noticed that Wolf's surly companion was hitting on Ella

Langer. Finding Jimmy Benton, the top Fletcher's Gear model, I offered him my congratulations while covertly watching Fletch talking with Trent.

What on earth could those two have to discuss? I'd hung out with Trent during my second year at Parsons until I realized he'd ripped off several of my designs. I'd never expected to see such an unpleasant blast from the past at one of my shows. Who the hell had let him in?

And although Wolf had stated that he wanted to back off from the litigation, AnnMarie hadn't mentioned any formal proposal from his lawyer.

So two of my enemies looked thick as thieves, thieves who wanted to steal my company. I rubbed the back of my hand against my side, involuntarily reliving Fletcher's caress. His gall amazed, confused, and frightened me. Though he appeared to be normal, he was someone for whom normal boundaries of behavior didn't exist. He was unpredictable, and that bothered me. A lot.

When would this all end?

Several days later I sat at my drafting table, sipped coffee and read industry papers' accounts of the show that bothered me even more. A photo of Fletcher Wolf kissing my hand overshadowed shots of my clothing, outfits we'd painstakingly stitched for months.

The caption was even worse. *Wolf Eyes New Prey. Will corporate raider Fletcher Wolf, scion of the toolmaking family, shift gears to head into high fashion?*

Another read: *Haunt Couture: Cara Fletcher puts on a show to remember in the spooky environs of the Cloisters. Influenced by tarot cards, Robin Hood and Renaissance angels, the show attracted fashionistas as well as corporate raider Fletcher Wolf. Wolf's attendance prompted speculation . . . related story page one of business section . . .*

Fletcher Wolf had garnered more attention than my designs, damn him. That wretched photograph had run in no fewer than four papers. My resentment grew as I read that the takeover rumors had sparked a rise in Fletcher Tool and Gear stock. Shouldn't I get a cut? I wondered.

Well, it didn't matter. Ann had assured me that since I owned my company one hundred percent, no one could ever take it from me against my will. Orders were coming in at a brisk clip, staving off financial collapse. With luck, AnnMarie would quickly deal with the lawsuit, and the irritating Fletcher Wolf would soon be gone from my life. And, hopefully, from my dreams.

I shoved the Wolfman out of my mind and turned my attention to next year's spring line, which would be shown in early November. I'd learned that time was more precious than gold lamé and Chinese silks. After staff summer vacations stole productive weeks, the autumn would seem mighty short. I picked up a piece of charcoal and started to work.

Chapter Six

The day began innocently enough, though Natalie, excited because school soon would close for the summer, was more of a challenge than usual. Persuading Nat to get dressed, eat breakfast, and then get into a taxi in time to arrive at school before the first bell had been a chore. But I'd done it, so now I could relax during the cab ride to the workshop.

Reaching into my satchel, I took out my cell phone to call my parents. Carson Fletcher, my dad, answered.

"Hello, sweetheart! How's everything going?"

My heart contracted. Dad always sounded cheerful, but I knew that his MS had reached a more acute stage. "Everything's fine," I said. "You doin' okay with that wheelchair?"

"It's great. I feel like a butterfly just come out of the chrysalis, after being stuck with crutches for so long. By the time you send Natalie to us, the house should be completely retrofitted. You know, we hired someone to make all the doorways bigger and build a couple of ramps."

"Cool. But I won't be sending her. I'll be bringing her myself."

"Oh, good. When?"

"School's out at the end of the week. I'll bring her up Saturday, and we'll both be there for Father's Day. She'll stay for the next week."

"Why such a short time?"

"She's enrolled in computer camp and gymnastics for most

of the summer. Keeping her in a routine is important at this point in her life." Also, I didn't want to burden my parents with Natalie for too long.

"Can you stay over, sweetheart?" my father wheedled.

"Just for the night. I have the show coming up in early November. Time seems to move so fast once September rolls around, so I want to get a jump on things now."

"Honey, you work too hard. Don't make the same mistakes I did."

"What mistakes? You're a great father."

"I regret the amount of overtime I worked when you were growing up." Pain and doubt infused my father's voice. "I was too busy trying to make it. And now, time's so short . . ."

"You were around plenty," I said. "Don't worry about it. Umm, how's Mom?"

"She's fine. Jenna!" I could hear Dad calling to Mom. "Pick up a phone, it's Cara."

"Hi, sweetie!" My mother came on the line. "What's going on?"

"Everything's fine."

"How's the lawsuit?" Dad asked.

"Okay. The Wolf's called off his pack, at least for the moment. Last week, Ann and I signed an agreement to delay the case for a while."

I hadn't seen Fletcher Wolf when we'd signed the paperwork, which was just as well. He didn't belong in my life, regardless of the sweet memory of his tenderness when he'd kissed my cheek, and the sexy, sensual glint in his eyes when he'd given me those flowers the day he'd visited the workshop. His presence at my show had scared me, bugged me and, dammit, I just couldn't forget the stroke of his lips on my hand. I'd spent entire weekends with men who'd made less of an impression than had Fletcher. That really bothered me. I wanted to get him out of my head, but that seemed impossible.

"I'm glad the case has settled down," my mother said. "Now maybe you can relax a little and focus on your work."

"Exactly. Sales reports are great. There were massive advance orders for Fletcher's Gear. Even better than our projections, so that stores could stock up before Father's Day. If the Wolfman leaves me alone for a while, I'll make a dent into my debts and be able to pay AnnMarie's fees to get rid of the case. She's working on a game plan to handle Wolf right now."

Fortunately, I hadn't had other wet dreams involving Fletcher Wolf, so I was able to put the Fletcher Wolf problem into the correct perspective.

"Okay. How's Nat?" Mom asked.

"Excellent. We expect good grades this semester. We'll be down on Sunday, and she'll stay for a while."

"How about you? When are you going to take some time off?"

"I can't right now."

"Sweetheart, this isn't good," she said. "You haven't taken a decent vacation since you left school. And even then, you worked summers."

"I can relax later," I said. "Right now, I want to repay my loans and start making a profit. Then, I'll make as many licensing agreements as I can before I sell out. That way, I'll max out my financial potential. If I want, I can continue to design for the couture clients, but I'll have enough to retire from the mass-produced, ready-to-wear market. That's the plan, at least."

"If you say so, honey," my dad said. "You know that we're always here to help you."

I smiled. I'd never accept financial assistance from my father, who was on disability retirement, or from my mother, who devoted herself full-time to taking care of him. My seven-figure loans were too big for me to ever ask my parents for a bailout.

Nope, I definitely operated without a safety net, but I'd never let my parents know how close to the edge I danced. "Thanks, Dad. It's good to know you're in my corner."

"What have you found out about those phone calls?" my mother asked.

I winced, pressing my lips together. After Natalie had blurted out the story of the attempted break-in and the trap on the phone, we'd had a long talk about what Grandma and Grandpa ought to hear. It was a sensitive issue, since I believed that Natalie needed to talk with her grandparents about matters that troubled her. Still, she was old enough to handle adult information without talking to her grandparents about everything. At least, I hoped so. "Frankly, the phone company, the police and I are all stumped. The calls seem to come from various public phones all around the eastern seaboard, so it's not Kenney. It's probably just a glitch in the phone lines, and they're trying to track it down."

"What about the guy on the roof?" Carson asked.

"The good news is that the police don't think the phone calls have anything to do with the guy on the roof. But the downside is that there's nothing new. No prints, but he hasn't been back. Hopefully, it's all over. Whoops! Looks like the cab is at my workshop. I'll call back in a couple of days, okay?"

"Love you, honey!" My parents chorused.

"Love you, too. Bye, now!"

I clicked off my cellular, threw it into my satchel, paid the driver, and exited the cab. Then I noticed that my workshop's metal security door was ajar. What the hell?

Maybe Maggie had arrived earlier than I had. Unlikely, though, since she most often showed up at about nine o'clock. I usually got here first, at eight-thirty or so, depending upon the traffic, to disarm the security system and open up the workshop. That way, I could see which employees got to work on time and who lagged behind.

I walked inside.

It was as though I had stepped into an alternate universe. A chaotic, horrible universe.

My beautiful workshop had been trashed.

My entire body began to quiver uncontrollably. I couldn't breathe, but my pulse began to race. My hands seemed to lose all strength. My satchel fell from my sagging shoulder, landing on the floor with a thump.

Not a single piece of furniture remained upright. Every dressmaker's dummy had been upended, with torn scraps of partially sewn gowns and jackets hanging off them in shreds. Every computer monitor had been smashed.

I was in a state of shock. When I could, I went further into the room. My boots crunched on broken glass from the screens and slipped on rags and tatters of the expensive apparel which had comprised my spring line. The big ceiling fans spun, circulating both air and random shreds of ripped fabric. They swirled, a colorful mist in front of my eyes.

Everything went blurry and I swayed, dizzy. I clutched the nearest object—a metal pillar—for support. I heard my pulse, fast and loud, beating in time with the ceiling fans. Flashes of darkness and light alternated with the pulse beats. The world was going light, then dark, then light again. My head throbbed.

No. I can't faint, I told myself, putting my sweaty forehead to the cool metal. If I fall down, I'll cut my hands. I need my hands to work. Oh my God, who would do this to me?

Is he still here?

Terrified, I stumbled outside and somehow managed to find my cellular to call 9-1-1. I was still shaking when Maggie came about five minutes later.

"Cara! What's going on?" Maggie looked surprised to see me collapsed outside the atelier.

"Don't go in, Maggie, not before the police get here." My voice felt raspy. I struggled to find air, my throat too tight and tense for a single oxygen molecule to reach my lungs.

I dropped my head between my knees, again hoping I wouldn't faint. Dear God. Months of work, trashed. Thousands of dollars of equipment, gone. Records—oh, Lord, if he'd destroyed the computers, I wouldn't have any records of sales orders to send to the factories, or even copies of my drawings for the next show. Cara Fletcher Couture would come to a complete stop. I'd lose everything, and, despite insurance, would certainly have to declare bankruptcy. Except—

"Maggie!" I jumped up and grabbed Maggie's sleeve. "Do you have the flash drive backup to the computer?"

"Sure," Maggie said. "I download every night. You know that. What the hell's the problem?" She again reached for the door.

"Go in and look. But I'm warning you, it isn't pretty. And don't touch anything!"

After poking her head inside, Maggie let loose a truly admirable stream of curses. Despite my full-blown anxiety attack, I was impressed.

Maggie jerked back outside. "Who the hell did this?"

"I don't know. Kenney, maybe. Trent Whiting. I don't know!" On the verge of tears, I waved my hands around in panic and despair. All I had ever wanted was to make beautiful clothes. Why did so many people hate me? What had I done wrong?

"What about Fletcher Wolf?"

"Oh, no," I said. "He wouldn't do something like this. This doesn't seem like his slick, smooth style."

"I'm not so sure. Didn't AnnMarie tell you he's a corporate raider? This looks like a raid to me!"

"Where's that flash drive?" I asked. "I need to see it, Maggie, right now. Did you update it last night?"

Maggie took out her keychain, displaying a small, flat tab

linked to it. "Sure did, boss. Even if he wrecked every computer, all the data you need is right here. Every sketch, every drawing, every spreadsheet . . . and, better, every order."

"Insurance?"

"Ten million dollars worth. We're insured against every possible eventuality."

"So we're down, but not out."

Sirens screamed, heralding the arrival of two squad cars. I had calmed down enough to draw in a breath and to steel myself to give a police report . . . for the second time in less than three months. This is almost becoming routine, I thought bleakly.

Hours later, after the crime scene investigators had come and gone, I tried to send everyone home. I didn't want my employees to see me weepy and miserable. They refused, choosing to help me clean up the workshop. I could hear them downstairs, talking in hushed, serious tones as they righted mannequins, set up drafting tables, fixed chairs.

Much of the less expensive equipment could be salvaged. The vandals couldn't destroy the sturdy chairs and tables, but the computers were destroyed, especially after the fingerprint experts had dusted them with a fine, black powder in order to lift prints. Every machine in the shop was garbage, fit only for a dump, including expensive, top-of-the-line sewing machines.

Every fabric swatch, each representing hours of work, had been ripped apart and scattered. Every sketch for the next show was torn to shreds. It was a disaster. If this had taken place in September or, worse, October, the extensive vandalism would have forced me to cancel the show, which could have destroyed Cara Fletcher Couture. With no new designs, there would be no new orders and, therefore, no company. As it was, we had a lot of work ahead of us, months of work that we'd already done once but would have to do again.

Maggie had gone to negotiate with the insurance company while I walked around the place with a police detective. The roar of a newly purchased Hoover wet-dry vac, sucking up broken glass and fiber strands, occasionally interrupted our conversation and contributed to my pounding headache.

"Let me show you this, Ms. Fletcher." Detective Briggs led me to a storage closet on the ground floor, where we kept unused bolts of fabric and trim samples. He pointed upward to the metal box housing the building's security system.

I could see that the wires inside the open box had been severed. "Cut off at the source. But how did they even get in to cut the lines?"

"As with most of these systems, there's a programmed delay," the detective said. "It allows you to enter the building and disconnect the security system via your code, or a key, without setting the system off. In this case, it seems as though the perpetrator, or perpetrators, knew enough about the system to enter by shooting through the front door lock, and to disable the system within the thirty-second delay period." Pausing, he took a deep breath. "Ms. Fletcher, you have to face the fact that this may have been an inside job."

"An inside job! That would mean that someone working here wants to hurt the company. I don't believe that. Jobs in this business are scarce. I treat my employees well. What about the theory that a business rival did this?" I avoided mentioning either Trent Whiting or Fletcher Wolf without more proof. I didn't know much about the law, but slinging around accusations to the police without proof was wrong.

Briggs hesitated. "That's a little out of my league. I suppose it's possible. Anyone with knowledge of security systems could guess, with a reasonable level of certainty, where the main coordinating box of the system would be located. Most people and businesses do put them in closets.

"But let me show you something." He led the way over to a dressmaker's form. I thought all my tears had been cried out, but I again became weepy as I looked at the dummy.

This particular mannequin held the remains of a yellow silk gown, its fluttery edges trimmed with Esme's embroidery in the vivid jewel tones I adore. The tiny, exquisite stitches had taken months.

Now, the bright silk was scored in a dozen places, with slashes so deep they carved rents into the dummy's padded body. Detective Briggs ran a thoughtful hand over the wreckage.

"There's anger here, Ms. Fletcher," he said softly. "This is a personal attack on you and your work. Watch your step."

Chapter Seven

AnnMarie Slye's office looked like her: sleek and powerful. Furnished with polished metal and glass, it had an impressive view of the East River. Dressed casually in a poet-style blouse and jeans, with hair tinted dark to match my mood, I squirmed in one of the uncomfortable, high-tech chairs as I tried to explain my worries to Ann and her investigator. "I don't want to sound as though I'm paranoid, but I'm really frightened. If I weren't heavily insured, I'd have to declare bankruptcy. Even so, there are losses money can't compensate."

The private investigator AnnMarie had hired, Shila Chong, nodded. "Many of my clients talk about the loss of a sense of security stemming from an invasion of this sort."

"Yes," I said with relief. The woman seemed to understand my concern. "And, combined with the other events like the attempted break-in and the phone calls, I'm beginning to feel, well, hounded."

"Now, this suspect you mentioned?"

I paused, wondering if I was making a big mistake. "I need absolute discretion."

AnnMarie interrupted. "As my subcontractor, Shila's bound by the same privilege which restricts me. Don't worry. This conversation is confidential."

"The prime suspect is a man named Fletcher Wolf, or someone working for him." Prime suspect, indeed! I hoped I didn't sound corny, but the situation did have elements of a

Perils of Pauline melodrama. "Wolf is suing me over the use of the name of my sportswear division. A few weeks before this vandalism, he toured my workshop. He could have spotted the security box then. And we talked about this particular dress." I took out a color photograph of the ruined canary silk on the slashed mannequin.

"Hmm," Chong said. "The majority of crimes are committed by males between the ages of fifteen and thirty-five. That would fit."

Ann frowned. "Wolf has occasionally used questionable tactics to take over other corporations, but I doubt that he'd stoop to this level."

"What questionable tactics?" Chong asked.

"There are rumors of corporate espionage and spying, but they're only gossip. He usually creates a situation where the target has no choice but to bow down. Buy-outs are his specialty."

"Who is this Fletcher Wolf?" Chong pushed back a lock of her black hair.

"That's the question, isn't it?" I managed a bit of a smile. "Every time I try to categorize our Mr. Wolf, he seems to change into something, or someone, else. He seems to have the iron hand in the velvet glove routine down pat."

"Wolf is the CEO and part owner of Fletcher Tool and Gear," Ann said. "His company is aggressive enough that he's gained a name as a corporate raider. I must admit he has a reputation for ruthlessness."

"And who else could it be?" I asked rhetorically. "Okay, I don't have a great relationship with my daughter's father, but he lives on the West Coast. And there's . . ." I bit my lip, realizing that perhaps there were more people out there who hated me than I had previously thought.

"What?" Chong asked. "Who?"

"Someone from my past showed up at my April show," I said. "A creep named Trent Whiting, who's currently using the name Trent Nevada."

"Trent Nevada?" Ann snorted with laughter.

Chong smiled. "What makes you think he could be responsible?"

"Nothing, really. But it seemed strange. He hasn't had access to my atelier, so he wouldn't know how to disarm the security system, or even where it is. And Wolf does. Did." I rose to pace.

"I don't mean to pry, but have you ended any relationships recently?" Chong asked. "Stalking and vandalism are typical bad acts of a jilted boyfriend. Some men just can't accept rejection."

"I'm too busy these days to date." I didn't want to tell Ann and her investigator that the only man other than my father who'd touched me in months was Fletcher Wolf.

Chong pursed her lips. "I'll check out Whiting and your ex . . . what's his name? Kenney Madden. But Wolf seems the most likely suspect. Have you talked with him about this event?"

"No. The last thing I want to show is weakness. That would be fatal."

With a glance at AnnMarie, Chong tossed a portable phone to me. "Call him. Let's see how he reacts."

I pawed through my satchel for Fletcher Wolf's business card. "I'm not sure that I really want to do this. There's no proof."

"But he's an adversary who knows the location of the security box. He or someone he employs could easily make the crank phone calls, too," Chong said.

"That's true," I said, anger flooding me. "He frequently travels from Wilmington to New York. Also, he's got hundreds, possibly thousands, of people working for him. What do you think, Ann?"

AnnMarie shrugged. "Wouldn't hurt. Use my speaker phone."

I punched the numbers of Fletcher's office into the phone with staccato stabs of my finger, as though I could stab the vandals through their dark, cruel hearts.

"Fletcher Tool and Gear, may I help you?" an aggressively perky voice chirped.

"Yes. May I speak to Mr. Wolf?"

"Which Wolf?"

I was momentarily startled. "Er, Fletcher Wolf, please."

"Who may I say is calling?"

"This is Cara Fletcher." After I was put on hold, I said to Chong, "There's more than one Mr. Wolf. Please check this out. Ann, your dossier didn't mention more than one Wolf."

Ms. Chong nodded. "I'll get on it as soon as I'm back in my office and fax you what I find out. You still have a fax, don't you?"

"Nope. Better messenger it over." I waited on hold with one knee bouncing restlessly, in time with my heart.

"Cara Fletcher, as I live and breathe."

Damn him, that Virginia accent was as sexy as ever. I repressed the heat sweeping my body at the mere sound of Fletcher Wolf's voice and said, as coldly as I could, "Mr. Wolf, I don't want to sling accusations, but . . ."

"But what?" Fletcher prompted after a pause. "Hey, are you on a speaker phone? Your voice sounds hollow."

"My atelier was vandalized last night, and I'm being harassed," I explained in a rush. "Frankly, you're the only person I can think of who wants to hurt me."

"I don't want to hurt you, Cara. Quite the opposite. Harassed? Are you all right?"

I couldn't help thinking of the kiss we'd almost shared, but told myself to cut the crap. "Oh, please. Let's not mince words. You're suing me, costing me thousands of dollars. I know you're unhappy about the Fletcher name, but I demand that you confine this war to the courtroom. If you and yours disturb my peace again, destroy my property again, attack my business again, I can't answer for the consequences."

"Exactly what do you mean, Ms. Fletcher?" His voice was cold as a corpse.

"Let your imagination run riot, Mr. Wolf. I'm not going to let you or anyone in your employ destroy everything I've built during the last ten years. Do you understand me? Just stay out of my way, and we'll all be happy."

"I'm an honest businessman and don't engage in dirty tricks to get ahead. Your case stinks and I'll blow you out of the water the next time we're in court."

"You lost last time. Are the use of tactics like vandalism and harassment the way you even the score?"

I heard his heavy, angry breathing. "Is this how you repay me for a continuance? I'm trying to calm this case down, not fire it up."

"You requested the continuance. I merely agreed. I'm sure you had your reasons. Did you need extra time to arrange to have my workshop destroyed?"

"For the last time, Ms. Fletcher. I did not destroy your workshop. I did not order anyone to vandalize it. And, for the record, I'm sorry it happened, but I'm not responsible."

"I don't believe you." Damn it, I could hear the beginnings of hysteria sharpening my voice, shrill and high.

"There's nothing I can do about what you think." And with that, Fletcher hung up on me.

After more inconclusive discussions, I returned to my workshop, my brain in turmoil. The more I thought about it, the more I doubted that Fletcher Wolf had anything to do with the vandalism. Maybe I was blinded by lust, but I didn't see him as two-faced. Complex, yes, but hypocritical, no.

But he wasn't the only Wolf in the pack.

I struggled to put aside my worries for the rest of the day, hoping for a productive afternoon. All went well until a heavy pounding on the workshop's metal door blasted apart my concentration. When it finally popped open, Natalie, dressed in her school uniform, confronted the intruders. "What the hell are you doing here? Get out! Haven't you done enough?" She tried to slam the door shut.

Fletcher shoved his foot inside before Nat could close it. "You shouldn't use that word, young lady."

Natalie turned, screeching, "Mo-om!"

I leaned against a pillar and watched Fletcher haul a companion into the workshop. I wondered who he was, but really didn't care enough to ask. I set my hands on my hips, preparing for battle. "It's okay, Nat," I called down to my daughter. "I don't expect you to be able to guard the door against the wolf and his pack mate."

Fletch raced past Natalie, shoved through my cadre of workers, and shot to the foot of the spiral stairs in three seconds flat. My breath caught in my throat and my heart pounded. What had I done? What was I in for?

He took the steps two-by-two, dashing to the top. The heavy pound of his shoes slammed through me like bombs dropping on a defenseless city.

He grabbed me by the arms. "Now," he said through his teeth, "I want you to look me in the eyes and tell me you think I vandalized this workshop!"

"I didn't lie to you!" I yelled back, glaring into his fiery amber gaze. "Look at this place! Don't act as though I'm nuts, don't condescend to me, and don't tell me what to think! And don't assault me!" I stamped down hard on his shoe with my heel. I was wearing the red and black leather boots I'd worn at the April show, and they had nice high stiletto heels.

I nailed him on the instep. Small satisfaction if he'd been the asshole who'd trashed my workshop, and if he wasn't responsible, he deserved it anyhow.

Yelping in pain, Fletcher let me go and jumped back. "Dammit, Cara, can't you wear normal shoes? Why the hell do you cram your feet into those ridiculous boots?"

A giggle interrupted his tirade. "That's what I told her." Natalie entered the loft behind Fletcher's unknown companion. "She'll never get anyone nice if she wears stuff like that."

I compressed my lips into a thin, tight line. "Natalie, please get your book bag and start your homework, pronto. Use one of the empty desks downstairs."

My daughter's body language expressed the sentiments of children all over the world when excitement is in the air. Something was going on with the grown-ups in the loft, and she wanted to be there. She took a few tiny steps in the vague direction of the staircase as her eyes darted from one adult face to the next.

I wasn't having any of it. "Now, Nat."

"You heard her," Fletcher said. "Where's your bag?"

"Don't tell me what to do," Natalie snapped. "You're nothing to me."

"Natalie." I struggled to maintain control, but my voice rose. "Now, I said."

Nat poked out her lower lip, but found her bag, which sat by the teal leather armchair, before slouching down the stairs.

As soon as she left, I turned on Fletcher. "Do not," I said through gritted teeth, "do not, under any circumstances, ever attempt to discipline Natalie. You know nothing about my child. Leave her to me, okay?"

"Just trying to be helpful." Fletcher shrugged.

"I don't need your kind of help."

"I didn't vandalize your workshop, but I see that someone

did." His gaze took in the unnatural emptiness of the atelier. Gone were the trashed mannequins and the destroyed machines. I'd even had to lay off some of my people, which made me feel even worse about the situation. He continued, "It wasn't me. Damon, my brother, is here to tell you that we haven't been to New York all week."

He gestured to a slender man who greatly resembled him, except younger, with sable hair and eyes as green as today's contact lenses. Instead of a business suit like his brother's, Damon wore jeans and a black leather jacket, which gave him a dark and dangerous look.

"Ah, yes. Damon." I said sweetly. "Or should I call him 'Damon the delinquent'? I heard about Damon from the investigator I had to hire. She found that dear Damon has a criminal record from eight years ago for stalking and vandalism. I take it back, Fletcher Wolf. I'm sure I did, indeed, wrongly accuse you. Your delinquent brother is now my prime suspect. Where were you two nights ago, Damon Wolf?"

Damon Wolf went white to the lips. His fists clenched, and every muscle in his taut body tightened even more. For the first time, I feared for my safety, but Fletcher intervened. "Hey, Big D, I'll handle this. Go down to the car. I'll be right there."

Damon gave me a long, thoroughly nasty scowl before he stomped down the stairs. If looks could kill, I'd have been pushing up daisies in seconds flat. Concern crossed Fletcher's face, quickly repressed, and that bothered me even more. Did Fletcher know something about his brother's hot temper that I didn't?

An uneasy silence reigned until the slam of the metal front door told us that Damon had left. Fletcher immediately started in on me. "Look, you don't have the monopoly on anger and guilt-tripping. Just to let you know—not that it's really any of your business—Damon's arrest when he was in college stemmed from a situation with a girlfriend. The young lady became pregnant. Rather than marry my brother, which was what he wanted, she instead chose to terminate the pregnancy. Damon didn't take it very well. Yes, he did vandalize her car, trying to prevent her from getting to the clinic where she got her abortion. Yes, he stalked her. He followed her to the clinic. He's not proud of what he did, but my brother's no criminal."

Shit. I'd totally misjudged the situation, and Damon. I turned and sprinted down the stairs. Though my high, spiky heels weren't designed for running, I nevertheless took the narrow metal staircase as quickly as I could, then dashed outside, letting the metal security door fall closed behind me.

I found Fletcher's car easily. Parked less than a half block away, the long, shiny limousine stuck out like a sleek black panther in this scuzzy part of Manhattan. To my surprise, Damon wasn't alone. Ella Langer, her blonde hair teased to a cloud, stood with her back to me. Even so, I knew who it was; Ella had a distinctive body and stance, one that had made her one of the most successful plus-sized models in history. From my angle of approach, I could see Damon's green eyes riveted on Ella, who was dressed in a peach linen suit and heels.

Then his gaze met mine, and his eyes turned chilly as an icy mountain stream.

Turning, Ella stretched out her arms. "Cara, darling! I came over as soon as I heard."

I gladly fell into her warm embrace. "Bad news travels fast. Who told you?"

"Andrea Covarrubia. I'm so sorry. You must be devastated."

I tried to smile. "I've had better weeks."

"But the fall show will go on, won't it?" she squeezed my hand.

"Oh, yes. We have plenty of time. This setback won't destroy us." I looked past her to Damon, whose scowl would have suited a death-row inmate about to sit in the chair.

"Oh, good." Her relieved expression said it all. I could expect a parade of models rolling in to politely ask if a source of income had dried up. I couldn't blame her. Though she was at the top of her corner of the profession, I doubted that she earned as much as her skinnier colleagues, regardless of her talent and sweet nature.

"All right," she continued. "I'll just run along. I'm sure you're very busy. Lunch next week?"

"Love to." I let my smile fade as Ella flagged down a cab and left.

Alone with another of the mysterious Wolf clan, I had to face Damon. According to the investigator, even a third Wolf ran with the pack, Griffin. Although he wasn't on the suspect list, I hoped I'd never meet Wolf Number Three. The first two Wolf brothers were trouble enough: thorny, prickly, difficult, unpredictable menaces.

Damon, a younger version of his brother, leaned against the hood of the limo, staring moodily into space.

I hesitated. What approach could I take, after having said something so unforgivable? "He told me. I'm sorry."

His scowl deepened. "I'm none of your business, and I don't need your pity."

His fury felt like a slap to the face, but perhaps I deserved it. I held myself steady as I said, "You don't have it. I like to think of myself as an honorable person, Mr. Wolf. I'm merely doing what's right." I turned and went back into the workshop. My conscience was cleared but I still had a mystery to torment me. If not the Wolf or one of his littermates, then who?

Looking up to the loft as I reentered the building, I inadvertently met Fletcher's eyes. As usual, they revealed nothing, but the strong lines of his face seemed softer, as if he sympathized with my plight. Why? I approached the steps to my office with a mounting sense of confusion and helplessness roiling in my belly. Another panic attack threatened, and I fought to keep my mental balance.

I passed Natalie seated at an empty desk, working on what must have been one of her last homework assignments of the school year. "Good girl, Nat," I murmured and stopped to stroke my daughter's hair, which had fallen out of her French braid. I started to fix it. "I'm sorry I yelled at you, sweetheart."

"It's not your fault. He's to blame." She jerked a thumb up to where Fletcher stood, scrutinizing the scene with the attitude of a sultan surveying his domain. When our eyes met, he smiled down at us and disappeared.

"I'm not so sure. I'm starting to believe that neither Fletcher nor his brother is responsible." I finished the braid and wrapped her scrunchie around the end.

"He sued you. He wants to put you out of business. If not the werewolves, then who?" She fiddled with the braid.

"I don't know, sweetie. But we'll figure it out, you and me. Okay?"

"Okay." Nat turned back to her homework, but I could tell she wasn't in a positive frame of mind. When she chewed the end of her braid, she wasn't happy.

I clumped heavily up the metal stairs, and when I reached the top, I thought I could see Fletcher moving away from Maggie's desk toward my drafting table, eyeing today's design. But he had a distant expression in his eyes that suggested to me that he wasn't admiring the feather-trimmed evening suit I'd created. What had he seen on Maggie's desk?

This could be serious. Maggie was my executive assistant and ran everything pertaining to the business end of Cara Fletcher Couture. I didn't particularly want Fletcher Wolf in possession of any potentially damaging information about my company, from which money had been draining like a dam's glory hole.

I strolled over to check, finding nothing amiss on Maggie's desk. Briefcase closed, laptop shut with no lights flashing, no papers strewn around her desk with red figures marching in bleak columns.

"So what happened?" he asked.

"I apologized, he was surly, and so's Natalie." I let myself collapse into the cracked leather chair near Maggie's desk.

"He certainly isn't more upset than I am. Look, you just can't call people up and make wild accusations, no matter what your attorney says."

I felt red embarrassment flush my face and neck.

He noticed, of course. "Gotcha, honey."

I narrowed my eyes and pressed my lips together. He sat down beside me, perching on one of the wide arms of the chair. "How much did you lose?" His voice was soft.

My body jerked with shock before I could control myself. "I'm not sure I should discuss this with you, Fletcher."

He smiled. "I'm glad you used my first name. Did you know it's the first time?"

I closed my eyes. "No, I haven't thought about that."

"My nickname is Fletch. Feel free to use it."

"Whatever." I flapped a limp hand in the air.

"Tell me." He rested a warm palm on my shoulder, and I didn't flinch at his touch. He felt good . . . too good. "How much did you lose?"

I glowered at him.

"I can find this out if I want. Secondly, of what use could this information be to me in the context of our case? Come on. Tell me."

I sighed. "Peace of mind, worth billions. Equipment . . . I'm not sure. Eighty thousand or so. The books . . ." I rubbed my face. "There were some expensive items there." I waved at my now-empty bookcase.

"Oh, all your beautiful books. I'm sorry."

He sounded sincere, and his empathy touched me. I tried not to cry. "I had antique tarot cards, signed volumes by Cartier-Bresson . . . oh, perhaps ten thousand? Clothes for the fall show, worth easily over a hundred thou."

"That much? I had no idea."

"Well, yeah. Think about it. I've got twenty people. The designs and clothes made during the last six weeks were trashed. It's simple mathematics. I'm not counting overtime, my time, or Maggie, either."

"Where is Maggie, anyway?"

"Out purchasing new computers."

I let myself slump back into the comfy old chair. Part of me knew that revealing my vulnerability to Fletch was a big mistake, and more of me didn't care. I just didn't have the energy to fake womanpower at this moment.

I closed my eyes, and a finger stroked my jawline.

My eyes popped open.

His golden gaze was steady, calm. "Do you remember when we nearly kissed?"

My heart jolted, banging against my ribs. "Yes," I whispered.

"Then how could you think I'd tear this place apart?"

Mind blank, I didn't have a word to say.

"I've let this situation ride for too long. You need a reminder." Slipping his hand over my nape and into my hair, he eased my head back, tilting my chin toward his lips. Our eyes met; his gaze was gentle, yet mesmerizing. His other hand trailed along my collarbone, exploring the neckline of the poet's blouse.

My skin tingling, I sucked in a breath.

He teased one button out of its hole and helped another slip free, then slid one finger between my breasts.

The tingle became a sizzle. I lifted my face toward his and kissed him.

Heaven, the warmth of his mouth on mine. Then a more intense pleasure as our lips opened, and we began to soul-kiss as naturally as children licking lollipops.

I grabbed his lapels to bring him in closer. Our tongues met in a languorous dance, and my sex-starved imagination took flight. I pictured myself seated on him in the comfortable old chair, my legs spread wide over the padded arms, while he rocked in and out of me, deeper and deeper, with his golden eyes reaching inside me, deeper and deeper . . .

My body clenched with need, and my hips involuntarily bucked. A husky moan broke from his throat. Jolted out of my X-rated fantasy, I pulled away.

He looked as startled as I was. He'd shared my intensity, and I bet he'd been as shaken as I by the kiss.

"Remember." He strode toward the stairs. Before he left, he turned and winked at me, jaunty as a sailor on leave.

I chuckled. The man sure as hell didn't lack gall. My instinct that he hadn't been the culprit behind the vandalism firmed into a certainty. But he had a reputation for boldness and manipulation, didn't he?

I don't really know him, I thought. He could be the kind of nutcase capable of ordering the destruction of the workshop and then kissing me as though he was a diabetic and I the insulin he needed to survive.

I'd never been kissed with such intentness, such savagery. His mouth devoured, devastated . . . The caress of his fingers, the flick of his tongue in my mouth . . . I closed my eyes, unable to resist wondering if he were as talented in bed as he was out of it. Good God. This man had the potential not only to rip my world apart, but to tear my heart into tiny pieces that could never be put back together. If he wanted me, he'd have me. My body would never resist his if he truly wanted to seduce me. I'd fall like the proverbial virgin on prom night.

Chapter Eight

It took a whole lot of effort, screaming and cajoling, but I had managed to hustle Natalie out of bed early enough to catch the train to upstate which would leave Penn Station at seven-forty in the morning. We'd showered the night before, with me adding purple streaks to my black hair. I wore matching contacts for a fun, witchy look.

Clutching her pack, Nat leaned against me while we waited in the long line for tickets at seven o'clock. I had just my satchel, because I planned to stay only one night. For that, all I needed were fresh panties, extra socks and another top. I'd wear the same black skirt and sandals two days in a row, and could borrow toiletries from my mom. Nat, who would stay longer, wore jeans, a denim jacket and had God-knows-what stuffed into her pack. I hadn't time to monitor what she'd picked, figuring it didn't matter. The Finger Lakes aren't a Third World country, and if she needed anything, we could buy it for her.

Penn Station, always crowded, looked like a "Where's Waldo" picture this Saturday morning. The schools had closed for the summer, so I bet that folks wanted to leave the city for vacations. Because tomorrow was Father's Day, a lot of people planned to go out of town to see their dads.

New Yorkers came in all shapes, sizes, colors and cultures, and there was at least one of each type or more at Penn Station. I checked out kids in leather billed caps, like baseball caps, glittering with fake bling. A new trend? A street person ambled past, keeping a weather eye out for station security. The scent of pastries wafted from a vendor's stand, making my stomach rumble.

Finally at the head of the line, I fumbled for a credit card.

The woman behind the window tinkered with some of her electronic playthings and, after a few moments, said, "I'm sorry, ma'am. The credit limit to this card has been exceeded."

"What? You must be mistaken. I pay this card off monthly and I haven't used it for weeks."

"I'm sorry, ma'am, but I can't accept this card." The woman handed it back. The plastic clicked against the shelf separating us.

"I don't get it," I muttered as I put the card back and pulled out another. "Okay, no problem. Try this one."

The woman went through the same routine while I found one of my purple pens in the satchel. Ready to sign the slip, get our tickets and board the train, I could already taste the excellent coffee I wanted to order in the club car to sip as we watched the countryside go by on the way to Syracuse. "Umm," I hummed, imagining the flavor of fresh French roast.

"I'm sorry, ma'am. You're over the limit on this card, also."

"Huh?" What the heck? "That's not possible. I don't use this card at all!"

"What's going on, Mom?" Curious, Natalie leaned over to see.

"Nothing you need to worry about, honey." I found a third card and handed it over. Same routine, same result. Amazed, angry and suspicious, I checked my watch and, aware of the murmurs and mutters in the restless queue behind me, said, "Let's use cash. It'll clean me out, but we need to get this train. It's the only one for hours."

As Natalie trotted behind me to the platform, my mind seethed. As soon as we sat down, I took out my cell phone and punched in the investigator's phone number. I left Shila a voice-mail message, marking it urgent, with my cell phone number and my parents' home phone number as well. But I didn't want to wait until Monday to contact the card companies, so I entered the 800 number on the back of one of the cards.

After waiting several minutes, I realized that customer service might not be open on a weekend. I punched in the number to report a lost or stolen card. Maybe someone there would help me. I hoped I wouldn't become stuck in the maze of a voice-mail system.

Only a few minutes passed before a pleasant-voiced fellow came on the line. "Your card number, please?"

I wondered how the majority of callers would respond to the question. Wasn't this the number for lost cards? I told him my name and card number, then explained the situation.

"This is quite common, Ms. Fletcher," he said. "We urge all our customers to avoid inadvertent dissemination of their card number."

I could hear soft clicks, as though he tapped on a computer keyboard.

"Is there any way someone could have gotten hold of your number in the past few days? All these purchases were made by phone since Wednesday."

"No. Yes." The knowledge of how this latest disaster had been orchestrated burst on me like a stink bomb exploding. "My workplace was vandalized Monday night. When I came in on Tuesday, every piece of equipment and paper had been torn apart, including the stuff in all the desks. The vandal must have found my credit card information." My back molars ground. This criminal had made my life a living hell, and I'd get him.

"You'd better cancel all your cards," the man said. "We'll excuse the debt if you send us a copy of the police report."

"No problem. Believe me, my investigator will be calling you to get all the information you have on these charges. We need to get to the bottom of this. But how could they have run up these huge bills in such a short time? They maxed out at least three cards with five figure credit limits!"

"Let's take a look at these charges. Airline tickets, jewelry, even a motorcycle . . . there's some expensive items here."

"Are the phone numbers available?"

"Yes, and the addresses, too. But they're all different."

"You don't sound surprised."

"I'm not. The thieves get the card numbers and sell them. Credit card theft is a huge industry."

My mom, Jenna, picked up Natalie and me in Syracuse, and after a brief visit with my dad, I headed out for a walk to relax. My parents lived near the shore of Owasco Lake, and visits always calmed me down. Maybe it's the negative ions around water, but there's something about the Finger Lakes area that just makes me a happier gal. I'd had a great childhood roaming the woods near my house. I bet it's one of the reasons I'm creative. I had a lot of free time to play, fantasize and dream.

Later, Mom and I drove to Ithaca to a farmer's market to buy strawberries for the special brunch we planned for Dad on Father's Day. I love farmer's markets, and this day was particularly beautiful. The weather had turned sunny and mild, with the warmth bringing out the scents of the berries and other fruits. The mid-seventies temperature brought a lot of people outdoors, so we were part of a happy crowd in search of flowers, fruit, or just a snack.

I reached a display of honeydew melons and stopped. The delicious aroma of ripe fruit invaded my nostrils, a sweet flood. Where on earth had the vendor found them? They certainly weren't in season yet in upstate New York.

I hefted one of them in each palm, trying to decide between

the two melons, and sniffed the stem end of each. Both smelled succulent and tasty. Though of a like size, the one in my left hand was heavier, meaning that it would probably be juicier. Smiling, I got in line and waited for my turn to pay.

I finally started to relax. It only took getting out of town for a few hours. Maybe Mom and Dad are right, I mused. I ought to take a vacation, just hang around the lake for a week or so—

I stopped, the honeydew still held poised in one upraised hand as the short hairs at my nape prickled. The haunting sensation was, to say the least, unwelcome.

I dismissed the feeling. Not here. Not now. Impossible.

Mom nudged me. "Hunk alert!"

I stared. " 'Hunk alert?' Where did you learn that phrase, Mom?"

"Never mind. Just look at that man. He's ogling you as if you're the last woman on earth."

I lifted my gaze to meet a pair of familiar, yet disconcerting amber eyes. Fletcher Wolf regarded me from across the fruit stand with a small smile twitching the edges of his mouth. I looked away from that disturbing sight, then back. I couldn't help noticing that his faded jeans outlined an impressive bulge right where it ought to be. I yanked my attention back northward to the T-shirt which outlined every sculpted muscle, while I involuntarily relived our kiss just a few days before. His male scent, the gentle caress of his fingers on my neck, his mouth on mine . . . the memory shuddered through my body as though he were making love to me.

Damn him, his stare was downright proprietary. He stripped me with his smile, making an electric tingle run through each of my nerves from top to toe, something which only Fletcher could do. My nipples beaded although the day was unseasonably warm, rasping pleasantly against my shirt. His scrutiny dropped to my chest as I replayed one of my favorite fantasies starring

Fletcher Wolf. In it, he started with my breasts, nipping at the hardened tips before moving to my belly. Then he kissed all the way down, lingering between my thighs for a long, long time.

I started to sweat as though I were coming, and truth to tell, I was close. I lost my hold on the melon's smooth skin. It dropped to my feet and cracked open with a wet, ripe *splat!* The blank space inside my skull turned blue as I mentally muttered every four-letter word known to humankind.

Mom grabbed my arm. "Are you okay?"

"Yeah, I'm fine." Wrenching my gaze away from Fletcher's, I found a couple of dollars in my pocket to give to the fruit seller.

I looked back at Fletch, whose smile broadened. *He's enjoying this, the rat.*

He escorted an older woman around the crowded stand toward us. She was dressed in a tailored mauve shirtwaist and a charming, old-fashioned straw hat with a matching ribbon. They were trailed by Damon and another young man I didn't know. He had a pleasant, open face and wide brown eyes.

"Cara, I'd like you to meet my mother, Veronica Carter Wolf." Fletcher's voice flowed smooth as molasses flavored by the delicious Virginia accent I loved. "You've met Damon, and this is my youngest brother, Griffin. Mom, Griff, this is Cara Fletcher."

"Pleased to meetcha." Griffin, who offered a gentle handshake, had a younger, less confident man's shy sweetness. I smiled at him, wanting to put him at ease for no reason I could identify. He just seemed nice.

I had a far different effect on Veronica Wolf. "Cara Fletcher? The clothing designer? I'm more than happy to meet you. Your suits are marvelous." Her gaze traveled from the purple streaks in my hair to my purple eyes and on down to my gauze lavender tunic, which topped a black skirt I'd pieced out of floaty bits of silk.

I smiled. "Thank you. This is my mother, Jenna Fletcher.

Mom, please meet Fletcher, Damon and Griffin Wolf, and their mother, Veronica Wolf."

"You didn't mention your friendship with Cara Fletcher," Veronica said to her eldest son, plunging full tilt into the conversational gap. I liked her accusatory tone, and really liked watching Fletch squirm. "How did you meet?" Veronica asked me.

I looked the woman right in her hazel eyes. The day had taken an unanticipated but delightful turn. "Your son is suing me for fifty million dollars, ma'am," I said politely.

Veronica glared at Fletch.

"Anything to make the acquaintance of this pretty lady," he drawled.

That was really too much. "A simple 'hello' would have been fine, Mr. Wolf. And what brings you to Ithaca, ma'am?" I asked, attempting to shut out Fletch by turning toward his mother.

Veronica puffed up with pride. "We're here for the commencement exercises. Griffin received his doctorate of veterinary medicine from Cornell yesterday."

"Congratulations, Griffin. That's a great accomplishment." I was telling the truth. Cornell was one of the toughest universities in the country, and a D.V.M. from Cornell was special.

Mom echoed my good wishes to Griffin. "So you're spending the rest of the weekend packing?" she asked.

"Yeah," Griffin said. "We'll be headin' out tomorrow. We thought we'd take a break this afternoon, since we've been at it since six o'clock."

"Where will you practice?" Mom asked.

"At our family horse farm, Darkrider Farm, Virginia. That's what I've always wanted to do."

"Really?" Miffed, I realized that here was another factoid about the Wolf pack that AnnMarie's dossier and Shila Chong's investigations hadn't revealed.

"I've never visited Virginia. It must be lovely," my mom said to Veronica and Griffin, as Fletcher slipped between me and the rest of the group.

His eyes flirted. "An unexpected pleasure to see you. Do you and your mother often visit Ithaca?"

"Not together, though I imagine Mom gets here more often than I do. My parents live near Owasco."

"I'm glad to hear it's your family and not some other interest that took you away from Manhattan."

"What?" I stared at him. If he only knew. All I needed was a wimple to complete a nun's outfit, even though my randy thoughts wouldn't fit a chaste woman of the church.

"Why not? Do all the men in New York need glasses?"

"Oh, please. Quit flirting. You're suing me. You're not my buddy, my pal, or my friend. You just confuse everything when you pretend to be interested."

He laughed, his eyes twinkling like sunlight on water. "I'm not faking anything. Just you wait, everything's gonna turn out all right. You'll see."

I'd trust a predator to chase prey, but not to catch a meal by licking it to death. Despite the sexual tension that crackled between us, this leopard wasn't going to change its spots. Fletcher wanted to tear out my throat, but I had no intention of being his entree du jour.

"One day I'll find out what you truly look like." His hungry glance again swept me from top to toe.

"Fat chance," I said.

Veronica touched my arm. "It was very nice meeting you, dear, but we must be going. And don't worry about that nasty lawsuit. I'm sure it's all a mistake." Her voice grated as she glowered at her son.

I gathered that Fletcher had learned his daunting behavior at his mother's knee. I didn't bother suppressing my smile, realizing that she was about to nail his ass. Perhaps then the lawsuit and Fletcher Wolf would recede into my past and fade to a vaguely unpleasant memory.

Ten days later

At the gym after a long day of work, my mood matched Godzilla on a rampage. I'd received a Notice of Deposition that very morning, along with a demand for full financial information. AnnMarie Slye had told me that the demand could be limited to just the Fletcher's Gear division, but even so, the Wolf at the door would have far more information about the financial instability of the company than I wanted him to know.

The familiar aerobic exercises in my kickboxing class didn't take much attention to follow as I stepped, hopped, kicked and twirled. My mind ran like a mouse in a maze as I sweated my way through the routine.

What was Fletcher's angle now? When he'd looked at me at the farmer's market, he couldn't have been more blatant if he'd hired a skywriter. He wanted me in a way I'd never been desired, wanted all of me. I didn't want to be controlled by Fletcher Wolf or anyone else. Or did I need him in the same mad way?

Then he'd had the gall to tell me "everything's gonna turn out all right." Oh, really? For whom?

After the class ended, I went to the locker room and stripped off my sweaty T-shirt and shorts. I shivered in the cool air as Natalie, finished with her gymnastics class and shower, headed out. "Got money for the juice bar, Nat?" I asked her.

She fished in a pocket of her backpack. "Yep. I'll see ya out there." She left for the waiting room where I figured she'd follow her post-workout routine of a bagel at the juice bar while I swam and showered.

The litigation was turning me inside out, but Nat seemed unaffected, at least for right now. Her summer computer camp was full of other preadolescent byteheads, and she seemed to revel in the environment. She was making new friends, some of whom were—eek—*boys* she met at the coed camp. Though I was edgy about my daughter entering a world potentially full of spin the bottle and rainbow parties, I knew the step had to be taken. Computer camp had turned out to be perfect.

With Natalie settled for the moment, I decided to take my time. I pawed through my gym bag and put on a red maillot I found crammed at the bottom. I didn't often have time to swim, but always found the heated water calming. After I swam, I relaxed some more in the steam room and the Jacuzzi until I hauled my prune-y, wrinkled body to the showers.

The women's locker room, which contained the steam room, showers and Jacuzzi, was quiet; I'd outlasted everyone else. It was late, long after all the evening classes had finished. Even the die-hard workout freaks had gone to dinner or to congregate at the juice bar to flirt and gossip. I bet I was alone in the facility except for the staff at the faraway front desk.

That was the way I wanted it. Since Natalie's arrival, I'd rarely been alone. Although I'd die for my daughter, I still missed quiet times.

But after I shut off the shower, I heard footsteps. Damn. Couldn't I have a moment of peace, entirely alone?

Apparently not. I tried to stuff my resentment, telling myself that others were allowed to use the gym. But then I heard laughter. Husky, deep *male* laughter, along with clattering and banging, as though an intruding man tested the metal locker doors.

My flesh chilled despite the steam left in the stall from the shower. I grabbed towels off of a nearby hook. Wrapping one around my wet brown hair and the other around my torso, I mentally reviewed my options. Men didn't belong in the women's locker room. Should I see who it was and what he was doing? "A-hole," I muttered.

But dressed in only two small towels, I didn't have the Amazon attitude required for a confrontation. On the other hand, could I hide in the shower stall forever?

Heart pounding, I slipped out of the shower as stealthily as I could. If I could get to my locker quickly, I could use my scissors to hold off anyone stupid enough to mess with me. Or I could call for help. Come to think of it, wasn't there a phone in the locker room connected to the gym's front desk, for emergencies? In my opinion, a man in the women's room constituted an emergency. At least it was something I could legitimately complain about without seeming like a kook or a fraidy cat.

I took a deep breath, but still quivered with fear. Creeping out of the tiled area toward the carpeted hall lined with lockers, I was careful not to slip. I wanted to meet any stalker present in the locker room while upright and vertical. Sprawled on the floor was not an adequate defensive position.

Nerves shuddering with dread, I rounded the corner and caught sight of the lockers. One of them had been pried open, and stuff was strewn around the carpeted floor. "Dammit to hell!"

Though I'd told myself to be sneaky and quiet, I couldn't stop swearing loudly and at length. Of course it was my locker. Of course it was my satchel that had been searched and its contents scattered.

I grabbed the scissors, every muscle poised and tense. Again I heard that irritating, mocking jeer. The sound seemed to recede. A door slammed. Had the laughing thief left?

I tried to relax, but my fingers shook from the adrenaline rush as I gathered my things. My mood flamed to anger when I realized that my wallet was missing.

Damn, damn, damn. As I searched for his card, I wondered if

Detective Briggs would think I was a professional victim, a crank, or just plain jinxed.

Chapter Nine

The stalker was driving me clinically bananas. Okay, I was already a little nutty, but matters were getting worse.

At least no credit cards had been in my wallet—what for? They'd all been canceled, and no replacements had arrived yet from the credit card companies. Still, I'd kept all kinds of important items there. ATM and library cards, New York state driver's license, photos of my family. Assorted business cards, including those of Detective Briggs, AnnMarie Slye, Fletcher Wolf, and Shila Chong. The loss of a wallet-sized copy of my parents' wedding picture hurt a lot, along with the few, precious school photos of Natalie I'd begged from Kenney over the years. On top of that, my purple eel-skin wallet had been a high school graduation gift from my mom and dad.

The next morning, after spending several annoying hours at the department of motor vehicles, I sat at my desk and tried to gather the missing pieces of my life while Maggie compiled the financial information Wolf and Muckenmyer had demanded.

"The problem here is that I'm not sure where Fletcher's Gear ends and the rest of Cara Fletcher Couture begins."

I put an obstructionist bank teller on hold. "What did you say, Maggie?" Today, I saw that my normally immaculate assistant wore her hair clumped at the back of her head in a sloppy chignon. Stray wisps stuck out, making Maggie look as though she'd gone crazy with hair gel and an electrical outlet.

"I don't know what to give AnnMarie. For example, we

ordered fifty grand of this raw silk for men's sports jackets, but you didn't like the color, so they ended up as trousers and vests for Comfort Zone. How do I count that?"

The teller came back on. "One minute please," I said into the phone. I cupped my hand over the receiver and said to Maggie, "Just print everything out and messenger it over to AnnMarie. She'll figure out what to send and what to throw away. Write her a note about it."

I switched gears. "Yes, a new ATM card with a different number," I said to the teller. "Why do I have to close the account?" I couldn't stop my voice rising along with my temper. If I had to open a new account, I'd have to take a taxi over to the bank to sign new signature cards, then come back. Another hour or more stolen from my life while I still struggled to reconstruct the outfits that the vandal had destroyed. At the rate things were going, our fall show would be in January.

Sensing defeat, I sighed. "Okay, I'll be there in a half hour. Please have everything ready. Thank you." I clicked off. "Bitch," I snarled at the receiver before asking Maggie, "Anything else?"

"Nope. See you later. I'll be taking an early lunch."

"Adam, again?"

"Yes, Adam and Andrea are taking me to the Modelshop Café."

I raised my brows. "Hot stuff! Well, have fun." As I left for the bank, I contemplated the concept of Maggie Andersen and Adam Covarrubia. Talk about an odd couple! But that was fine, especially since Adam had appeared upset when he'd asked me out and I'd refused. For one thing, I didn't like him, and also, Natalie didn't need to see me with Adam, a freak from the word go. This was not the example I wanted to set for my daughter. Then I'd picked Jimmy Benton for the Fletcher's Gear ad campaign, a choice Adam couldn't have liked. If he was getting it on with Maggie, he must be happy with the situation, I reasoned as I hailed a cab. Fine. I didn't plan to climb the ladder of success while pushing others off of it, unlike a certain wolf I could think of.

I brooded some more about meeting Fletch at the Ithaca Farmer's Market. He'd looked great in jeans, dammit. I hadn't been able to avoid checking out his lower body. He'd amply filled out the crotch. And the view when he'd turned to leave . . . oh, yeah. Lean, perfect buns. Yep, Fletcher Wolf was one hell of a man, from top to toe. And entirely forbidden.

I couldn't completely eliminate the possibility that Fletcher caused all my current hassles, not just the lawsuit. When strung together, each simple crime became part of a series of carefully planned, well-orchestrated events. Perhaps he intended to break down my resistance, leaving me too weak, mentally and financially, to fight the lawsuit. Such a plan showed intelligence and ruthlessness, traits which he exhibited to an alarming degree. Most exasperating was the sexy, flirtatious act he put on whenever we met. No doubt he intended to further confuse me. Unfortunately, he was succeeding all too well.

I shuddered, remembering a psychology experiment I'd read about in high school about operant conditioning. Pigeons, trained to retrieve kernels of corn by depressing a lever, were later subjected to electric shocks along with the corn. The birds given random shocks continued to push the lever for a longer period of time than the animals that were consistently shocked. The poor pigeons were trapped in a cycle of fear and indecision, both attracted and repelled by the alternating stimuli.

I wanted to convince myself that I didn't crave the corn. Just as well that the thief had stolen Fletcher's business card. I didn't want his phone number. Too tempting.

My fruitless train of thought continued all the way to the bank, through the transactions, and back again to the atelier. I paid the driver and got out in front of the workshop. Thank

God I kept a cash stash at home or I wouldn't have been able to do anything. Now, I was halfway to resurrecting my life.

Inside the heavy metal door was yet another unpleasant surprise. Detective Briggs and several of New York's finest overran the workplace. They wore grim expressions.

"Detective, how nice to see you again." I pasted a gracious smile onto my face and headed toward the detective, right hand outstretched. All the while I wondered: What's he doing here? He can't have come out because of a stolen wallet!

Another officer clicked a handcuff onto my proffered wrist. "Cara Linda Fletcher, you are under arrest. You have the right to remain silent and not incriminate yourself. Anything you do say can and will be used against you in a court of law. You have the right to the presence of an attorney before and during any questioning. If you can't afford an attorney, one will be appointed for you free of charge. Do you understand your rights?"

Mouth agape, I was now certain I was losing my mental marbles. I sensed them, a jumble of brightly colored glass spheres bouncing around in the toilet bowl of my mind, ready to be flushed down the tailpipe of my rocking, rolling emotions to the sewer where I kept my nightmares.

I stared at the cuff on my wrist, then at the officers' somber faces. A tense, silent group of my employees awaited my reaction.

I lifted my chin. "May I ask what this is all about?" I fought to maintain dignity in the face of a rising tide of disasters which seemed destined to overwhelm me. I wouldn't be overwhelmed, dammit. I'd . . . I'd . . . whelm. Or something.

"Do you wish to make a statement?" the arresting officer barked.

"Yes, as a matter of fact I do." Pausing, I took a deep breath and drew upon all of the New York grittiness I'd acquired from living in the toughest town in the world for fifteen years. I got right into the officer's face. My mouth was bare inches from his and I glared into his eyes. "I hereby state that you are surely the biggest donkey's ass who ever lived. Now, please tell me why you have engaged in this exceedingly unwarranted action? How dare you come into my shop and treat me like a criminal?"

My voice rose as I let loose all the bottled-up rage and frustration I'd developed during the past weeks of torture by the vandal. "Just who the hell do you think you are? Release me immediately or my attorney will turn you into a small greasy spot on the ground. That is, after she takes your job, your home, your savings and your pension!"

"Okay, lady, that's enough outta' you. Take her away." He twisted me around to click the other cuff over my free wrist.

Before the arresting officer could drag me off to the pokey, Briggs laid a restraining hand on his arm. He turned to me. "Ms. Fletcher, Vice busted a motel room last midnight that was being used to sell drugs. Someone rented it using your name. Your driver's license and other identification were found there. How did that happen?"

"I have no idea," I said through a clenched jaw. If this kept up, I'd have to get caps because my teeth would be worn to stumps. "But if you'd bothered checking your own records, you'd know that I reported the theft of my wallet and ID cards last night at about eight o'clock. If you let me go, I'll show you my temporary license."

An "I told you so" look stole over Detective Briggs' face. "I'll make the call." He raised his brows at the arresting officer.

A bum came into view. How on earth had he gotten in? This one looked like the lowliest street person from one of the Bowery alleys. He even smelled of garbage, but when he passed me, smiling, I saw that his teeth shone white, straight and even, a sure tip-off that he wasn't a tramp at all. He elbowed the arresting officer in the side in a familiar fashion, then whispered in his ear.

"You don't say." The officer's eyes narrowed as he regarded me.

"Yep, sure do." The plain-clothed investigator retreated.

"What?" I asked.

The arresting officer slowly withdrew a key from his belt to unlock the cuffs. "You have a friend, Ms. Fletcher. I'm reliably informed that you were in your home by nine P.M. last night. Sorry, ma'am, but this was a big bust. Twelve ounces of coke and five of heroin."

"I don't do drugs." I rubbed my wrist.

"Her story checks out." Detective Briggs had returned from making his call. "Carlene Keith in the theft unit filed the report at 2200 hours last night."

"May I have my stuff back?"

"You have a temporary ID already," Briggs said. "You don't need the DL back."

"You said 'other identification.' I want everything back. Was there a purple eel-skin wallet? Some pictures?"

"I don't know."

"Look, I suggest you find out. I'd like to remind you, gentlemen, that I'm the victim here. I've been stalked. This workshop has been vandalized. Someone tried to break into my home. Someone has been harassing me with phone calls. Someone ran up fifty thousand dollars on my credit cards." Sick, but I almost enjoyed the self-righteous anger flowing freely through my body. "This has been going on for months. It's cost me over a quarter of a million dollars and is driving me and my child nuts. I'm the victim here, and from my perspective, your department is doing a piss-poor job. Now get out of my shop."

Applause from my coworkers and employees burst out spontaneously as I showed the officers out and slammed the door shut with a resounding bang. Remembering the mysterious undercover detective, I tore it open again almost immediately. He seemed to be both friend and foe. He'd rescued me from a trip to the slammer, but because he knew where I'd been the previous night, he was keeping me and Nat under surveillance. I didn't like that. No, I loathed that. Plus, it scared me.

I looked up and down the street, but it looked deserted except for police piling into unmarked vehicles.

Who the hell was he? I shuddered. Who the hell else out there was spying on me, hating me, stalking me? I headed to a phone to report this latest trauma to AnnMarie and Shila.

I didn't really care about what I was supposed to wear to the deposition at Muckenmyer's office. To hell with them all, I thought as I pulled on my denim skirt, which today fitted loosely onto my hips. No pantyhose because the early August weather was stiflingly hot and humid. I slapped a pair of blue contacts into my eyes and didn't bother with makeup. After dragging a brush through brown hair, I went to the kitchen.

Fragrant wheat toast popped out of the toaster with a metallic jangle. Nat spread it with her favorite peanut butter and jelly. I poured myself French roast from the preset automatic, popped two tranqs, and managed light chatter during breakfast. Even if my world was crashing down around my ears, Natalie didn't need to worry.

The entire year had been a financial disaster, and I couldn't figure out why. The reports Maggie churned out reflected ever gloomier news. She had no explanations, leaving me stumped. The clothes sold well—all divisions, all year—so poor sales figures didn't provide the answer. Sure, marketing had been costly, and the lawsuit and the vandalism hadn't helped, but there was no good explanation why Cara Fletcher Couture had, in just a few months, turned from an up and coming concern into a financial black hole.

Maybe it was all my fault. Organizations functioned from the top down, and my personal issues, starting with the trauma of the traffic accident, continuing with the hassles with Kenney, the stalking, the attempted break-in, and the thefts, had left me numb. Yeah, I went to work every day and turned out designs which my employees claimed were gorgeous, delicious, inspired even, but I knew I could and should do better. I stood at the top of the hierarchy. Everything came from me. If there was a multi-million dollar deficit, I had to shoulder the blame.

With breakfast over, I dropped Nat off at computer camp. Only then did I allow myself to slump in the back of the taxi heading for Muckenmyer's office. Despondency flowed through me like a sluggish, stagnant stream. I'd worked so hard. How could I have screwed up so badly?

Seated at a conference table in Michael Muckenmyer's office, I caught sight of myself in a wall mirror and winced. I looked like crap warmed over, especially compared to Fletcher Wolf, natty today in a summery linen suit with a pastel shirt and tie. Crisp, calm, self-assured and, despite the light clothing, mega-hot.

AnnMarie, imperturbable as usual in a navy suit which set off her platinum hair, started off the meeting on a jarring note. "Mike, I don't understand what's going on. This is supposed to be a deposition. Where's the court reporter?"

Mike steepled his fingers. "I have canceled the deposition."

Great, just great. I stood. "I suppose that means I can leave. Ann, please bill Mr. Wolf and Mr. Muckenmyer for your preparation time. Good day, everyone."

Fletcher got to the door before I did and touched my arm. "Please don't go."

Startled by the neediness in his voice, I stopped. What the

hell was going on?

"It's time we talked turkey about this case," his lawyer said.

I sucked in my lips. "It seems to me that you've dragged me here under false pretenses, wouldn't you say? Ann, what do you think?"

"I would have preferred notification of a change in plans. Mike, you're aware of the preparation a depo requires. If you have a settlement proposal, we're willing to listen despite your discourtesy." Ann turned to her paralegal, who still lugged several notebooks. "Dirk, you can return to the office."

Though reluctant, I sat, while Fletcher let out his breath with a whoosh. Relief? I frowned. What did he have planned? I was sure it wouldn't be pleasant. Again, I felt like prey.

"It's my fault," he said. "I didn't tell Mike until this morning that I wanted to call off the depo and confer instead." I glared at him, as did Ann. He added quickly, "I really think it's for the best." He shot me his stunning smile.

I frowned in return.

He didn't look the least put off. In fact, his smile grew.

"Fine," AnnMarie said. "What's your offer?"

"Initially, we'd like to review the situation and the evidence," Mike said. He sat back in his chair and assumed a professorial tone, as though he lectured a classroom full of law students. He had the look, complete with the glasses and the tweedy jacket, down pat. A-hole.

"First, we learned that Cara Fletcher, without engaging in a trademark or copyright search, began using the Fletcher Gear name approximately one year ago. Fletcher, here, received notification when he viewed a television commercial aired during the football playoffs early this year. Suit was filed less than ninety days later, defeating any contention of delay."

"We did do a search. It didn't reveal that 'Fletcher's Gear' is copyrighted or trademarked, though 'Fletcher Tool and Gear' is.

We didn't see a problem, and still don't. Plus, we haven't alleged delay," AnnMarie said, sounding testy. "But now that you've mentioned the issue, is there any reason Wolf didn't contact Cara Fletcher Couture to attempt to settle this issue before filing?"

"He did phone, as you well know. His efforts to discuss the matter were rebuffed."

"He didn't discuss anything," I said. "He threatened me, so I hung up on him."

Muckenmyer raised his brows. "We were persuaded that attempts to settle would be useless. Of course Cara has the right to use her own name, and acquiring proof that the interests of Fletcher Tool and Gear due to the similarity of the names were damaged would take time. Suit was filed within three months of the football commercial, which itself generated immediate problems for Fletcher Tool and Gear. Numerous confused customers called to order T-shirts, pants, and other products." Mike waved his hand in the air before he reached into a folder and extracted two sheets of paper. "Here's a compilation, week by week, of inquiries to Fletcher Tool and Gear for clothing. Mr. Wolf had to add two additional phone operators and lines to handle the load at an estimated annual cost of fifty thousand dollars."

I shifted in my chair and glanced at Fletcher. "That's peanuts to Fletcher Wolf."

He didn't say anything, but Mike lifted his eyebrows. "Fifty thousand dollars may be peanuts to you, Ms. Fletcher, but my client hasn't built up his company by tossing money away. Believe me when I tell you that you have caused a great deal of disruption to Fletcher Tool and Gear."

"Are you saying that fifty thousand dollars will make this case go away?" I asked. That was do-able. That would be nice.

"Hardly." Mike smiled, sharklike. "The problem you created

is ongoing, and increasingly expensive as you willfully continue to exploit the Fletcher Gear name and expand production."

"The judge said I could use my own name!"

"True," Mike said. "But he never said you could use the Fletcher's Gear name, and he reserved a ruling regarding confusion to the public due to the use of similar names. As you know, Ann, we commissioned a poll of past and present customers of Fletcher Tool and Gear."

Mike reached into his folder again and withdrew two bound reports. I gulped against a rising tide of bile flooding my throat. I had a feeling that the reports contained very bad news for me. Why else would he provide them?

"The data indicate that over fifty percent of Fletcher Tool and Gear customers believe that Mr. Wolf now manufactures T-shirts and sportswear in addition to gearshifts and precision tools."

I glanced at Ann. We had a trick or two up our sleeves, also. "This is an impression no doubt fostered by Mr. Wolf himself. Ann, please show Mr. Muckenmyer the orders from Fletcher Tool and Gear as well as the other materials."

Ann slowly opened her gray leather briefcase, milking the moment. With a dramatic flip of her hand, she tossed several eight-by-ten color glossies onto the polished wood conference table.

A wince crossed Fletcher's handsome face. The photos depicted his brother, Griffin, with his hands on either side of a pony's head, gentling it while Fletch himself sat on a split rail fence, grinning. The shot clearly depicted the Fletcher's Gear logo on the front of the T-shirt he wore.

"Looks pretty good on you, Mr. Wolf," I said, smiling. "Maybe I should hire you for the next ad campaign. By the way, Mr. Muckenmyer, sales figures show that Fletcher Tool and Gear purchased twenty thousand dollars worth of product from my company. That's a lot of T-shirts. Seems a mite inconsistent."

AnnMarie took over the argument. "Unclean hands, Mike. Fletcher Tool and Gear cannot, in good faith, complain about Fletcher's Gear while making volume purchases thereof."

"Mr. Wolf really didn't have a choice. He'd alienate his customer base if he didn't make some attempt to meet their demands. We're sure the court will accept this explanation. You can't claim bad faith when a businessman merely gives the customers what they want."

"Yeah, but why's he wearing my shirt?" I asked.

"I like your shirt," Fletch said calmly. "And I like this photograph. Is this my copy? My mother will love this shot of Griff. You remember my brother Griffin, don't you, Cara? You met him in Ithaca in June."

Ann nailed me with a hard, level stare. Her brows lifted so high they merged with her clipped, silvery bangs. Consorting with the enemy, said her steely gaze. I squirmed then relaxed as Muckenmyer shot Fletcher an equally nasty scowl. Fletch kept a mild smile on his face as he watched the interactions.

He was amused, the wretch. More than anything else, that scared me.

Fletch continued, "Griff helps out at the Assateague Pony Penning, when the wild ponies of the barrier islands are given exams by local vets, and excess stock sold at auction. We go every year. It's an exciting event. Surveillance, huh, Cara?"

I couldn't meet his gaze, but stared straight ahead. "I'm being stalked and victimized. It isn't fun."

"Yes, and it's cost you a lot of money. Upwards of a quarter million, right? But that's not the end of your financial problems." Fletch nodded at Mike to continue.

"The documents discovered to us were both complete and

informative." Mike opened a notebook, removing a stack of papers.

"Let me see that!" Seated between the attorneys, I was in an excellent position to grab the stapled stack from Mike. "Good God, Ann, you gave him everything!" Jumping to my feet, I glared at her. "I'd like an opportunity to speak with my attorney privately."

Mike waved his hand. "You can use my office. It's at the end of the hall."

I stalked out, Ann following.

Chapter Ten

Slamming the door of Muckenmyer's office shut, I wheeled to face my lawyer. "Ann, you sent him everything! Didn't you read Maggie's note?"

"I'm sorry, but I don't know exactly what happened. I was in trial in D.C. on a major patent case when the response to the document demand was due. One of the other attorneys in the firm took care of it. He must not have seen the letter. What did it say?"

I sagged into a chair, drawing a deep, shuddering breath. "I couldn't figure out exactly what they wanted, so we sent everything over to you. All of our financial reports and current records. The note told you to cull out the parts relating to Fletcher's Gear and to send only that!"

Ann swore. "How bad is it?"

"Awful. He knows exactly how vulnerable we are right now. Things are worse than ever, and I'm clueless. I just don't know where the hell the money goes. Maggie doesn't have any explanations, either. The clothes are selling like hotcakes, but we're more in debt than ever."

"This is bad. Everything we've learned today erases the advantage we had by winning the first hearing."

"He's closing in." I couldn't keep my voice from rising in panic. "He'll bring me down as though I'm a crippled doe."

"Cara, I'm sorry, but try to be calm. We're anticipating a disaster which doesn't yet exist, and may never. Let's just go back in there and listen to their settlement proposal. Avoid reacting in any way. We'll tell them we'll consider their offer and get back to them in a few days."

I made a point of stepping back into the conference room with a straight back and squared jaw. Finally, I wished I'd worn a suit. My casual garb may have affected the tenor of the meeting. Eying Wolf and his attorney, who sat with similar expressions of watchful patience, I changed my mind. The fanciest outfit wouldn't have made a difference. They'd meticulously crafted their presentation. Nothing had been left to chance.

After Ann and I sat, Mike picked up from where he'd left off. "We were about to embark upon a discussion of the precarious financial condition of your company, Ms. Fletcher."

"The financial condition of Cara Fletcher Couture is not your concern," I snapped, feeling like a caged tigress. "Get to the point. What's your settlement proposal?"

"In a moment. First let's discuss your losses, which are, er, stunning. Although you've sold ten million dollars worth of stock during the first two quarters of this year, you were unable to make a dent in your indebtedness of four point five million. Although payments are current, your debt actually grew to five point two million. The fact is, Cara Fletcher Couture is unable to prosper long term and, at this moment, won't survive a direct frontal attack."

I tried not to throw up as Muckenmyer brutally described what I already knew. The financial health of the company had gone from unhealthy to terminal. As he droned on, I began to loathe his professorial smugness. "Fletcher's Gear is the most successful line that your company produces. You're to be congratulated, Ms. Fletcher. In less than a year, your men's sportswear division has garnered an appreciable market share in a targeted, upscale group. However, we believe that we can show that the popularity of the Fletcher's Gear line is not just due to the admittedly high quality of the clothes and the designs. The fact that the Fletcher Gear name was recognized by a large portion of the public contributed to the success of the clothes. Mr. Wolf intends to share in that success."

"If all I have are debts, Mr. Wolf is welcome to share in them." I kept my fists under the table. I might clobber one of the lawyers if I didn't keep myself under control. How could Ann have screwed up so badly?

Mike Muckenmyer ignored my comment. "Structurally, it's not possible to split off the Fletcher's Gear line and eliminate it, partially because it's so successful and also because of the integrated structure of your company."

"The structure of my company is, again, none of your concern."

I had been uneasily aware of Fletcher hovering around this meeting, present but not quite participating. What's his game? I wondered yet again. Now he moved restlessly, spoke impatiently. "Mike, we've been arguing for what seems like hours. The only people who gain are you and Ann. Let's end this, now."

I tensed as Muckenmyer tossed a sheet of paper at me. I recognized his rudeness as a deliberate ploy to make me feel small, to demean me. What a jerk.

"Here's an estimate of the annual value of the Fletcher's Gear name to Cara Fletcher Couture, based on the comparative net sales of Fletcher's Gear and the other divisions. One million dollars, every year, give or take a few grand. So the damages to Fletcher Tool and Gear are one million dollars annually for an unknown period of time. That's legal damages, Ms. Fletcher, not damage or hurt in a literal sense."

One million dollars! The man was daft.

"Here's our settlement demand." Michael Muckenmyer lounged back into his seat. I leaned forward, then caught myself looking too eager. I made a show of flipping back my hair as I propped my elbows on the table.

"We will license the Fletcher Gear name to Cara Fletcher Couture for an annual fee of one million dollars, rising to one point three million in five years. Thereafter we'll renegotiate based upon the same comparative sales data we've used today."

I laughed with disbelief, then rose. I bit my lips, trying to avoid letting loose every colorful expletive I'd learned from Manhattan's endearing street people. "If that's your best offer, we're outta here. Come on, Ann." I turned and made for the door, my vision clouding with tears and shock. That rat bastard knew I couldn't do it!

As I touched the doorknob, Muckenmyer spoke again. "Ms. Fletcher, I imagine you don't relish the thought of adding to your debt load. But consider this: purchasing the name is productive. You spend money, you make money. The tens of thousands you waste on this litigation is unproductive and, in the end, futile."

Compressing my lips, I tugged open the door, eager to leave before I fell into complete hysteria. As I stepped out, I heard Ann say, "Mike, for how long is this offer open?"

In the hall, I fumbled for a tissue and dabbed my eyes while I listened for Muckenmyer's response. "Until midnight tonight."

"What?!" Ann's voice jerked up so high it squeaked. In another situation, I would have thought it funny. Instead, I walked away while she continued to protest. "You know we need more time than that to evaluate the proposal and run the numbers. Forty-eight hours at minimum!"

"There's another alternative." Fletcher's soft, southern tone intruded like a gentle summer rain during drought. "Ann, sit back down."

I stopped walking. That voice. That beautiful voice never failed to grab me by the guts.

Fletcher stuck his head out the door. "You too, Cara. Come back in, honey."

Honey. I frowned. *What's that devil up to now?* But I allowed him to take my elbow and, with an almost courtly grace, reseat me at the table. Fresh out of good ideas, I felt that an alternative—any alternative—would be welcome, regardless of the source.

Fletcher poured a glass of water for me, offering it with a tender smile. "There's no need to fight, Mike, and there's no need to destroy Cara's company. We all know she can't afford to pay me a million dollars a year. That's an absurd demand."

I blinked. Perhaps there was some hope, if client and attorney didn't agree. Maybe a chink had developed in the armor-clad fastness of Fletcher Tool and Gear's case in the form of a dispute between Wolf and Muckenmyer. A small thread of excitement began to wend its way up my spine.

Fletcher wandered the room, ending up at the window. He stared out a moment as though marshalling his thoughts. He turned. "Cara, I have a lot of respect for you. I have a lot of respect for the clothes you make." His molasses voice hardened. "I do not respect the way you do business."

Youch. That hurt. "I'm an honest person, Mr. Wolf. What's not to respect?"

"Most people are in business to make money. You're losing money, year by year. It's not the clothes or the designs." He sat down across from me, pinning me with those amazing eyes. "Now, I can't make clothes. Hell, I can't even design tools or gears! But I do know how to make money."

I wasn't impressed. The man had mastered the game, but big deal. "What's your point?"

His intense gaze touched me, withdrew, touched me again, palpable as his hand on my arm. "We can make this a win-win situation for everyone. Do you know what a joint venture is?"

"Umm, when two people get high on pot?" I dredged up a weak smile.

"Very funny."

"Sorry. What I know about high finance could be written on a Chiclet leaving room to spare."

"Precisely my point. You're an artist, not a businesswoman."

"That was supposed to be Maggie Andersen's job." I slouched into my chair, sighing.

He shook his head. "Your personal assistant is out of her depth."

"She has an MBA from Harvard."

"So what? A lot of people do. That and a dollar will get you a cup of coffee at a cheap diner. She has no track record." He leaned forward. "But I do."

"What do you mean? I wish you'd stop beating around the bush. What, exactly, do you propose?"

"Accept my financial expertise in exchange for dropping the lawsuit and a small stake in your company."

"What?" I jerked upright. "You want my company! This is what it's always been about, isn't it?"

"It's a great solution for both of us. I can turn your firm around, but I won't do it for free."

"Corporate acquisitions, didn't you tell me, Ann? At our first meeting, you said Fletcher Wolf is a corporate raider."

Fletcher beetled his brows, anger shadowing his features. "That's an unfair accusation. Every firm we've acquired has prospered. I haven't put a single employee out of work. I don't steal companies and suck them dry. I do the opposite."

"What about my job? If you own my company, what happens to me and my designs?"

"I won't own your company. I'd be willing to limit the deal to only Fletcher's Gear for the first year, with an option to renegotiate annually. When you see what I can do, you'll be more than happy to turn the entire business over to me." He gestured expansively. "As for you and your designs, I'd consider you the most significant asset of the company. True talent is a precious commodity. Think of yourself as a flower, Cara. You need room to grow, unfurl your petals. I can clear the clutter out of your life. Pull the weeds, so to speak, and give your talent space to bloom. That's the essence of joint venture. It's a team effort."

"This seems very vague." Rising from the chair, I began to pace back and forth, feeling trapped by the uncomfortable realities of the situation. I couldn't help my suspicions, sure that Fletcher hadn't become successful by being the touchy-feely cultivator of talent he wanted to appear. He radiated "predator," not "nurturer."

He shrugged. "Right now, yes. That's a valid point. How about this? I'll retire your debt or pay it off within three years."

Turning, my mouth dropped open. "The entire company's debt? All five million?"

"Five point two, actually, but what's a couple hundred grand between friends?"

"What's the catch?" I studied him, totally perplexed. I was as far out of my world as Twain's Connecticut Yankee at King Arthur's court.

"No catch, but if that's part of the agreement, you have to let me be CFO of your entire company, not just Fletcher's Gear."

"What?!"

"As I said, I can turn your company around, but I won't do it for free. And, to be honest, you have no alternative. You can't recall thousands of pieces of clothes and put new labels in. Plus, you spent more money on a print ad campaign using the Fletcher's Gear name. My name."

Another voice distracted me from my focus on Fletch. Muckenmyer. "I'm gonna win this lawsuit, and you'll lose so big your company and your dreams will be destroyed. Fletch is right. Settle or die."

Fear clawed at reason, reducing my world into a tight little tunnel with failure and bankruptcy at one end and Fletcher Wolf at the other. I took a deep breath, banished panic, and leaned on the window frame. "This is a big step for me. I've never thought about sharing my company with anyone. Letting the wolf in the door isn't part of my plans."

Fletch grinned without appearing insulted by the jab. "Most companies aren't owned by just one person. Mine included. You already share power and decision-making with Maggie Andersen, who, quite frankly, isn't competent to run your firm."

"Maybe." I felt like a starving woman offered rattlesnake stew. The stuff seemed strange; I didn't want it, but consuming the foul potion was inevitable. I guessed I'd pick up the fork and chow down, but I didn't want to commit myself right away. "How long do I have to consider this?"

"I don't know about you, but it's almost lunchtime and I'm tired of being in this stuffy office. Mike, why don't we get a bite to eat? We can talk some more, maybe hammer out some details."

I hesitated, seesawing between distrust and doubt on the one hand, and a dawning sense of hope on the other. True, I'd been disappointed and mystified by the quarterly reports. But why would Fletcher Wolf want to take on the problems of a small, struggling company whose product was so far outside his expertise?

I needed space, a moment of privacy to collect my thoughts and perhaps get some advice from people I could trust. "Where's the women's room?" I asked Muckenmyer.

"I'll go with you," Ann said.

Fletch rolled his eyes. "Women," he remarked to his lawyer.

"Can't go to the gal's room alone, always got to be a social occasion."

Mike nodded solemnly. "It's programmed into the chromosomes."

I used the facilities, then washed my hands. "Well, Ann?"

"It has some possibilities. We can tweak the specific terms so they're more favorable to you."

I tore off some paper towels. "I need additional input. Could you excuse me? I need some privacy for a few minutes."

She stepped out, and I retrieved my cell phone to call my parents. Funny how we turn into little kids under stress, but I needed my dad's level-headedness in a crisis and my mom's clear common sense. I got them on the line and explained the situation, minimizing the danger to the firm as best I could. I didn't want to worry them, but they needed enough facts to advise me.

"Remember, honey, you've never enjoyed the financial aspects of the business," Dad told me.

"But I'm afraid he'll steal my company right out from under me." I tried not to sound teary.

"Can't your lawyer prevent that?" Mom asked.

"She thinks she can, but she's really botched this case. What if she messes this up, too?"

"Has she made other mistakes?" Dad wanted to know.

"No, she's been great."

"Then trust the expert you hired," Dad said. "Put limits into the joint venture agreement that'll protect you. You might even consult another firm for a second opinion."

"That's a good idea." I found myself calming down. Dad had that effect on me. Always had. "I guess I just have to decide what I want."

"Honey, you've always said you just want to design and make

beautiful clothes," he said.

"Fletcher and his family seemed so nice," Mom chimed in. "If he can make life easier for you, why not? You can always leave and design for another company if you want."

I sighed. "I'm scared."

"It's okay to feel scared, honey." Mom, the pop psychologist.

"Just don't let your fear freeze you," my father added. "Consider this carefully. We'll be here if you want to talk again."

"How do you think this will affect Natalie?"

"If he can lift some of the burden off your shoulders, you'll have more time for Nat," Mom said.

"She's been uptight lately, because I'm so stressed, I guess." My belly churned.

"It seems to me that this joint venture thing could help you on all levels, honey. It wouldn't hurt you to have a man around, you know."

"Oh, Dad!" My voice rose in exasperation. "That's not a concern right now. I can't think about a relationship with everything else that's going on."

"It doesn't hurt to look around," my father said. "Jenna, didn't you say this fella's pretty good-looking?"

"Oh, Dad, stop it." I giggled, a little hysterically, and my parents joined in. Bless them for making me laugh. "But the whole idea was to be independent. Now some guy is going to be taking care of me."

"Sweetheart, be realistic. We live in an interdependent world," Dad said.

"And you told me that one day you'd sell your company or license your name. It's just happening faster than you thought," Mom said.

"Would you feel better if Fletcher Wolf were a woman?" he asked.

"Maybe," I answered. "But that's sexist, isn't it?"

"Yep," Dad said.

" 'Fraid so, honey," Mom murmured.

"I don't want to, but I guess I'm gonna bite the bullet and do it," I said. "I guess."

"It'll be okay, honey." Dad sounded confident and comforting. "Just bring the contract to Banner and Crayton in Syracuse and have them take a look at it. Make sure you know what you're getting into before you do it."

"I love you. Thanks for being here for me."

"Love you, honey," my parents chorused.

I took a deep breath and went back to the conference room. Fletcher smiled at me as I entered. "Ready for lunch?" he asked.

"Yep," I said.

"Okay. Cara, why don't you ride with me, and we can talk some more. Mike, we'll meet you and Ann at, umm, that sandwich shop near the park where we ate yesterday." Fletch grabbed my elbow and swept me out before Ann could say a word.

Fletcher's driver opened the limo door and held it, waiting. Fletch climbed in. Seated, he looked at me, his eyes glimmering from the dark interior of the limo.

Wolf in his lair. I hesitated and he beckoned me with an outstretched hand.

What was it about this man that made me so confused? The way he held my hand made me feel both secure and threatened at the same time. His plans for my business would result in bailout and takeover. The wildness in his eyes promised erotic bliss coupled with masculine possession.

Did I want to belong to Fletcher?

I settled on one side of the bench seat, a safe two feet away from him. He smiled at me and my heart jumped into my throat, blocking my breath.

The driver closed the door, shutting me in, alone with Fletch.

"Sam, take us to that place we ate at yesterday," Fletcher said, as the driver seated himself behind the wheel.

"Yes, sir." The limo glided into the traffic.

Depressing a button, Fletch raised the smoked glass panel between driver and passengers, still smiling at me. And why wouldn't he smile?

He'd set me up, totally. I'd been played by a master. Perhaps a takeover of my company was what he'd planned all along. *The sandwich shop where we ate yesterday* . . . where they'd probably hammered out the details of this morning's meeting.

"You do realize what this is about, don't you?" he asked.

"Yeah." I dropped my head into my hands. He was going to take everything away from me. Everything I'd wanted my whole life. I'd worked my ass off, and now Fletcher Wolf was a hair's breadth from taking it all.

I swallowed, feeling ill, then managed to raise my head. "I don't know if I can agree to the proposal."

"Why not? It's a perfect solution for both of us."

I closed my eyes. Hot tears lurked behind my lids and jammed my throat. Damn. I would not, could not, shame myself by crying in front of this man. Thank heaven I'd taken an extra tranquilizer. I'd have melted into a full-blown panic attack if I hadn't.

"Talk to me. Tell me."

I opened my eyes, willing the tears back to their ducts. "I don't know if I can explain."

"Try. Even if you reject this proposal, I have the right to know."

I fiddled with the heavy seam running down the side of my denim skirt. "When I was a kid, other girls dressed their Barbies in store-bought outfits, but I made mine."

"Is that so?"

"Yeah. I would rip out seams, add accessories, paint the fabric, even sew totally new costumes. I made Hippie Barbie, Disco Barbie, and even Punk-chick Barbie."

He shouted with laughter. "That's great. I wish I'd seen that. What did she look like?"

"Punk-chick Barbie had a neon-green Mohawk and a camo mini. Hot-pants Biker Barbie had a black vinyl jacket and boots. Corporate Clone Barbie . . . well, you can imagine."

He grinned. "Do you still have them?"

"Nope. I put the Barbies in an art display at my elementary school for parents' night. The owner of a local gallery saw them and gave me a show. He sold every one." I paused, recapturing my pride and self-possession. "I was eight."

He sat back. "All right, I'm impressed. What drives you?"

"I don't know." I hesitated. "I just know I have to succeed my way, alone."

"No one does it alone."

I leaned into the seat. "Baloney. You're alone. It's lonely at the top, but you like it there, don't you? We can't work together. We'll fight constantly."

"Listen, it'll work. I'm committed to you, Cara Fletcher."

What the hell was he saying? Though scared of what I might see, I dragged my gaze to his.

His eyes blazed, golden and bright with determination. "I'm committed to your talent and your company. We'll make it work. We'll be . . . we'll be . . . just like Adam and Eve." He winked.

With so much at stake, I wasn't going to flirt. "They got thrown out of Eden."

"Romeo and Juliet."

"They died, Fletch."

He threw his arms out wide. One of them hit the window. "There's just no pleasing you, is there? So we'll be like Lucy and Ricky!"

I was overcome by giggles. "You better hope not! Remember what Lucy did in the candy factory?"

He laughed with me, a good sign. "Don't worry. Cara Fletcher Couture will hum along like a well-oiled machine with me at the helm."

I calmed down. "You have a lot to learn about the couture business."

"I have the best teacher in the world." He caught my hand and kissed my fingers.

Shivers ran down my spine. What the hell was that about? I pushed him away. "Cut it out. Don't try to fool around with me while you're stealing my company."

"You don't get it, do you?"

"What I get is that you're trying to get my company through me."

Fletch laughed. "You have it bass-ackwards, honey. I'm trying to get to you through your company."

"Huh?"

"Think about it. You and me. Working together, with each other, for each other."

I clutched my hands together in my lap and closed my eyes. Confusion mushed my thoughts. Who was he kidding? "Please. This is too much. I just can't think about that right now."

"Fine. Think about this." He came in close and fast and kissed me.

Oh God, I loved his mouth. This man was the best kisser in the world. My heart danced with hope and my body thrummed with pure lust. My fate was signed, sealed and delivered. I'd have my hands full with Fletcher Wolf in my life. Complex and demanding, he'd challenge me on every level: intellectual, sexual, and, God help me, emotional. His need to run the show no doubt matched mine.

Both Fletcher and I needed to be on top. Who would win?

Pushing aside my questions, I slid one hand into his hair and grabbed his lapel with the other to pull him closer. He stroked my breast, and everything in me sparkled. I purred with pleasure, and he answered with a growl from deep in his throat. He played with my nipple, which peaked in response.

The limo stopped. He slid away from me, leaving me breathless and bereft.

Sam opened the door.

"Think about it, babe. What use do I have for a clothing company?" Fletcher stepped out of the limo, extending a hand to help me out.

I took it, still befuddled by the unexpected make-out session. "That's what I've been asking myself. I just can't figure you out."

"I'm a man. Males are really very simple. You'll like this place," he added as he escorted me into the café. "The sandwiches here are great. I promise not to order beef."

Chapter Eleven

"Do you know what you've done?" Maggie slapped a copy of the joint venture agreement onto her desk. "Do you think he'll be satisfied with just CFO and fifty percent? Wolf will rip this company right out of your hands!"

"Don't be paranoid, Maggie." I left my drafting table to pour coffee into a battered ceramic mug, one of Nat's best creations. She'd whimsically added pink elephant's ears and a trunk to the gray pottery. "This deal's solved a lot of problems for us. He'll take care of the money I owe. Even better, no more lawsuit."

"He'll poke his nose everywhere. It'll spoil everything!"

"Why? This company is about designing clothes. How could he mess that up? You've read the contract. He has no say, none, regarding any design. So what could be the problem?"

"He's a corporate raider, and you're nothing but his cash cow."

I raised my eyebrows, trying not to feel bothered or bovine. "If he can make life easier for all of us while we make clothing, more power to him."

"I don't like it."

"I'm sorry you feel that way, but it's done. Because of the debt load, I really didn't have much choice. Besides, I have a show to put on, remember? I'm tired of side issues stealing my attention. I have to focus on Nat and clothing. Wolf will help me do that."

Maggie looked at me with narrowed eyes. "That was supposed to be my job."

"What?"

"Taking care of the details so you could focus." She paused, as though waiting for encouragement.

Well, none would be forthcoming. I wouldn't sugarcoat the truth to her; she'd fallen down on the job. Maggie's failure had weakened the company to the extent that I'd been forced into the joint venture with Wolf. The company had been my baby. Mine, not Maggie's. I hated the situation, but the deal was done and I had to live with it.

Her lips tightened into a thin line. "I'll clean out my desk right away."

"I really don't think that's necessary. You're still my personal assistant. He's CFO, which means he'll oversee finances. That's all."

"So what am I supposed to be doing?"

"Look, Fletcher knows nothing, zip, zero, about the fashion business. He can't do what you do. Who's going to arrange marketing, deal with personnel, help me put on the runway shows? You, that's who." I eyed Maggie, hoping her ego wouldn't become a problem. "So now that the joint venture agreement's been signed, life will settle down around here, okay?"

While Maggie freaked, I worried. What changes would the Fletcher Wolf Era bring?

I avoided contact with Fletch after the day of the settlement conference, preferring to conduct negotiations away from his disturbing presence. The memory of his kisses still burned. As far as I was concerned, he was one hundred percent off-limits, even if he could make my body sing with joy.

Because he'd be working with me, ignoring him would be tough, even impossible. I dreaded Monday morning, which would be Day One of the Fletcher Wolf Era.

When Natalie and I left our brownstone to hail a cab, I saw a familiar black limousine parked in the street. I realized with a jolt that Fletcher brought surprises even at the early hour of eight o'clock.

Sam, who'd been leaning nonchalantly against the back fender, sprang to open the door for us. "Good morning, Ms. Fletcher, Miss Fletcher."

"Who are you?" Natalie asked.

The sandy-haired young man extended a hand to her. "I'm Sam, your driver. May I take your bags?"

Looking bemused, Natalie handed Sam her backpack and her gym bag, which he put into the trunk of the limo. If I hadn't been so outraged at Fletcher's high-handedness I'd have laughed at the dumbfounded expression on her face. Because of Kenney's antics, she'd grown a tough shell around her emotions faster than a hen produced an egg at laying time. She didn't expose herself to strangers, but Sam had cracked her open merely by shaking her hand and ushering her into a limo. Taking my gear, he closed the door behind us.

"Good morning, Cara, Natalie." Emanating from behind the *Wall Street Journal,* Fletcher's mellow southern bass filled the limo's interior. He folded his newspaper, putting it on the seat beside him. "Juice?"

The car sped off while Fletcher opened a small refrigerator in the front area of the limo to pour orange juice.

Natalie took the glass from Fletcher's hand. "Where are we going?"

"Computer camp, of course." Fletcher lifted the newspaper back into place, concealing his expression.

"How do you know where it is?" I asked.

The paper lowered. Fletcher raised his brows. He tapped on the partition dividing passengers from driver. It opened. "Sam, what's your schedule today?"

"Eight-fifteen. Drop Miss Natalie at computer camp at the

Midtown Teen Center. Eight-thirty, Ms. Fletcher's workshop, the Bowery. Noon, take you and Ms. Fletcher to lunch. Three-thirty, pick up Miss Natalie, get her a snack, and take her to an afternoon activity, her choice. Five P.M., pick up you and Ms. Fletcher."

"Thank you, Sam." Fletcher smiled at us.

"This really isn't necessary," I said.

"Oh, but it is. Your habit of using taxis is extremely wasteful."

"With all due respect, how I get to work is not your business."

His brow raised again. "Does Cara Fletcher Couture pay for your transportation?"

I pursed my lips.

"Gotcha, honey." The *Wall Street Journal* elevated once more, rustling as Fletcher turned a page.

The limo stopped for Natalie to get out. I noticed through the open door that Sam watched Natalie until she'd entered the building.

Alone with Fletcher in the cozy confines of the limo, my nerves tightened. Fletch tended to get touchy-feely at the oddest times. But how bad could that be?

When he'd kissed me in the limo after the settlement conference, I'd melted right then and there. Next he'd gotten out of the car and continued talking all through lunch about the deal in such a cool, rational way that I'd been convinced that he wasn't half as attracted as I.

Although he'd implied that the only reason he wanted the company was to get into my Victoria's and find out my Secrets, I didn't believe that for a second. Okay, I'm cute, but not the kind of wildly sexy and beautiful that drove men to extremes. And Fletcher Wolf, who no doubt had girls and money galore, wouldn't go to so much trouble over me. Take away the magic hair, changeable eyes, and nice clothes, and what was I? A skinny, pale woman with no chest or hips to speak of, with a troubled child in tow and a demanding career. Five million dollars was a lot to pay for a quickie, and he'd never implied that he looked for a permanent relationship. What did the man really want?

I'd never have a romance with a coworker. That was just plain stupid. What if the affair went awry? I had Trent Whiting—oops, Trent Nevada—to remind me of how stupid that could be.

A botched relationship with my CFO . . . The consequences were too dreadful to contemplate. Despite the price I could pay, I was tempted. Oh, yeah, was I ever. The memory of Fletcher's touch lingered. One smile from this man and my brain spun off into crazy dreams and risqué fantasies.

My pulse leaped at Fletcher's sudden movement. He rapped at Sam's partition again. "Stop at the next store you see, please."

"What now?" I asked. "This stop isn't on the schedule."

He raised his brows at my sarcasm. "I prefer fresh cream in my coffee."

"Oh, there's Coffee-mate or something at the atelier. Don't worry about that."

His eyebrow twitched for the fourth time that morning, and it wasn't even eight-thirty. Would he set a record?

After the limo stopped in front of a corner store, he left for about two minutes, returning with a small carton in hand. What was this business about fresh cream, anyway?

Nope, I couldn't fool with Fletcher, the man with the thirty-page prenuptial contract as well as a gazillion personality quirks. Besides, Nat didn't like him, and Nat came first.

More surprises awaited me when we arrived at the workshop. Fletcher carried his briefcase and a laptop while Sam unloaded a top-of-the-line coffee maker, a grinder, a jug of distilled water, and a large bag of beans. I hadn't any idea that Fletcher was so persnickety about his coffee, but here was the living proof.

After I climbed the steel stairs to the loft, I was met by another unexpected sight. A huge old desk occupied most of the available space in the area. Wooden and battered, it sported an unsightly stain on one corner. Even more damaging to my state of mind, it sat less than three feet from my drafting table.

"Wh-when did this get here?" I sputtered.

"Over the weekend. Can't work without my desk. Sam, put the coffee pot over there." Fletcher nodded his head toward the long table under the loft's windows. He turned. "Good morning, Maggie."

Maggie, at the workshop unexpectedly early, left her desk to stalk over to the table where her java already brewed, filling the air with a sweet scent. She picked up the bag of beans Sam had set next to the new, boxed coffee maker, and read the label on the sack. "Zanzibar coffee? Who the hell heard of coffee from Zanzibar?"

I winced. Maggie the mouth rides again!

Fletcher took off his jacket, exposing wide shoulders, a starched white shirt, suspenders printed with cute little horseshoes on a pale yellow background, and a matching tie. My mouth watered at the sight while the artist in me saw that the yellow picked up golden flecks in his ancient amber eyes.

He draped the jacket over the back of the leather executive's chair behind his desk. "It's part of Tanzania, and their coffee is very good. Special, in fact. Would you care to try some?" He poured beans into the grinder, flipping its switch on and off several times.

It sounded as though he was making an effort to get along with Maggie. Good.

"No, thank you." Maggie used a sickly-sweet tone of voice that I knew all too well. "Too exotic for my blood. Like to try some of my Irish pecan vanilla-bean creme Frangelico?"

I hid my grin behind the drafting table.

He looked as though he had eaten rotten eggs, but said, very politely, "No, thank you." He turned away to pour the ground coffee into a filter, muttering, "Frou-frou coffee."

They were about as subtle as a sucker punch. And if looks could kill, ol' Fletch was in a coffin with the priest saying a eulogy. I wondered how I could function in the incredibly hostile atmosphere. Didn't these two realize how much I had to do in the next ten weeks?

The china cup Fletcher unwrapped bore his company's logo in gold leaf. Good Lord. He placed his cup and saucer next to Natalie's elephant mug while the Zanzibar coffee brewed.

I left the safety of the drafting table to pour myself a cup, picking the elephant mug.

He bumped against me. "Sorry."

He didn't sound apologetic. I became sure that the bump was intentional when he rubbed his hip against mine. He took the mug out of my hand to serve me the Zanzibar roast. Lucky thing he did, because my hands had begun to quiver with a palsy of some sort. Damn. How did he do that to me?

"What if I'd wanted the flavored coffee?" I asked.

"You don't. You told me that you prefer plain French roast." He handed me the mug, smiling into my eyes.

"Thanks." My heart pumping, I fled back to my refuge behind the drafting table, amazed that he'd remembered a stray fact that I'd mentioned months before. What was he doing to me? What had he already done? My giddy excitement reminded me of my first ride on a roller coaster. If he was this distracting for the entire day, I'd never get anything done.

And then there was Maggie, whose glower reminded me of the Wicked Witch of the West. Being in the same room with the two of them was like cuddling with a couple of angry porcupines.

One of them would break, and I was pretty sure it wouldn't

be Fletcher. Maggie would simply have to get used to the situation. I liked her, but truthfully, she hadn't been competent to run Cara Fletcher Couture when it had expanded into ready-to-wear. Would she quit? The timing would be unfortunate, but Fletcher's takeover resulted in Maggie's demotion.

Lunch, thank goodness, was uneventful. Maggie trotted off at twelve to meet the Covarrubia twins someplace hip and trendy while I stayed in the loft to work, having asked Sam to bring me a sandwich. I didn't know where Fletcher went, and at that point I didn't care.

The afternoon turned out to be just as annoying as the morning. Maggie still grumbled, and Fletcher's attitude toward her didn't help. Her frequent absences and his southern courtliness disguised mutual suspicion blending into outright animosity. I had to put up with their immature shenanigans all day long. I spent most of the time hiding behind my drafting table, waiting for them to duke it out.

Natalie came in at five, voicing my thoughts like a carnival mind-reader. "Is all this new furniture yours? I thought you weren't gonna be around much."

"Natalie!" I wanted to crawl under a desk.

"It's all right, Cara. I understand that Natalie's going through a difficult period now."

She scowled. If Fletcher didn't stop talking down to her, life would be difficult indeed.

Fletcher addressed Natalie. "I'm sorry to disappoint you, but I have a lot to do around here."

"Yeah. I heard that you lost your lawsuit, and you have to pay my mom five million dollars."

"Is that so?" He looked at me. That eyebrow again.

"So I guess we have to put up with you."

I gasped. "Natalie, apologize to Mr. Wolf right now!"

"Sorry, Mr. Wolf," Natalie chirped, without a shred of guilt or shame. She flounced downstairs.

"Fletch, I apologize," I said. "But I'm not sure that we can expect more than that, at her age."

He shrugged. "You can't." He picked up his briefcase. "I'm done for the day. Ready to go?"

I returned my pens to their box, then slid the design I'd completed that afternoon into a portfolio case. "Yep." I followed Fletcher downstairs to snag Natalie and Sam. We all piled into the limo.

Surprise jolted me yet again when Fletcher got out of the limo at our health club and took a workout bag from the trunk. "Where are you going?" I demanded as Sam helped me out of the car.

"To work out." Fletcher slammed the trunk closed.

"What?"

"Why do I repeat myself so often when we're together? I'm beginning to think that you don't listen to what I say."

"I'm listening. Did you join this gym?"

"Yeah. I thought it would be convenient. Do you lift weights?"

I swallowed further surprised exclamations. With his fit, muscular build, I'd known at least subliminally that Fletch had to exercise, but I hadn't expected him to work out at our club.

I looked over to scope out Natalie's reaction, but having retrieved her gym bag, she hurried toward the door of the club. She liked to be on time for her gymnastics class, since tardiness earned a latecomer twenty push-ups for every minute late.

"No, I don't lift weights," I said. "I take an aerobics class and occasionally swim." I grabbed my gym bag and my satchel.

"See you in, oh, about an hour and a half," Fletcher told Sam. "Is that enough time, Cara?"

I nodded, and he walked with me into the gym.

The eyes of the woman behind the counter widened when she saw us. "Hi, Cara. Who's your friend?" Vicki reached for my membership card.

"Vicki, this is Fletcher Wolf. He's a new member. Do you have your card yet?" I asked Fletch.

"I have a temporary. Can I get a locker?"

"Sure," Vicki said. "Cara, Natalie didn't give me her card."

"Oh, she didn't want to be late. I'll put her stuff in my locker after she changes." I took a key from the woman while Vicki, a flashy redhead who wore a blue, thong-style leotard and little else, surveyed Fletch while licking her lips. *Boy, that's tacky. I sure hope he doesn't like tacky! Hey, am I jealous?*

Fletcher, who seemed to be unaware of Vicki's interest, squeezed my shoulder. "I'll see you back here in a while, honey." He headed to the men's locker room without a glance at her.

"You've been holding out on me," Vicki said. "When did you get a boyfriend?"

How would it feel to be Fletcher's girlfriend? Pretty good, I bet. The heat in my lower body cranked up a few more degrees. "He's not my boyfriend. I just work with him, that's all."

"I bet he doesn't think so. When he does the squeeze and calls you honey in front of witnesses, he's staked out his territory for sure."

"He's interested in business, not me."

She laughed. "Yeah, right."

"I'd better get changed and go to class." Uncomfortable with the conversation, I went to the women's locker room and stripped. I tugged on spandex tights while wondering if there was some truth to Vicki's observation. Slowly but surely, Fletcher Wolf had taken over. Since I'd first heard the name just six months before, he'd demanded and gained entry into my workplace, my health club, my entire waking life. He even showed up when I visited my parents.

I stepped into a leotard. If this day were any example, I'd be seeing him morning, noon, and night. The only hours without

Fletcher were those in my townhouse, but that wasn't entirely true, was it? He'd haunted my fantasies since our first meeting, in the hallway of the courthouse, before I'd even known who he was.

I pursed my lips and laced up my aerobic shoes. I couldn't deny that since he'd turned from predator to partner he'd become a lot more likable. The suspenders were charming, and so were his silly little habits such as the coffee, which I'd learned he drank with just a drop—no more—of the fresh cream that he bought on the way to the atelier.

I'd never dreamed that Fletcher had such an array of bizarre personality quirks, but he liked things to be just so, precisely placed in some order, the mechanics and logic of which seemed to be hidden to all but Fletcher himself. His favorite saying seemed to be "Organization is the key to success!" Maybe he was right. The haphazard way I'd run the business hadn't benefited anyone.

I'd miss the luxury of the limo on days when Fletch went to Delaware. Besides, since we'd negotiated the joint venture, the vandal hadn't bothered me. The hang-up calls continued, but that could've been a glitch in the phone lines. The truly bad stuff seemed to have stopped. I hated to think that the presence of a man in my life scared the perpetrator away, but that was a possibility in this backward, sexist world.

Perhaps there was a closer connection. Maybe the harassment had ceased since I now danced to the tune the harasser—Fletcher—played. I loathed that possibility, but returned to it over and over again, the way a child tests a bruise to see if it still hurts.

As I walked from the lockers to the aerobics room, which already boomed with the sounds of the hip-hop beat played during workouts, I couldn't resist peeking into the weight room to check out Fletch. Oh, my. There he was, all juicy and sweaty on a rowing machine, wearing a ragged, torn T-shirt with the Phillies logo atop very short shorts. The muscles I'd admired in Ithaca bulged and strained as he worked the machine. "Whoa," I breathed. Did he prefer briefs or boxers? Not much room under those little red shorts for either. I craned my head to get a better view.

When we met in the lobby after we'd finished our workouts, I couldn't overlook the jaunty way he wore his suit, with the jacket and tie draped over his shoulder and the collar unbuttoned, revealing a V of dark, masculine hair. What did he look like naked?

Oh yeah, Fletch was impossible to ignore.

The next day, the August sun heated humid Manhattan like a sauna. The air conditioning in the atelier labored and everyone dressed down, especially the denizens of the loft. I wore a loose, unconstructed dress. Fletch had replaced his suit with a much more casual outfit. Shorts exposed brawny, tanned legs while his T-shirt set off the broad shoulders and rippling pecs I'd seen flexing on the exercise machine. He'd tied his long hair back into a short, neat ponytail, which should have looked dopey but somehow made him even sexier. I wanted to free that wild hair and run my fingers through it, feel it stroke my naked body.

Damn. I had it bad for this man.

"Hey, Cara, when were you planning to break for lunch?" he asked. "There are some figures here that I want to discuss over a sandwich in the park."

I looked up from a mannequin on which I'd draped several different weights of silk blended with linen. If I went heavier, I wouldn't have to line the textured, cream-colored fabric. But how might that affect the flow of the garment? "What time is it?" When working, I generally didn't notice the passage of time, or much else.

"Eleven-thirty. If we leave now, we can beat the crowds and

get lunch early."

"Okay." I slid off my stool and rounded my shoulders a couple of times, doing shrugs to release tension.

"Maggie, can you come with us?" Fletch asked.

"Sorry. I have a lunch date. See you in an hour." She took her purse and left.

"She's certainly hot to help out." He moved behind me and rubbed my sore shoulders. Nice.

"I can't really blame her for her attitude. She feels that every irregularity you find in your review of the company's books is a criticism."

"She's unprofessional. We'd achieve more at a faster clip if she'd cooperate."

"Mmmm, that feels good," I said, changing the subject.

"You know I can make you feel much better than that," he murmured into my ear. His warm breath tickled pleasantly, sending a hot shiver down my spine.

I frowned. "Forget it. I have an example to set for a twelve-year-old."

"That's a good point, but when will you allow yourself to have a life beyond Natalie?" Stepping back to his desk, Fletch opened his briefcase and began to stuff some papers into it.

Stifling a sigh, I followed him downstairs. "Nat needs me right now. She's going through a very difficult period."

"She's an adolescent. She'll be difficult until she's twenty-five."

"Please don't force me to tell you one more time that Natalie is not your concern." Exiting the atelier, I stepped around a derelict, slouched against the wall.

"She hates me, doesn't she?"

I sighed again as Sam opened the door of the limo for me. "That's not the issue."

"Isn't it?" Climbing in after me, Fletch kissed me.

I kissed back, but dragged my mouth away after the briefest touch of lips. "I don't quite trust your intentions."

"I have the best intentions in the world, honey. And to prove it, I'm going to fix your company for you. Look at this." Releasing me, he pulled a sheaf of papers out of his briefcase. "While we were negotiating the joint venture agreement, I had a couple of long lunches with the CFOs at a few other couture houses. I think I've figured out a way to cut costs in a big way."

"Oh, really? That's good news." Excited, I hoped that the gamble—the joint venture—would pay off quickly. Fletch was a genius if he could turn the company around so fast. Then I could get rid of his distracting presence in my workplace, at my gym, in my life. "How?"

"By hiring offshore factories to make the ready-to-wear apparel. Look at these figures for Kidstuff and Comfort Zone. They're less expensively priced lines, so I think we should look to Asia and Latin America for our manufacturers."

My good mood crashed. "I've always used union labor here in the U.S. It's something I feel very strongly about."

"Look, I'd never accept any diminution of quality. But we can get clothes made overseas for a fraction of what it costs us now. This one change will bring you from red to black within one year, two at the outside."

"I won't allow sweatshop labor, and that's final."

"I'm not talking about sweatshop labor."

"Hey, I've read about what happens overseas. Little kids are paid pennies a day. No. No way."

"You're jumping to conclusions. Who said anything about little kids or sweatshops?"

"Listen. This is my company, my name is on the clothes, and I won't allow it." I rapped on Sam's window. It lowered. "Sam, stop the car."

"Here, ma'am?" Sam pulled over on Centre, near the Brooklyn Bridge.

Fletch raised his voice. "Sam, do not stop the car here. Cara," he said through his teeth, "this isn't a good place to stop. We're practically in Brooklyn. Where do you want to eat lunch, the Gowanus Expressway?"

Sam sped up and turned on Park Row.

"Any place will do, as long as I don't have to debate this any longer." I folded my arms.

A muscle in Fletch's jaw jumped before he took a deep breath. "I do not propose the use of sweatshops, child labor or grossly underpaid workers to make our clothes," he said, in very precise tones. "The adverse publicity could be horrendous."

"Our clothes?" The nerve of the man.

"Yes, dammit. Our clothes. I own half of this company. Please don't forget it."

"You've made it impossible for me to forget." I steamed with resentment. I'd agreed to the joint venture and done my best to live with it, but some issues just weren't negotiable.

"I'm trying to work with you. When I make a suggestion, I'd appreciate a fair hearing and a little respect." He shoved his papers back into his briefcase. "Sam, stop the car."

"Yes, sir." Sam pulled over near City Hall Park.

After getting out, Fletch stuck his head through the open car door. "We'll discuss this again when you're more rational."

"I'm totally rational, and it's insulting for you to imply otherwise." My voice rose along with my temper. "Tell me something, Fletcher."

"What?"

"Do you object to underpaid Third World labor because it's morally wrong, or because of the negative publicity?"

He hesitated. Got you this time, I thought.

"They're inseparable. Sam, take Cara to wherever she wants

to go, and pick me up here in an hour."

"Yes, sir."

Left alone in the limo, I fumed. Why did men always imply a female is irrational if she disagrees with their oh-so-holy opinions? *Next he'll ask me if I'm premenstrual when I object to some other misbegotten proposal he invents!*

"Where to, Ms. Fletcher?"

I slumped in the seat. "Battery Park, Sam."

I stared at New York Harbor, ignoring the hordes of Manhattanites and tourists that crowded the park at lunchtime.

Had I made a mistake with this joint venture scenario? Like a large sun with a minor planet in orbit, Fletcher had come to dominate and overwhelm every aspect of my life. There's a price to pay for everything, I knew, but . . .

The Statue of Liberty seemed to float above the harbor, an ironic sight considering the changes in my life. I'd traded my independence for financial stability. According to the joint venture agreement, Fletcher didn't have to discuss the issue of factories and labor with me. He could have the clothes made wherever he pleased, without my permission.

Yet, he'd asked, and had wanted to discuss the matter, and I'd been a total bitch about the issue. Okay, it was important, but I'd have to get used to a fifty/fifty power split, and that meant compromise.

I took in a deep breath. Okay. Fletch had given by consulting me. I'd give back, and if that meant an apology and a lunch of roast crow, I'd pick up the knife and fork and chow down.

Chapter Twelve

The limo slid to a stop at the same corner where Fletch had walked out an hour before. I popped out of the car to give him a sheaf of flowering greenery. "I'm a doofus. Forgive me?"

He smiled. "Dogwood, the Virginia state flower. It's out of season by several months. Where did you find it in New York City?"

"Oh, I won't reveal all my secrets, but I wanted to find something special. Roses would have been too mundane for you."

He grinned, no doubt recognizing the line he'd handed me months before. "Thank you. No one's ever bought me flowers before."

"Really?" I raised my brows. "I assumed you'd be inundated by bouquets from grateful women." I got back into the limo, sliding along the leather seat.

"Whatever gave you that idea?" He followed me.

"You're not exactly bashful."

"Depends on the lady. You inspire me." He slipped an arm around me. "Are we friends again?"

"Yep. And I promise to listen to your ideas. But I really feel strongly about this issue."

"Your concerns are valid. I'll do some research, and we may have to do some on-site factory visits to make sure the workers are treated fairly. Deal?"

"Deal."

"Seal it with a kiss?" He bent his head toward me.

I raised a hand. "Fletch, come on. We were doing so well just being business associates."

"You think a romance is incompatible with a professional relationship?"

"God, yes. I'd never be so dumb."

"Is Miuccia Prada dumb? Her husband runs her couture house, and they're gazillionaires, as you'd put it. If you can't trust your honey, who can you trust?" He moved closer. "I can make you eat those words."

I narrowed my eyes at him. "Please. I've already eaten crow and groveled once today. Isn't that enough?"

He chuckled. "I suppose so."

After the limo pulled up in front of the atelier, he helped me out and followed me up to the loft, then booted up his laptop while I returned to work. A few minutes later, he said, "Hey, Cara."

"Yeah?" I looked up from uncapping a felt-tipped pen.

"We're due a shipment of samples from Italy. Someplace called Prato. Where's that?"

I came over to scan his screen, noting a red-flagged entry. "Prato's a few miles from Florence."

"Florence?"

"Yeah. It's been a center for textile mills for centuries, since the medieval era. Most couture fabrics are milled in Italy, many in Prato. When are the swatches due? Seems to me they're way late."

"They were due to be received and approved before the end of July, so they're at least three weeks overdue. What's going on?"

I frowned, thinking. "All the Italian mills close for the entire month of August. It's an ancient tradition. If we didn't get the samples August first or thereabouts, we won't get them until after Labor Day. This isn't good. I can't think how I overlooked this."

He gave me an apologetic smile. "You've had a few distractions lately. I wonder why they didn't arrive on time." He tapped the eraser end of a pencil against his teeth. He looked over at Maggie's desk. Empty, but she wouldn't give him any answers, in any event.

"Beats me. Check out when they were paid," I said with a faint smile. "Money's been tight around here, you know."

He sighed. "Guess I'll have to follow the paper trail." An hour later, he asked, "Can I interrupt you again?" He stroked my shoulder with one of the flowering branches I'd given him.

Out of the corner of my eye, I noticed Maggie, who'd returned, watching us flirt. Fletcher had the gall to wink at her.

I chuckled. "Sure, you can interrupt me any time."

"Let's take a walk."

What was up? I put on a big straw hat against the August sun and went with him. As we left the atelier, I saw that Sam still hadn't left to pick up Natalie. Fletcher led the way to the limo, which I appreciated. The Bowery wasn't the best place for a stroll.

Walking on Fletcher's left, I tripped over the extended legs of one of the neighborhood's more fetching denizens. Fletch's hand shot out, steadying me as the bum drew in his legs. The derelict laughed.

I glared. "Hey, you."

"Gotta handout, lady?"

"If I did, I'd give it to someone who needs it. You may smell, look, and dress as badly as the average scumbag, but you're no street person, dude." I nudged his ankle with the toe of my sandal.

The bum lifted his bottle, gulped, and burped. "Says who?"

"Says I. Your teeth are a dead giveaway. They're perfect."

"Maybe I'm a recent addition to the down-and-out brigade." He shot an uneasy look over my shoulder, meeting Fletch's gaze.

My suspicions grew. "Oh, please. I demand to know why you're stalking me, or I'm going to call the cops, right here, right now." I pulled my cell phone out of my satchel.

Fletch cleared his throat. "Show's over, Tony."

"Guess so." The derelict jumped to his feet. "You can put the phone away, lady. I work for your pal, Mr. Wolf."

My jaw slackened and my hands lost their grip on both phone and satchel.

Fletch smiled blandly. "Life's full of surprises, isn't it? Cara, meet Tony Ramirez, head of security for Fletcher Tool and Gear." He helped me pick up my stuff.

Ramirez bowed from the waist, the courtesy at odds with his two-week beard and greasy, torn clothing. An older man, Fletcher's security specialist had dark hair flecked with gray. "At your service. I worked for the New York City police for twenty-five years before I retired to work for Mr. Wolf. I still have some useful contacts."

"He's been keeping an eye on you since after your workshop was vandalized," Fletcher said.

My jaw tightened involuntarily. "Whatever for?"

"Making sure you're okay." Fletcher opened the limo door for me. Angry, I didn't want to get in there with him, but if I resisted, I'd be just as rude as he was.

"Nice to meet you, Ms. Fletcher." Ramirez resumed his post, leaning against the wall near the metal security door of my building.

"Thank you," I said through gritted teeth as Fletcher shoved me into the limo.

Sam shut the door on us, and Fletcher wasted no time in raising the glass partition which separated driver from passengers. No doubt he'd figured out what was coming.

"No wonder you knew our schedule. You've been watching us. How dare you?"

"Honey, it was for your own good."

"You are incredibly patronizing. Can't you just mind your own business?"

"If I minded my own business, you wouldn't be here. You'd be in jail, facing felony drug charges."

"Oh, please. They would have found out that I reported the theft of my ID before the bust went down."

"I saved you a lot of trouble." His voice rose. "Should I have let you rot in the slammer? A night or two in jail with Manhattan's most wanted might have sweetened your temper."

"You are unbelievably deceptive. Remember the settlement conference at Muckenmyer's office? You had the gall to get on my case about keeping you under surveillance. When were you going to tell me you were doing the same thing?"

He waved his hands around. "I just never found the right moment, but I'm not sorry I butted in. After I heard about the vandalism, I couldn't just sit back while you were being hurt. It made me crazy. I had to do something."

"So why have you dragged me out here? I have a lot to do, you know. I have no time to drive around scenic downtown Manhattan or meet your assorted employees."

"You need to calm down before I talk about this new issue. Do you want a cold drink?" He took a soda out of the limo's fridge.

I grabbed it and popped the can's top. "I'm perfectly calm. Just spit it out, okay?" I snapped.

"All right, I will. A lot of paperwork was lost when the vandal destroyed your workshop," he said. "I've been unable to recreate the most recent transactions with your mills in Italy."

I swallowed. "What's the big deal? We have computer records, don't we?"

He hesitated. "Yes, but if there's a dispute going over international borders, the computer records won't help us. I think we should go to Italy to check this out."

"Italy? I don't have time to go to Italy. I have a runway show to put on in just ten weeks."

"I don't understand. Don't other couturiers go to the mills for regular inspection trips?"

"True. But I've never felt I could take the time."

"You close the atelier for Labor Day weekend, don't you?"

"Ye-es." I sipped from the can.

"What do you and Natalie normally do for holiday weekends? Go upstate to visit your parents?"

"Yeah, well . . . I guess I could take the time away, but I wouldn't feel comfortable sending her alone on the train. I know her father might, but I'm more careful." I couldn't keep the bitterness from my voice. Nat had been shortchanged, and I wouldn't let her down. Not for anything.

"Maybe your parents could come to the city."

I shook my head sadly. "Not very easily. My dad's in a wheelchair. He has MS. Didn't you know?"

"No, I didn't. I'm sorry." He touched my hand and muttered, "So much for Mike Muckenmyer and his fabulous dossier. No wonder you and Nat spend your free time upstate. How about this? Sam can drive Natalie to Owasco for the weekend, if she wants."

"I guess."

"Or I can see if my mother is willing to come up from Darkrider Farm for Labor Day. She likes to shop in Manhattan. Better yet, we can send Natalie to the farm for a few days. Does she like horses?"

"The only horses Natalie knows are the ones that pull the

carriages at Central Park."

"Yeah, but most teenage girls are mad about horses."

"She does love animals. Umm, I think school is supposed to start the week after."

"Even better. We can put her on a plane at JFK when we leave, and pick her up there when we return. She'll have a special little vacation on a horse farm to tell all her friends about when she goes back to school."

"I don't know."

"I do. You've got to stop babying Natalie. She has to grow up, do new things, and learn to be more independent."

I fiddled with my hair, blonde today, and ruminated about Nat, Kenney and the whole damn thing. Nat was probably more independent than I liked to think about. "You're probably right, but I hate to leave. Time always seems to run so short. As soon as the fabrics come in, we have to make the factory prototypes and get them shipped. The weeks always seem to compress between Labor Day and Halloween."

"But it sounds like you can't get much done without the samples. Plus, if we're on site, you can make your decisions right there instead of in New York. You'll gain about ten days."

"Not really. The light's different in Italy."

"I don't understand. Same sun, isn't it?"

"Yeah, but I promise you, a lemon-yellow linen in Italy looks mustardy in New York. The light's clearer there. I can't explain it, but I know it's true."

"Then we can bring the swatches back home with us and fax them your decisions. Either way, you gain a few days and I can make some useful contacts for us in Italy. So how about it?"

"I guess so. It shouldn't take too long, huh?"

"No. If we leave Saturday morning, and return Tuesday, you miss only one day of work here. We'll be a little jet-lagged on Wednesday, but we can handle that."

"Why would we leave Saturday? No one in Italy works on Sunday."

"Jet lag, honey. Sunday will be an adjustment day for us, and we can do a little sightseeing. You're an artist. Don't you want to see the Uffizi, the Pitti, the Ghiberti doors and Michelangelo's David?"

I chuckled. "Okay, you got me there, partner. The way to an artist's heart must be through her eyes."

"Good." Fletch sat back as Sam stopped the limo and Natalie got in. "I'll get onto the Internet and make the arrangements as soon as this young lady decides what she wants."

"What young lady. Me?" Natalie darted a suspicious glance at him.

"Nat, I'm going away on business over Labor Day weekend. What do you want to do? You can stay in Manhattan, go to Grandma and Grandpa, or go to Virginia." I offered her the can of soda.

"Virginia? What's in Virginia?" She took the soda can to drink.

"My family's horse farm, Darkrider Farm." He smiled at her. "How'd you like to ride real Thoroughbred hunters, Nat?"

She tipped her head on one side. "That'd be cool. I like animals."

"You do? I'm surprised you don't have a dog or a cat," he said.

I kicked him to shut him up.

"Oh, that would be irresponsible," she said. "For one thing, the birds wouldn't like a cat, and a dog would get lonely 'cause we're gone all day long. Nope, birds only. We kill fish."

"Then you'll have fun on the farm. We have horses, dogs and cats. Probably a few rats and mice, too," His tone was wry, and I gathered that the rodents were uninvited. He continued, "My brother Griffin is a vet. He can tell you all about them."

"Your brother's a vet? No kidding!" She looked starry-eyed.

I smiled. "Natalie wants to work with animals when she grows up."

"Okay, Labor Day weekend's settled," he said.

"What about Grandma and Grandpa?" she asked. "They're used to seeing us on holiday weekends." She sipped the soda, then handed the can back to me.

I was gratified by her concern. "Grandpa had a good week, so maybe we can have a weekend to do something a little different. Remember, honey, Sam can drive you upstate if that's what you want. It's up to you. Do you want to talk to Grandma about it?"

Nat chewed on the end of her braid. "I don't want to hurt their feelings, but I really want to see the horses."

"Don't worry about it. I'll handle Grandma and Grandpa, and you'll fly down to Richmond out of JFK at the same time we leave." I glanced at Fletch.

"I'll arrange everything."

CHAPTER THIRTEEN

As Natalie boarded the flight to Richmond, my heart clenched a little. Irrational, I knew. Nat had flown across the country alone several times; her deadbeat father hadn't been willing to go to the trouble of accompanying her on her few trips out to see me or my parents, and I hadn't been able to spend the money or, later, to take the time. However, I guess I just couldn't help feeling a pang or two as I watched my baby fly away on a jet plane, even though I knew she'd be okay. One meeting with Veronica Wolf and the youngest Wolf, Griffin, had told me Nat would be safe and secure in their care.

Besides, Natalie needed to grow up whole and independent. This flight alone to Richmond was an important step for both of us. Well, okay, more for me than for her.

Turning to Fletch, I beamed at him to disguise my teary eyes. "I guess it's time to make our way over to our terminal."

Our flight was scheduled to leave at eight in the morning, and we'd cut it close. But now I watched Fletch settle into his seat as though transatlantic journeys on luxurious private jets were commonplace. He handed his jacket to a flight attendant, who also took my straw hat.

Fletch quirked a brow at my hair. "That's what they call fire-engine red, isn't it?"

I grinned at him. My flaming head surmounted a calf-length, flowing summer dress in a yellow and green flower print, with a white bolero jacket to keep me from the chill of overly air-conditioned planes and airports. The contacts today were leaf-green, matching the dress. "I hear that there are hordes of tourists in Florence. I didn't want you to lose me in the crowds."

"No chance of that, honey, no matter what color your hair is." Opening his briefcase, he took out the morning's editions of *Wall Street Journal* and *Investor's Business Daily*. "Window or aisle?"

"Oh, I don't care. Isn't the view mostly ocean?"

"For the most part, but we should also have a nice view of the coast and countryside before we land. How about this? You take the window seat, and I'll look over your shoulder."

"It's a deal." I found a pen and drawing paper, then stuffed my satchel under the seat and buckled the safety belt.

I'd traveled by plane before but I'd never seen the level of service the private jet provided. We didn't have to stay belted into our seats, but could move around and lounge on sofas, if we preferred. Which we did. Neither of us wanted the heavy breakfast the attendants offered, preferring our usual French roast coffee and orange juice, followed by fresh croissants. Sprawled on a love seat, absorbed in his reading, Fletch looked as comfortable with his coffee and newspaper there as he would in my atelier. An adaptable man, I thought.

Several hours later, the coast of Europe came into view, and I used the private jet's bathroom to freshen up before landing at the airport near Florence. Life with Fletcher was one unbroken, luxurious cruise. It certainly felt better to be Fletcher's pack-mate than his prey, I thought, remembering our first, disastrous dinner. Chuckling, I sat down next to Fletcher and buckled myself in before landing.

"What's funny?" he asked.

"I was thinking about our disastrous dinner."

"You're not holding a grudge about that, are you?"

"Oh, no. I don't hold grudges. Waste of time. I was just realizing how far you and I have come."

He smiled, the golden flecks in his eyes glimmering. "I can take you even farther, if you'll let me."

"How far might that be?"

He sat back and buckled up. "You tell me, Cara Linda Fletcher. Where do you want to go in life? I'll help you get there. What do you want? I'll get it for you."

I was startled by the turn the conversation had taken, but conversations with Fletcher often twisted and turned unexpectedly. That was part of the joy of Fletcher. One had to learn to ride the wave, so to speak. He generally sounded authoritative, and so now he spoke with total assurance, which I found both exciting and disturbing. I had no doubt he meant what he said, and that he could deliver. But at what price?

"I don't quite know. All my life, I've only wanted to make gorgeous clothes."

"But what about love? You're a very beautiful woman." Fletch's hand shifted to touch mine. One finger stroked the sensitive skin on the inside of my wrist.

The delicious tingle was fraught with a mixture of nerves and pleasure, but I didn't move my arm away. "I don't think about that, and certainly not since Natalie came to live with me."

"Huh?" His finger stilled. He stared at me, his amber eyes blank and wide.

What didn't he understand? "I said, I don't think about relationships much and certainly not since last Christmas. Natalie's father dumped her and she needs me."

His chuckle was rueful. "I didn't know. I thought she was just the average, umm, how can I say this? An average adolescent."

"The average bratty adolescent, you mean. No, she has a little more than that going on. Plus, there are those panic attacks. Don't you remember?"

"God, yes, I remember. How could I forget? It reminded me

of my father."

"What about your father?" Sensing that something important was buried in this subject, my belly tensed.

He spoke in a flat, emotionless voice. "You witnessed a fatal car crash. I found my father. He'd blown his brains out at his desk."

"Oh, my God!" I put my hand on his, squeezing tightly. I now realized what the stain on the desk had to be. "The same desk you use? But why? How do you—"

"So I'll never forget." His eyes, like ancient doubloons, looked metallic and hard.

"Forget what?"

"Anything. Everything. Listen, okay?" He shifted in his seat, facing me. "Fletcher Tool and Gear is a very old company, over three hundred years old. Fletcher's a family name, and the firm was started by one of the first blacksmiths in colonial Virginia. When the Industrial Revolution came along, we changed with the times, grew bigger, made different products. We survived the War Between the States by marrying into the Wolf family, wealthy merchants from the winning side of the Mason-Dixon line." He stopped speaking for a moment and blew out his accumulated breath in a sigh.

"Dad . . . I guess Dad didn't inherit the business gene. Oh, he tried, but he simply didn't have the knack. He never understood computer technology so he avoided it. His concepts of finance were a joke." Fletcher's tone took on a coldness I remembered from the settlement conference, when he'd judged my business practices as wanting. "He felt like a failure so he blew his brains out."

"Good God. How awful for your family."

"Yes. His entire identity had been so tied up in the business that when it began to slip away, he couldn't handle it."

I didn't know what to say. This old wound had festered for a long time, and perhaps never would heal. I pressed his hand with silent sympathy.

He lifted my hand and kissed my fingers. "I can't get over it. I'm still so angry at his selfishness." His voice was low and rough. "He had no idea how much we needed him. The sad part is that he wasn't a failure, as far as we were concerned . . . until he left."

"All of you had to fend for yourselves." I shook my head in disbelief. "Three kids and his wife."

"Yes. My mother's not stupid, but he'd never let her into the company. Griff was twelve and Damon seventeen. This happened at Christmas."

"Oh, I'm so sorry."

He gave her a bleak smile. "Our family's Christmases aren't very merry. I don't know what it is about the holidays, but apparently the suicide rate goes way up. Anyway, I had just begun my last year in college for my business degree. Fortunately, I'd trained myself to take over."

"What happened?"

"I found out later that Dad had let multiple competitors invade our market niche, and we'd shrunk from a respected regional concern to a failing company mired in nineteenth-century notions. So I took a big chance. I mortgaged our only remaining asset, our home, Darkrider Farm, and purchased a small firm that made precision tools used in laser surgeries. I knew from research that these operations would become a big business, because the technology had become accessible to doctors performing facelifts and eye operations."

He took a deep breath. "I gambled, and I was right. Next I looked at computer components. It didn't take a wizard to figure that tools to repair computers, copiers and the like were in short supply. So I refinanced the mortgage on Darkrider Farm and kept going."

"But that's why Damon had such a bad time."

"Yes. I didn't have time to feel abandoned. My mother didn't fall apart, but she retreated with Griff into their private, horse-dominated world. Damon went to college as planned, but now I realize he felt totally adrift. He became one of those guys who drank too much, partied too much, and spent a lot of time looking for love in all the wrong places. He's better, but he's still hurting, and very, very angry."

"What about you?" I asked. "And what's the lesson of your father's desk?"

"That was when I started turning gray, at the ripe old age of twenty-two." He shoved back his hair.

"That's the silver lining, so to speak. It's very sexy."

Fletch grimaced. "Makes me feel old."

"So you're human, after all."

He barked out a gruff little laugh. "I never pretended I wasn't."

"And the desk?"

"Ah, the lesson of the desk." He squeezed my hand. "The lesson, to me, is not to be selfish. Not to become so invested in business and forget what's really important. So don't work too hard making those clothes you love so much. Designing is great but it's just a job."

I took a sip of the Perrier the flight attendant gave me. "You're right, I suppose."

"You suppose? Aw, come on. You take care of your parents. You dote on your child. Family's where it's at, honey, and you know it."

"So how come you don't have one of your own, Fletch? Who cares for the caretaker?"

He looked blank for a moment, then stroked his chin while running his golden gaze over me. "I never thought about it. Maybe that will change. And you?"

I shook her head. "Nat's enough for now. More than enough."

"Nat might be happier with a man around."

I frowned. "Maybe, but if you're applying for the position of surrogate father you'd better stop talking down to her."

He groaned. "I don't know what it is about your kid, but every time I open my mouth around her I seem to stick my foot in it. And wiggle the toes for good measure."

"She's tough, I'll admit." I sighed.

"I'm sorry about Nat. Maybe I can figure out how to deal with her without acting like a buffoon."

He pressed a kiss onto my wrist. The hum of the plane's engines changed to a screechy whine as the craft braked for a landing. "Now it's time to forget about all that. We're about to land with two days of freedom in Tuscany."

"Two whole days?"

"A day and a half. It's dark outside, but it's daytime in New York City. Plenty of time to play."

Fletcher tucked my arm into his and walked to the counter where we'd get our passports stamped with the proper visa. Pulling my passport out of my satchel, I flipped it open to my photograph and vital statistics. He peered over my shoulder.

"Ah, the truth revealed. Brown hair and hazel eyes."

I glanced at him. "You're still obsessed by that? I'm the one who's supposed to be fascinated by appearances."

"I'm not obsessed." He sounded defensive. "Merely very interested."

"Buona sera," he said to the man who stood behind the counter. The inspector, a small chirpy fellow with a clipped moustache, looked me over with a gleam in his eye. I ignored the gleam and handed my passport to the inspector with a smile.

"Ah, Cara Linda Fletcher," he said in strongly accented English. "Cara." He looked at the passport photo and then back at me. His brows lifted so high that he looked like Marcel Marceau in a uniform.

Small wonder. Today, I didn't look much like the drab girl in the passport photo. I hoped that in the post-nine-eleven world of heightened security concerns, my fondness for hair coloring and contacts wouldn't land us in trouble.

The inspector checked me out again, a lascivious twinkle appearing in his brown eyes. "You are Cara Fletcher? Your *passaporto,* it says brown hair and hazel eyes."

"I dyed my hair and have contact lenses. See?" I popped out my left lens and blinked at the inspector, whose eyebrows jerked skyward. I guess I looked pretty bizarre, with one green eye glaring like a "go" light. I fumbled in my satchel and found a lens case. I put the left lens away, then took out the right, blinking some more with relief.

After putting the case away, I rubbed my eyes. "Eye-gasm," I said to Fletch with a grin, wondering if he'd get the joke.

"Eyegasm, eyegasm," the inspector muttered, clearly as lost at sea as the Flying Dutchman. He shrugged. "Hokay, *mia* Cara. You pass." He stamped my passport.

"No," Fletch said, pointing at his own chest. "*Mia* Cara!"

The inspector laughed, white teeth vivid against swarthy skin. "Hokay, hokay, *la mia Carissima!*" He turned his attention to Fletch, whose passport merited no more than a cursory glance.

"What was all that macho chest-banging about?" I asked as we went to find our luggage.

"He was making a pass at you. I warned him off."

"Huh. I've been claimed, like real estate in the Oklahoma land rush."

"Something like that. Take my briefcase, will you?" He hefted my tapestry garment bag over one shoulder and took his suitcase with his other hand. "Let's deal with customs and get a taxi."

"Why did he call me *Carissima?*"

"You know what your name means, don't you?" We walked through the gate marked in both Italian and English "nothing to declare," and left the terminal.

"No, I never thought about it."

Fletch put the bags in the trunk of a taxi, then followed me into the backseat. "The guide I have says that Cara means 'dear one.' In Italian, *issima* is a superlative. So when he called you *Carissima,* he called you 'dearest one.' "

"He called me his dearest one? Whatever for?"

"Honey, this is Italy. He was flirting. So then I made sure he knew whose girl you are." He slipped his arm around me, kissing my forehead.

Leaving aside my past doubts, I cuddled into his chest. He felt great. "Time to play, you said?"

Even after we'd found the hotel near the city center and unpacked, it was still only eight o'clock in Manhattan. Having sat all day, I felt restless and ready to explore Florence after midnight.

I was excited by fantasies of what the night could bring. Fletcher had made his intentions extremely clear. I wanted him too, but then again, I was in Florence, one of the great cities of the world, and for only a few days. I wanted to explore. Sex could wait.

"It's late. We might have a hard time finding someplace to eat," I said to Fletch as we met in the living room of the two bedroom, two bath suite.

Seated on a red and gold brocade sofa, Fletch waved a copy of *Let's Go* in the air. The Fodor's and Michelin guides sat on an inlaid coffee table in front of him. "Never fear, Fletch is here. All the answers are in these books."

"Three books for three days! Where's your sense of adventure? You want to play, but you're planning our every move. Let's just walk out and see what we can find."

"Yeah, but we could wander around this city until dawn and starve to death."

I shoved the coffee table aside and grabbed his hand, tugging him off the couch. "Come on, you big bad wolf. Let's go explore. Bring a guide you can stick in a pocket."

"All right." Grabbing the smallest booklet, he locked the door of our suite behind us.

The hotel, a converted palace, had only one suite on each floor, so I bet I wouldn't wake anyone else up with my chatter. I couldn't help myself. The place was incredible, with unbelievable detail work.

"My bathroom has gold-leaf fixtures and malachite sinks. The bathtub is marble!"

"Yeah, they kicked ass on this place. Look at the moldings at the ceiling." Fletch pointed upward. "I bet they had to replace and repaint everything." He pushed open the glass and brass revolving doors, and we merged into the warm Tuscan night.

Though late, the streets were busy with sightseers sporting cameras and T-shirts emblazoned with their previous ports-of-call. The Florentines were harder to spot, but I imagined that the elegantly clad men and women without tourist trappings were the locals.

I adored the cobblestone walkways, the old buildings, which had stood for centuries, and, surmounting it all, the massive orange dome of the Duomo, dramatically lit against the dark shield of the night sky. Like moths to its bright flame, we wandered through the narrow streets toward it. I led the way, laughing when I made a wrong turn into a dark, twisted alley, stinking of generations of Tuscan garbage. The ancient city, fantastic and picturesque, gave rise to wild fantasies of cloaked Medici assassins accosting their prey in dark corners while beautiful, exotically dressed women met their lovers in the moonlit gardens.

After crossing the square, I gazed at the Gates to Paradise, breathless with admiration. "What I would do to make something so extraordinary."

"Why, Cara Fletcher. I had no idea you had such lofty aspirations. I thought you were strictly a buttons and bows kinda gal."

I swatted his arm lightly. "Everyone wants to make an eternal mark."

"We're in Florence, the birthplace of the Renaissance. I bet everyone gets bit by the art bug here."

"Maybe." Dropping my serious mood, I pulled at his hand. "Come on, there's lots more to see." I zipped across the square to a brightly lit trattoria. "You hungry, Fletch?"

"For you," he murmured.

I ignored him. I wanted some of that famous Italian cuisine. I read the menu posted outside the restaurant. "*Anguille*. What's that?"

"Eel."

"Eel! Yuck. How do you know?"

"You scoffed at my guides, but I read the glossary in the back of the Michelin."

"I bow to your superior knowledge, oh my partner." I gave him a mock curtsy. "Let's go in."

After I sat down, I took a sip of Chianti, closed my eyes, and pointed randomly at the menu. He glanced over and guffawed.

"What?" I asked.

"Have fun, honey." He laughed harder as I ordered *triglie alla livornese*. Okay, so I mangled the Italian. Fletch, that coward, ordered only carpaccio and a salad.

My food arrived. Fish, but not just any fish. Whole fried fish, but the thin breading had partially fallen off them. The glassy eyes of three dead mullet seemed to stare up at me. Eek. I gulped.

He couldn't help rubbing it in. "Would you like some of my carpaccio?" He waved a forkful of raw beef in my face.

I shoved his hand away. "Wretch. You saw that coming, didn't you?"

"I have to get you out of the country more often. This is very entertaining."

I stuck a fork into the nearest fish. Bringing a bite to my nose, I sniffed it before I chewed and swallowed. "Needs lemon, or maybe some tartar sauce."

"Not very Italian."

"But I'm not very Italian."

"When in Rome, pretty lady." He played with his salad, offering me a bite.

"We're not in Rome, Mr. Wolf." I ate the greens and daintily touched my lips with a napkin.

"Oh, so we're back to Mr. Wolf. Well, Ms. Fletcher, I must say I'm really enjoying this evening."

"You have that look in your eyes again. Am I still prey?"

"I'm definitely on the prowl, honey, and I expect happy hunting."

I giggled into my wine glass, feeling a little high and reckless. "You're right. Take me on a plane, ply me with champagne and wine in an exotic port . . . and I'm yours to command."

Desire flared in his eyes. "Good. Let's get the check."

Whoa. This could be . . . serious.

CHAPTER FOURTEEN

Fletch guided me down the dark, quiet street, his hand firm on the small of my back. I shivered at his touch, thinking about Fletcher, sex, and the unexpected revelations he'd shared.

His father's suicide forced me to see him in a whole new light. I could now accept the lawsuit because I understood why he'd moved so aggressively to protect his family and their company. Easy to understand his reflex to defend, exercised so frequently during the last thirteen years. Twenty-two was young, far too young for Fletcher to have taken on responsibilities which would have overwhelmed a lesser man.

He'd been forced to take frightening risks with his family's future. Brave and bold, he'd overcome all obstacles to achieve a startling level of success.

I could almost forgive him for suing me for—yikes—fifty million dollars. Fletcher, deeply loyal, wouldn't have hesitated to take me and my company apart if it had proven necessary. The solution he'd orchestrated had its occasional frustrations, but I had to admit that I was far better off with Fletch as an ally rather than an enemy.

"Males are really very simple," he'd told me once. I wanted to laugh at the memory. Nothing about Fletcher was simple. His past, his motives, the way he operated to get to his goals . . . all were as subtle and intricate as Esme's embroidery. Lucky for me that he'd decided Cara Fletcher Couture was a worthy acquisition. Or had he? "What use do I have for a clothing company?" he'd asked.

He reminded me of the drawings of the artist M.C. Escher. Your eye traveled up one twisting staircase only to go down or across another, in a never-ending spiral of trick-the-eye, fool-the-mind complexity. Fletcher fascinated me. No, there was nothing simple about the man, and he was now impossible to ignore.

He seemed totally fixated on me. That was more than a little frightening. He'd engineered me into the most romantic setting imaginable. How had I let him maneuver me into this situation? Alone in a foreign country, staying in a private suite in a Florentine palace with the most devastating, dangerous corporate raider on the East Coast, who had designs on me, my body and my company. He wanted me, wanted me badly, wanted me enough to take a five million dollar risk, just to have . . . *me.*

The stunning realization overwhelmed me, and I stumbled over a loose stone in the walkway.

He pulled me closer. "Are you feeling all right? You seemed shaky for a second."

"I'm fine." I put my arm around his waist, steadying myself.

I warned myself to be careful. I wanted him too, had wanted him since first setting my eyes on the mysterious, compelling stranger in the courthouse hallway. His presence in my life had become as indispensable as breath, and he knew it. Fletch had created a situation where, like the settlement conference, I didn't want to say no. He didn't need to force anything. Instead, he spoiled, indulged, and romanced me into submission.

Still in the throes of indecision—would I? should I?—I stopped to stare as we rounded a corner. The Ponte Vecchio lay before us, displayed across the Arno like a fabulous gift. Despite the late hour, the bridge was still lit by the windows of the shops built on it. The gentle sound of the water flowing calmed my nerves, and I was able to look at him. Fletch's chiseled profile, silhouetted by the bridge's lights, seemed to soften as he bent his dark head toward me.

He was so beautiful, inside and out, that I couldn't stop myself. I reached up, slid one hand behind his neck and pulled him down for a kiss. He responded immediately, urging me into a closer embrace. His tongue probed, plunged, probed again, turning me on, lighting a fire that only Fletcher could bring and that only he could quench.

My mouth was a live wire zinging pleasure through my body. I sucked greedily, curling my tongue around his, playing with him, needing to give him as much joy as he gave me with his slightest caress.

Breathless with excitement and anticipation, I broke away to draw in some air. He ran a fingertip along my bangs, ending at my earlobe, which he pinched gently, then took between his lips, nibbling. He feathered his lips along my neck, and I shivered again, bending back my throat. My neck is very sensitive, and I knew kisses there would take me even higher.

Dammit, he let me go. "That's the first time you kissed me." His voice was deep with pleasure.

"We've kissed plenty of times."

He shook his head. "I've kissed you. You've responded, but this is the first time you've kissed me. Do it some more, baby."

Grinning, I pulled his head closer and nibbled on his lower lip. He sighed into my mouth, his breath scented with Chianti. Yum. I kissed deeper, tugging on his suit jacket while he wrapped one arm around me. We began to walk along the riverbank toward the hotel.

I was overcome by a fever of anticipation and couldn't keep my hands off him. I undid two buttons on his shirt, slipping my hand into the slit to caress his chest as he pushed at the revolving doors of the hotel.

"Oh, Cara, you wicked woman." His voice dropped to a growl as he kept me close by his side.

The lobby, dark, quiet and a little scary, stifled my giggles. I rushed into the elevator, and he followed, attacking me again, hauling down the shoulder of my dress to expose more skin as the elevator slid smoothly to our floor.

Laughing, I flitted away from his grasp and hurried down the hall to our suite. Fletch fumbled with the large, ornate key. An eternity passed before the door swung open, an eternity in which my heart hammered and the blood rushed through my veins like Niagara.

Lit only by the moonlight streaming through the suite's open curtains, he slammed the door. Pulling me close, he tore at the buttons on the back of my dress while I tugged on his belt buckle. I pulled his zipper down and let his trousers drop to the floor.

So long, so long, it's been so long. The chant sang through my blood, running hot and wild as I jerked at the knot of his tie. Fumble-fingered, I let go, and he took over loosening the tie, smiling. I focused on ripping off his shirt as fast as I could. I wanted to see him naked. He toed off his shoes and stepped out of his pants.

He pulled me into his arms for a kiss, our first full-body-contact embrace. It was amazing. I adored the glorious feel of his naked flesh touching mine. I burst with awareness, brimming with want and need.

Nude except for lingerie, I tried to drag him to my room, but he resisted. What the hell? I laughed when I realized that he was trying to take me to his bed.

"I guess we have to decide which bedroom to use." He kissed my fingers, then nibbled with an exciting blend of savagery and delicacy.

"Let's try both. How big is your bed?"

Still holding my hand, Fletch went to check out my suite, heading into the bathroom first. "Oh, this is nice. I have only a stall shower." He turned both taps on the marble tub. "Did they give you any bubble bath?"

I rifled through the basket of toiletries the hotel provided. "No, but there's shampoo." I opened the small plastic bottle and poured the pink contents into the tub. Scented foam burst from the water. "Perfect."

"Let me get in first and you can climb on me."

"Sure, but there's plenty of room. I guess those ancient Florentines liked to bathe." Leaning over the rim, I poked a finger into the tub. "Youch, real hot. We'll have to let it cool down." I straightened up.

"I can think of something to do in the meantime." He nuzzled my neck and turned me around to face him.

His eyes had turned serious, dark wild honey with flecks of gold. He captured my mouth in a deep soul kiss that sought and reached right into my heart. "Love me, Cara." His lips flickered over my neck, and I groaned from want. He leisurely slid his lips down and along my shoulder, then lower to take my breast, sucking my nipple in and out of his mouth in a seductive, blatantly sexual rhythm. I felt as though I as going to explode from pleasure. One finger slid inside me in a slippery caress, and my moans increased.

Suddenly I was in the air, clutching Fletcher's shoulders as he carried me into the living room. My heartbeat tripled. He sat me on the couch and knelt in front of me, opening my legs with a gentle but persuasive hand. My flesh rippled, and I let my head fall against the back of the sofa.

He stroked through the curls at the notch between my thighs, fingering the moist folds. He tugged my hips to the edge of the sofa, then bent his dark head, the streaks in his hair showing silver in the moonlight. His tongue, warm and wet, touched me tenderly, and I shivered with anticipation and delight. Again, his finger entered me, and I sucked in a breath at the intrusion. Though welcome, no part of a man's body had been inside mine for a very long time.

He stilled, letting his finger rest in my sheath. "Cara, honey. How long has it been?"

A little embarrassed, I squirmed. "Not for a while. Not since Natalie came to live with me."

"What's that, eight or nine months?" I realized with relief that his tone wasn't judgmental. "I don't feel a diaphragm or anything inside you, baby. Are you on the pill?"

I appreciated the question, since I'd forgotten about the issue in the heat of the moment. "No."

He rose and looked around while I leaned against the brocaded back of the sofa and watched him. The darkness emphasized his innate wildness while the shifting moonlight made his developed muscles gleam like carved statuary, as rough and as beautiful as a Rodin sculpture. I was going to touch and caress each sharply cut curve and plane with my fingers, my mouth, my tongue. I was going to make love to every inch of his gorgeous self in every way I could think of.

"Where are my pants?"

"What do you need those for?" I laughed.

He found them on the carpet near the coffee table and fumbled in the pocket, withdrawing a small square packet. "For this." Opening it, he protected us both as he returned.

"And you?" I asked. I had to know. I'd die if I was just his bedmate of the week.

"Hmmm?" He kissed me intimately once again. The hum vibrated through his lips into my most tender places. I grabbed onto his shoulders for support as I softened, buckled. He hummed again, then pulled away. "Did you have a question, honey?"

I recaptured my breath and managed to speak. "How long has it been for you?"

He rocked back onto his heels. "You beat me out, but I haven't been with a woman since before I saw your cute little self prancing down the courthouse hallway in those high heels you like to wear." He chuckled appreciatively, and I gathered he'd liked those damn shoes.

"Really?" I was relieved, though I had figured he was unattached. We'd been together constantly for several weeks, and the only women who phoned him were his secretary and his mother.

"Really. I figured it was a while for you, too." His hand, busy between my legs, continued to tease and play with me. Pleasure, like bright shafts of color, tore through me. I couldn't focus on anything else and threw back my head, gasping in short, sharp pants. "You're nice and tight for me, baby. I want you so much, *Carissima mia.* Let me love you."

He positioned himself and slowly pushed in. I gripped his forearms in an agony of waiting, willing myself to relax and open to him. I assumed he'd be big, like the rest of his frame, but I'd forgotten the reality of a man's sex thrusting into me. The sense of fullness made me heat, melt, moan. Stretching, my body drew him in. I clung to him, moaning and shaking. God, I needed this, needed him.

He kissed my forehead, my eyes, my cheeks and then my mouth, lingering there, his tongue echoing his movements inside. "Oh, baby, I'm sorry, but I can't wait." He reached between us, stroking me again, forcing me higher, faster.

My mind went blank as I came, writhing in his arms. He let himself go, thrusting hard, gripping my hips, trembling with the intensity of his release.

Spent, we curled together on the couch until our bodies calmed. I loved this mellow bliss, and wanted it never to end.

Finally, I raised my head from its pillow on Fletch's shoulder.

My skin prickled with cooling sweat.

He kissed my hair. "How 'bout that bath?" Lacing my fingers in his, he led me to the bath. "You're right. This huge tub will easily fit both of us." Sticking a toe in, he said, "Come on in, the water's fine."

He leaned against the tub's sloping end opposite the taps, which seemed to fit his back perfectly. I didn't want the taps in my back, so I clambered in and adjusted myself on top of him.

"Comfy, *Carissima?*"

"Not bad."

He closed his eyes, and I felt his muscles loosen in the warm water. I picked up a washcloth and dragged it across his chest. He hummed with pleasure. I held the cloth high, letting water drip from it onto his nipples. They stiffened. I slid the washcloth over his belly, then down to his groin. He hardened in response and reached for me, but I wasn't going to make it so easy. I slithered out of his reach, laughing.

"Come here, you fox." He fluffed some bubbles at me. They caught on my breasts, and his gaze homed in on them. He sat up and flicked one of my nipples. I guess it didn't harden fast enough to satisfy him, so he took its tip between thumb and forefinger, squeezing and rolling until it pointed. The pleasure, slightly tinctured with a delicate ache, made me whimper with renewed desire. He tasted, sucked, then went for the other one. Apparently he believed in equal time for both breasts. He nibbled until I moaned and reached for him.

I caressed him through the cloth.

"Do you know what you're doing to me?" His sex, already swollen, hardened once more.

I tightened my grip. "Oh, I know exactly what I'm doing. Don't you think so, Fletch honey?"

He grabbed my hips and I yelped, dropping the washcloth with a splash. Taking it, he rubbed it between my legs, kneading the sweetest spot through the cloth. I was in heaven. Tossing it aside, he pulled me on top, and I eased down on him carefully. I was a little sore and didn't want to push myself. His face showed his impatience and lust, but I dragged out the initial entry. He could wait. I knew that the taunting and the teasing would make it even better. When at last he impaled me completely, I let myself sag onto his chest as I swiveled my hips around him. I gave him tight little tugs from the muscles that held him captive as I climaxed. He came so hard I thought he was going to hurt me, but somehow, I took everything he had to give and still wanted more.

The water had cooled when I untangled myself from his limbs and, stiff, climbed out of the tub. He opened one eye to look at me. I loved the drowsy contentment on his face.

"I'll never look at a bathtub the same way again." I wrapped myself in a fluffy towel, and offered him one.

He stood, and water slid down every shining, chiseled plane of his body. My breath caught in my throat as he reached for the towel and kissed my hair. "My bed or yours?"

Sunlight streaming through the yellow curtains awakened me. Seated on the side of our bed, Fletch pressed a phone to his ear with one hand and held one of his ever-present guidebooks in the other.

"Nescafé, per favore, e panna. No, no, caffe nero. La panna separamente, per favore. Sí, accanto. Miele a panino, uh, panini. Um, frutta." He flipped pages frantically while I struggled not to giggle. "Not *frutta. Frutti, um, macedonia di frutta.*" He put the phone down. "If we end up with dinosaur eggs for breakfast, I apologize. Next time, the Hilton."

"No way. Does the Hilton have brocade couches and giant antique bathtubs? I love this place."

"Then we'll come back every year. *Buon giorno, Carissima.*

Sleep well?" He leaned over and kissed me. It was a long, lingering sweet one.

Of course, I kissed back. "Mmm. And you?"

"Oh yeah, except that a wild woman attacked me over and over last night." He caressed my breast with a broad, open palm.

I grinned. "You didn't seem to mind."

"Oh, I didn't. But I didn't get much rest. I might have to stay in bed today just to make up for my lost sleep."

A few minutes later, a knock at the door signaled that breakfast had arrived. Fletcher grabbed the hotel's toweling robe before going to the suite's door. He returned pushing a cart loaded with fragrant food: coffee, rolls, honey, and fruit compote served in cut crystal bowls.

I sat up in bed, ignoring my nakedness. Last night's mullet hadn't hit the spot—nowhere near it, really—and I was starving. I let the sheet crumple around my waist as I reached for a roll.

"Slow down, my little piglet. You'll get food in the bed."

"So what? There's another one." I bit, letting crumbs scatter. The roll tasted delicious, crunchy on the outside, but soft and sweet within, redolent with herbs.

"Good point. I think I'll have my breakfast right here." He leaned over and licked crumbs off my nipples. They promptly hardened.

I dropped the roll.

"Tasty, but I can make it even better. Lie down, baby." He stuck a spoon in the crystal honey pot, then dribbled the gooey mess onto my chest.

"What are you doing?" Startled, I tried to get up.

His firm hand forced me back down onto the pillows. "I'm just making a little breakfast."

Something inside me shook, trembled. "This is too weird for me."

"Oh, come on. Where's your sense of adventure?" Using both

hands, he rubbed honey into my breasts, mixing it with the crumbly roll.

Whoa. Bits of bread rasped my nipples. Then Fletcher's warm, wet mouth sucked one tip hard and moved across my chest. His morning beard grazed the soft valley between my breasts while a sticky hand slid behind one knee, spreading me wide.

More honey dripped, this time onto the nest of curls at my delta. As the honey warmed with contact, it became slicker, hotter . . . like I was.

I stretched and arched. Random morsels of bread scratched my back, my thighs, as he kissed honey from between my legs. The rub of his tongue pushing a bread crumb across my most sensitive flesh took me out of my mind. Languid and soft, I opened myself to him as he rose above me, pressing his erection against me before he moved inside. He rubbed sticky hands up and down my breasts as he thrust. He sank in, gasping.

We spent the day in the suite—the Pitti Palace be damned. I couldn't get enough of Fletch, and he seemed to feel the same way. We finally ventured out at night to find more food. Besides, both beds were a mess and we'd used every towel; it was time to let the hotel staff clean up. At dinner, I was more cautious with ordering, and ate something I knew I liked, pasta *alla matriciana* while Fletch tried a mysterious dish called *carciofi*, which turned out to be roasted artichokes.

We walked for hours in Florence after dark, enjoying the mystery of the exotic streets. Missing the churches and museums, closed at night, we instead explored the outdoor beauties of the city: the Michelangelo Gardens, the Neptune statue, the Arno River.

On Monday morning, I saw that Fletcher's mood had changed. He was all business, I thought, watching him emerge from the shower and reach for his suit without a single caress of my breasts. So I put on a hat, dress and sandals, getting ready for the drive to Prato.

When we got there, I saw that the factory seemed old and shabby by American standards. "OSHA would have fits," I said to Fletch.

He grinned. "From what you've told me, this place wove cloth worn by Michelangelo and Raphael." He peered into a dim room which reeked of chemicals.

I could see a dyer at work, her stained hands dripping measured pigments into beakers of solution. "I wonder where they're expecting to meet us."

"Signor Fabrizio—perfect name, huh?—said to find our way to the office in the back. The swatches and the paperwork will be there."

As Fletch predicted, we found Signor Fabrizio Conti in a tiny, cluttered space in the very back of the factory.

"Ah, Signorina Cara, Signor Wolf, 'allo, 'allo, *buon giorno.* It is so nice to see the long-awaited Cara Fletcher, so brilliant, so lovely." He bowed to me while kissing my fingers with extravagant flourishes. He even winked at me while shaking Fletcher's hand. "Here are your swatches, Signorina. We were so surprised to receive your fax six weeks ago."

"Fax? What fax?" I asked.

"Eccola." Signor Conti went behind his desk to open a file labeled with my company's name. He removed a sheet signed with my name.

"That's not my signature," I said, dismayed. "Fletch, look at this. It's a cancellation order on my letterhead, but someone forged my name."

"*Sí.* But we noticed this was not your signature from the prior correspondence. So we phoned, and your Signorina

Andersen said the future of your company is in doubt. So we waited."

I exchanged a glance with Fletch. "Maggie and I never discussed this. Did she recontact you?" I asked Conti.

"No, but we close in August, as you probably know."

"I'll take these samples back to New York with me, and I'll fax or call later this week," I said. "We'll have to work fast to put the show on by November fifth."

"We can do it," the small Italian said confidently. "The delay, it does not matter. Because our other orders have been shipped, it is quiet, and we can, ah, how would you say? Focus on your job." He beamed at me.

I was relieved. Sort of. Who had forged my signature? Maggie?

"And now, Signor Wolf, would you like to check the papers?"

While the men looked through the file, I took the swatches over to the window to look at them in sunlight. I'd selected ice cream colors for the spring line: lime, peach, lemon, vanilla. They looked every bit as tasty as I'd planned. The men's fabrics were similar but with touches of olive and tan to "masculinize" the line. The linens, silks, cottons and feather-light gabardines were all superb.

"Cara, come look at this." Fletch had spread a sheaf of printouts on the desk, comparing them to Conti's documentation. "Do you have a highlighter pen, Signor?"

"Sí." Conti produced a thick yellow tube.

Fletch marked two lines on one printout and three on another. "See, here's our record of checks paid to Fabrizio," he told me. "They total $189,549 American, correct?"

I scanned the figures. The man must have an adding machine in his brain. "Do you have a calculator?" I totaled the numbers, then nodded.

Fletch reached for a small sheaf of papers from Conti's file.

"Here are photocopies of the checks paid."

"These numbers are completely different." I added the amounts hastily, then rechecked my math. "Fletch, Fabrizio was only paid ninety thousand dollars. Signor, I'm sorry. We owe you quite a lot of money, don't we?"

"But no, Signorina. Cara Fletcher Couture is an excellent customer. We have been paid in advance, as always. See, here are the transaction records. The deal was for ninety thousand dollars American."

"But . . . but," I stuttered. "Fletch, what does this mean?"

"Signor, excuse us for a moment." Taking my arm, Fletch led me to a corner of the office while the Italian tactfully withdrew.

"What is it, Fletch?" I asked. "What the hell is going on here?"

His face looked carved out of stone. "Cara, those entries were made by Maggie Andersen. I think she's been skimming."

"Skimming! But how? Why?"

"I'm not sure yet, but since she had total control over the company's finances, there are a variety of ways she could have ripped you off. All your hard-copy records were destroyed in the vandalism, so untangling this mess isn't going to be easy."

I felt the ground crumble beneath my feet, as though one of the foundations of my little world had turned out to be infested with dry rot. Maggie had been my mainstay for years. I found it hard to believe that she had been systematically stealing from the company. She seemed to work so hard, putting in long hours, coming through for the runway shows season after season. I hated to think of her as a thief, and surely Fletch understood that. "How long have you known about this?" I asked, trying to read the expression in his eyes.

Hesitating, he evaded my gaze. "I didn't really know until just now. I'd guessed a couple of weeks ago."

"You didn't say anything to me." I can't believe this, I thought. This man owns half my company. I've opened myself to him body and heart, and he doesn't trust me.

"I can't accuse anyone without proof. I suspected, but I didn't know."

Well, that was reasonable. Kinda. "You should have said something. Please don't withhold information like this from me in the future, okay?"

Stepping away from Fletch, I turned to Signor Conti, who fiddled with an elaborate-looking espresso maker which sat on a nearby table. "Fabrizio, thank you for helping us. Would it be too much to ask for a copy of your entire file on my company?" I wanted to check every transaction. My stomach churned when I realized that every deal made with every company would have to be checked. When on earth would I find the time and energy to deal with this?

My thoughts remained chaotic throughout the drive back to the hotel. It was a miracle that I didn't fall apart, given that I hadn't taken a tranquilizer for days. My food remained in my stomach, also, which was good, but I still had huge worries. Maggie a thief! "No wonder I can't make any money," I told Fletch.

He nodded. "I wondered why you weren't in the black. The product is excellent and priced appropriately for an upscale market. I'm not entirely surprised, though. Rip-offs are common in any business. Maggie's attitude—"

"Yeah, she was really upset by the joint venture deal," I said, remembering the conversation with my assistant. "She said, 'he'll spoil everything.' Now I know what she meant. I can't believe this. I thought she was my friend."

"Your coworkers and employees are just that, and nothing more. They're not your friends."

My heart contracted. "What about us?"

He slipped his arm around me. "We're special, honey, and you know that. Damon works with me, also. Obviously he's more than a coworker, too."

I eyed him, unsure what to believe. If Maggie could betray me, couldn't Fletcher? I mentally reviewed my entire association with Fletcher Wolf. Both predator and prey, he operated in a world in which I was as alien as a werewolf on Mars. I recalled the tête-à-tête I'd overheard in the restroom about his thirty-page prenuptial agreement. Although he'd murmured sweet nothings to me, talked dirty to me, moaned his release into my ears, he'd made no commitments and said no words of love, even though we'd scarcely gotten out of bed in two days.

What had I done? He'd turned my world upside down with the lawsuit and the joint venture. He made love to me until I could hardly walk, let alone think straight. Now he was accusing my closest associate of embezzlement. Had he seduced me to tighten his hold on me and the company, already knowing he'd force Maggie out? What if the printouts had been fabricated by Fletch himself?

"I don't want to fire Maggie."

Fletch stared at me as though I had announced that I wanted to sprout wings and fly to the moon. "Cara, she's a thief. She ripped you off for nearly a hundred thousand dollars, then probably destroyed your studio to cover her tracks. That cost you nearly two hundred thousand. And I bet the Conti deal is just the tip of the iceberg. Who knows how much she's stolen?"

"You're speculating. Nothing's been proven to my satisfaction."

"I don't want to pull rank, but I will if I have to."

"Are you telling me that I can't select my own assistant?"

"That's not the issue. I won't allow a thief access to your atelier. What if she sells your designs?"

I gasped as though punched in the belly. That awful possibility hadn't entered my mind. "But if we tip her off, we'll never know, and we'll never recover the money."

He paused. At least I'd made him stop and consider. "You're right. How 'bout this? You'll lose time, but let's close the atelier for the week. When we get back tomorrow, we'll go to the police and swear out a warrant. If we can get hold of her personal papers and her bank statements, maybe we can trace the stolen funds."

"Or prove her innocence," I said.

"I hope you're right."

I looked at him, raising my brows. "Oh, please."

"I really do, honey. I truly feel no animosity toward Maggie. In fact, I'm mystified. I know you're not stupid, and I'm sure you checked her out."

"Oh, yeah. All her previous employers were very happy with her. She left Claiborne only because she wanted to work for a smaller firm and get more responsibility."

"She may have figured there'd be an opportunity to steal at a less structured company. Or maybe when she got to you she saw she had the chance."

"Especially when I got the loans," I said thoughtfully. "All of a sudden, she had piles and piles of money to play with. I guess the temptation was too much." Suddenly, I felt as though I was a million years old. Or that I carried the weight of worlds on my tired shoulders. I dropped my face into my hands. "I know we'd talked about sightseeing, but I can't. Let's go back to the hotel. I want to lie down for a while."

Chapter Fifteen

"How could Maggie do this to me?" I asked Fletch as he sat on the suite's couch and punched buttons on his cell phone.

"I don't know, love. Some people are just selfish." He frowned, and I could hear a gabble of Italian issue from the receiver. He put down the cellie, sighed, then used the hotel phone to call the concierge and asked the hotel personnel to put the call through. While he waited, he said to me, "Let's not mention this to Natalie, please."

"Oh, no. I never discuss business with Nat. She doesn't need to worry about money."

The phone rang and he picked it up. "Hello? Oh, Damon," Fletch said into the receiver, apparently surprised to hear Damon's voice. "You sounded like Griffin. Hey, I thought you were in Wilmington." He paused as though listening, then told me, "He's visiting Darkrider Farm for the weekend." He turned back to the phone and said, "Marvelous. Listen, Big D, I need a favor. We think there's an internal problem with Cara's operation in New York, and we want to close the workshop for the week. Can you go to Manhattan, change the security codes and the locks? And talk to Ramirez while you're there."

A pause before Fletcher explained the situation. "It looks as though one of Cara's employees has been skimming. We want to check it out when we get back Tuesday before making any accusations. We'll still fly back on time, but we want the employees locked out for the week. Tell them that they have a vacation at half pay because Cara has decided to, umm, replace the air conditioning. And be very, very careful what you say to Maggie Andersen."

"Maggie?" Even though Fletcher held the receiver to his ear, I could nevertheless hear the shock in Damon's raised voice. "Cara's assistant?"

"Yes," Fletch said. "She's been handling the money. We're not accusing her, but she's definitely the focus." Then he looked visibly startled. "He wants to talk to you."

I understood his surprise. In the past, Damon and I hadn't gotten along, but this was different. "Sure," I said, reaching for the phone. "Hi, Damon."

"What do you think about all this?" he asked.

I appreciated the fact that Damon was checking with me. It denoted respect. "Fletch is right. Close the atelier for the week. Let's boot out the bad guys and get to work. I have only eight weeks to put on a show, and I have to hit the ground running." Another thought occurred to me. "Hey, can you do something else for me?"

"Another favor? You and Fletch are the most demanding bosses on the eastern seaboard."

I smiled, again enjoying his acknowledgment of my authority. "Hire me another personal assistant. Check her very carefully."

"You can trust me, Cara, but listen. Don't blame yourself."

"I'm at the top of the heap," I said grimly. "There's no one else up here to take responsibility."

"Stuff like this happens in every business. Tony and I will fix it." His voice was self-assured and confident, different from the angry man I'd known.

"I'm glad I can count on you. Please don't breathe a word of this to anyone, all right?"

I must have sounded embarrassed or uncomfortable because Damon said, "Listen, it's okay. You haven't worked with me before. Don't worry, I'm the soul of discretion. Not a peep to anyone. I'll arrange to have the AC replaced this week so everyone has a little extra vacation."

"Great. Umm, is Natalie there?"

"Mom will find her. Hold on. Natalie?" I could hear Damon yelling even though the sound seemed muffled, as though his hand covered the receiver. He returned. "She's outside with Griffin. I declare, that little girl's become my brother's shadow. Hold on . . . here she is."

"Hi, Mom!" Natalie's voice was cheerful.

A weight lifted from my chest. I'd been afraid that she'd be unhappy or frightened. I should have known better. Her father probably had left her alone or with virtual strangers for long stretches of time. "How are you, sweetie?"

"Great. I love Darkrider Farm. Veronica's really nice."

"What are you doing?"

"Griff gave me a horse to ride while I'm here and he showed me how to curry her and muck out her stall."

"Griffin has you cleaning out the horses' stalls?" I eyeballed Fletch, who shrugged. "Okay, as long as you're having fun. What time is it there?"

"Breakfast. We just got up. How's Italy?"

"Fun." I grinned at Fletcher, thinking about the kind of fun we were having together. "See you Tuesday night, sweetie."

"Love you, Mommy. Bye."

"Love you."

The phone clicked, and I turned to Fletch. "I hope you didn't have to talk with Veronica or Griff. She just hung up."

"It's all right, honey. What do you want to do now?"

I slumped, feeling defeated. "I don't know. I'm still trying to absorb this. Maggie's been with me for years. If she'd needed a raise, or a loan, I would have tried to get it for her."

"I can't look into her mind."

"The detective said that the vandalism seemed personal, that someone wanted to hurt me. I never saw that in her. She must be the greatest actress in the world."

"Maybe she's jealous. You're beautiful and talented, everything she's not."

"But it's not as though she isn't loved. She has a boyfriend," I said. "A famous, rich one. Adam Covarrubia. You met him, remember?" Fletch's brow furrowed as my thoughts raced. "Oh, my God," I breathed. "Adam. Adam and Andrea. Oh, my God."

"What is it?"

Outrage flooded my body. I lacked words, I was so angry.

"You know something. What is it?"

Trying to collect myself, I squeezed my eyes closed, then blinked. "Adam and Andrea Covarrubia are twins from New Jersey. They're models, way famous, at the Iman–Kate Moss level. There have always been rumors about Adam and Andrea but they're so good that everyone gives them the benefit of the doubt."

"What kind of rumors?" Fletcher asked. He looked tense. A small part of me was happy he was taking me seriously, but mostly, I was just pissed off and suspicious.

Not about him, of course, but I had formulated a theory that just might be correct. "That they're heroin addicts."

"And you hired them?" His voice cracked with disbelief.

"Fletch, they were only rumors. I used them in my shows because they brought a lot of publicity and attention, and I've never seen any evidence of drug use. At least none that I could prove. Shit." Restless, I rose and began to pace. "But it makes sense. If they're addicted to drugs, they'd need money no matter how much they earn."

"Is drug use common in the couture industry?"

"I can't speak for everyone, but the designers I know work so hard there's no room in their lives for drugs. The models are another story. There's a lot of gossip about the ways the models have to keep weight off—coke and meth as well as purging after meals." I stared out the window at the Duomo, flaming orange in the afternoon light.

He touched my arm. "Let's call the New York City police and see what we can start."

After more phone calls, I was thrashed and went straight to bed, even though it wasn't near to bedtime. Stress, suspicion and jet lag had caught up with me. After I awakened, Fletcher took me out to eat on the terrace of an outdoor cafe in Fiesole, high above the city. I watched the lights of Florence emerge from the dusk in the valley below. In the deepening night, the Arno looked like a dark ribbon flung across glittering silver sequins.

I didn't have much to say, but found myself touching Fletch often. I needed reassurance and contact to anchor me in a world gone increasingly skewed. I held his hand, caressed his thigh and played footsie, but somehow our eyes didn't meet. I was increasingly disturbed by the mixed signals.

I knew how I felt but didn't have a clue about his emotions, if there were any. He clearly wanted me and had for a long time. The intensity of his lovemaking left no doubt of that. But lust meant nothing to most men. Desire, possession, and love weren't always related, and Fletcher Wolf had always impressed me as a predator. From the moment he'd seen me, he'd schemed to take me and everything I had. Not only had he achieved his goals, but he was frighteningly close to stripping me of my closest associate.

But how could I blame him for Maggie's crimes? Sighing, I realized that the truth was hard, very hard to face. Maggie hated me. Did Fletch love me? I found my upper teeth dragging at my lips. Regardless of my own feelings, how could I trust anyone after how seriously I'd blundered with Maggie? I'd misjudged her so badly.

I raised my eyes to meet Fletch's. He watched me with that disconcerting golden gleam. I should have been used to that look, but my heart still lurched.

Good God. I loved this man, but had no idea what he felt about me or wanted from life. I was too damn scared of the answers to ask. I couldn't hear myself saying, "Fletch, do you ever want to marry? Have kids?" Most men took one look at Nat and ran as fast as they could the other way.

Who cares for the caretaker? The question I'd put to Fletcher haunted me. A lone wolf, he seemed content to run alone at the top of the pack, but that could be a mighty lonely place. If he chose that place forever, there would never be any room for me or my daughter in his life.

After we made love, he kissed me, tenderly cupping my breast as I continued to come. The trembling that seized me gentled into blissful afterglow as we cuddled.

"Here. I want you to have this." Rolling away from me, Fletch reached into a drawer of his bedside table to take out a small wrapped box.

Though still boneless with pleasure, I managed to sit up. The sheet slipped off me and bunched around my waist as I took the gift. Pulling off the purple ribbon and gold paper revealed a small velveteen box, the kind of jeweler's box which often contained a ring. Shocked, I inhaled in a short, sharp burst. "Fletch, I don't know what to say."

"Better save your acceptance speech 'til you've seen what it is." He leaned back against the pillows, smiling. His eyes held a mixture of lust, amusement, and something I was scared to analyze.

The box contained a cameo ring surrounded by tiny pearls

and set in gold filigree. "Oh, this is wonderful." A bewildering mix of surprise, relief, joy and disappointment tumbled through my heart.

I'd actually thought he'd propose. Good God. I'd become a fool over this man. Rattled by the situation, I wondered if I'd truly wanted him to propose. How would I have reacted? It was surely too soon for a declaration of undying love. But to be honest, wasn't that what I really wanted from Fletcher?

I remembered the thirty-page prenuptial contract and winced inwardly. No wonder it wasn't an engagement ring. If Fletcher ever proposed, he'd probably have his attorney deliver a diamond along with a contract delineating the rights and responsibilities of each partner in their relationship. Nope. No way. I wanted an old-fashioned marriage like my parents had, based on love and trust. I'd treat this romance for what it was: a fling. At some point, I'd find a way to tell Fletcher that, despite mind-blowing sex and burgeoning love, we couldn't continue our relationship back in New York.

But the cameo was a sweet gesture, and I appreciated it. Really. I took the ring out of its black velvet nest, trying it on various fingers.

"As luck would have it," Fletch said as the ring slipped easily onto the third finger of my left hand and stayed there.

I squirmed with embarrassment. What exactly did he mean? And did I really want to wear a ring on that finger? That was pretty possessive. However, did I want anyone else?

No, I didn't. "It's beautiful. Thank you."

"I picked out one just like it for Natalie. Call me corny, but I think that matching rings on you two will be cute."

"That's very sweet. Where did you get them?"

"On the Ponte Vecchio, while you rested."

"I didn't want to miss our last day of sightseeing, but I needed that nap."

"I'm sorry that today was so hard on you, honey." He picked up the purple ribbon from the sprawl of crackling golden paper.

"It's not your fault."

"I could have warned you. Let me make it up to you." Fletch slid closer, pushing box and wrapping out of his way. He passed the cut edge of the ribbon over my breasts, which hardened as he lingered on the nipples, teasing them into fullness. He ran the soft satin strand down my belly, bouncing it over my hip. "Open your legs." He trailed the ribbon between my inner thighs. My skin rippled like a lake swept by a summer breeze. Tossing the ribbon aside, he took me in an intimate kiss that went on and on until I thought the top of my head would blow off.

Covering me again with his body, he slipped inside as I opened, then tightened, gripping him with my knees and wrapping my legs around his waist. He groaned as he glided in and out in a rhythm old as life, yet new and fresh as morning in Eden.

"Oh, baby, we really messed up." Fletcher squinted at the face of his watch as morning sun shafted into the room between the heavy brocade curtains. "We'll never make our flight."

"What time are we supposed to be at the airport?" I stretched my arms up over the pillow.

"An hour ago."

"Oops."

"Oops is right. I'm sorry, honey. I forgot to ask the concierge for a wake-up call."

"This must mean you're loosening up. What happened to precise, punctual Fletcher, 'Mr. Organization is the key to Success?' " I laughed at the chagrined look on his face. "Hey, I thought you had a private jet."

"I don't own the plane, but I have shares in it. It doesn't

make sense for us to own a jet. Fletcher Tool and Gear wouldn't use it enough. We have to schedule use of the plane." He punched buttons and got through to the airfield. "Just as I thought," he said. "We can't leave today. Tomorrow morning at the earliest."

I reached for him. "Bummer. I guess we have to spend another day in Florence."

He groaned as I rolled him between my palms. "*Cara mia*, you'll be the death of me."

We had to wait until it was daylight in America to call Richmond to talk with Damon, but he'd already left for New York. Veronica told me she'd put Natalie on a flight to JFK on the same morning that we'd arrive.

The flight back the next day was uneventful, except for the discussion I dreaded. I waited until we were high over the Atlantic before raising the subject of our future.

I clinked my champagne glass against Fletcher's before taking a sip. Okay, it was a swig, then two. I hated to tell Fletch, who'd treated me like a princess, that our romance was over, and back in Manhattan we'd have to stick to business. I cleared my throat, preparing to speak, then took another swallow of champagne. So I'm a chicken. Squawk, squawk.

"Better go slow on that stuff, honey. It'll only be eight-thirty in the morning when we get back home. You'll have a whole day to get through, and you won't make it if you're sloshed." He peered at me over the rim of his champagne flute. "Hey, what's wrong?"

Damn him. How did he always know when I was bothered? "Umm, you."

"What now?"

I took another gulp of liquid courage. "We can't go on like this back home."

"Like what?" He twinkled, daring me to get graphic, the wretch, with a flight attendant hovering to fill our glasses or offer appetizers.

"Like, well, you know."

He tipped back his head to stare at the ceiling. "Don't know much right now, honey. For the last four days, I've been loved until my mind is blank." He turned back to me and smiled, baring his teeth, alpha wolf keeping his mate in line with the program.

"You are determined to make this harder than it needs to be, aren't you?" I spoke very precisely, feeling the effects of the alcohol.

Taking my hand, he put it into his lap. His bulging sex strained the cloth of his khakis. "How hard does it need to be for you, honey? And I know how you like it. Very hard, very deep and very long."

A flight attendant stopped at my side, and I felt a slow burn start in my cheeks. I snatched my hand away.

The attendant lowered a tray of caviar canapés toward me. "Hors d'oeuvres?" the lady asked.

"Two, please," Fletcher said, and she put a pair of the munchies on a china plate and set it on my tray. Picking one up, he held it in front of my nose, letting me smell the salty fish. "Open your mouth."

I didn't like to be told what to do, but I was hungry. The caviar, miniature bombs of briny flavor, exploded between my tongue and palate. The chopped egg mediated the taste. Yum. I sipped more champagne and realized I was lost.

"Now what did you want to talk about?"

I gathered my straying wits while I still could. "Us."

"Isn't it a little early to have a relationship talk? We've been lovers less than a week."

"Is there a schedule I'm supposed to follow?" How like

Fletcher. Everything on time and precisely organized.

"Of course not. Just relax and go with the flow." He waved his hand in the air.

"What about Natalie? I'm supposed to be setting an example for a preadolescent."

Fletcher chuckled. "Whatever you want, Cara. So we had an affair when we were in Florence that we won't discuss with Natalie. Does that make you feel better?"

"Well, yes, it does."

"Fine," he said. "Let's call it an affair so we don't have to worry about something as serious as a relationship." He snuggled closer to kiss my forehead, and then my cheek and mouth. "Hey, come with me to the lavatory."

"What's in the lavatory?"

"I want to join the mile high club."

"Fletch!"

"Come on, honey. Live a little." Leaning over, he unlocked my safety belt, then tickled my side.

I squawked, spilling champagne into my lap. The remaining appetizer fell off the china plate. Smelly caviar smeared my jeans.

"Oops," Fletch said blandly. "Guess we'd better get you to the lavatory to clean up." He gave me a grin and a little push.

Glaring, I hauled myself out of the seat and headed aft. Fletch, following, crowded into the restroom before I could close the door. Being a private jet, the restroom was larger than on a commercial airliner, but it was by no means huge. Its small size didn't seem to deter him. He knelt, licking chopped egg off my pants. I gathered his long hair with one hand to keep it out of the food and watched him with a growing sense of amazement and desire.

He rose. "Hmm. This space does present a challenge, doesn't it?" he said with a wink.

Chapter Sixteen

After our luggage was unloaded, we endured an interminable wait before Natalie, bubbling with joy, deplaned from her flight from Richmond. She'd had a great time, and I made a mental note to remind her to write thank-you notes to Veronica, Griffin and even Damon, who'd turned out to have an unexpected soft side.

The limo pulled up to the airport curb at precisely ten in the morning, New York time, but I had already tolerated a long day of travel. I could hardly wait to get home, take a shower, and slip into my nice, familiar bed. My nice, familiar, empty bed. Lovemaking with Fletcher had a major drawback: I didn't get much sleep.

As the car stopped outside our brownstone, I opened the door and sniffed.

"Pe-yew, gross smell, Mom," Natalie said.

I craned my head to search for the source of the stench. Nothing suspicious in the gutter. I looked up, and my mouth dropped open in horror. I squeaked and scrabbled for Fletcher's sleeve, tugging him out of the limo. Couldn't he move any faster?

"What?" He looked up. "Sweet Lord Almighty!"

The upper portion of the building was a smoke-blackened ruin. With mounting outrage, I saw that only our loft had burned. The other apartments seemed to be untouched.

Natalie jumped out of the car before I could stop her.

"Hillary! Chelsea!" she shrieked, dashing toward the building.

"The birds," I murmured. My daughter had a fondness for those lovebirds that was grossly out of proportion to their brains, looks, or personalities. "Nat!" I called. "They're with Tom and Ellie, remember?"

Natalie stopped. "Let's go see them right away, Mommy."

I hurried after Nat, who'd resumed her headlong flight into the charred building. But at ten in the morning on a weekday, I didn't expect to see either Tom or Ellie at home.

Natalie pressed her ear to their door. "I can hear them. I can hear Hillary and Chelsea talking." She banged the knocker.

Fletcher walked up and down the hallway. "Strange that only your place is burned, Cara." A strip of yellow crime scene tape with black lettering was strung up and down the hall, sealing off our loft. Holes had been chopped in the walls, presumably by the firefighters to release trapped gases. The corridor reeked to high heaven. "I have a very bad feeling about this."

"What happened to your fancy-schmancy security guy?"

"He's been overseeing the installation of a new security system in your workshop, not watching your place. We didn't think anything would happen here with you away."

Tom opened his door. Surprising, since I thought he'd be working. His bony frame was draped in his usual worn jeans and chambray workshirt. A frown flickered over Fletcher's features, replaced by a vague, pleasant smile as he advanced and extended a hand.

"I'm Fletcher Wolf, Ms. Fletcher's partner. When did this happen?" Fletch nodded at the extensive damage as he and Tom shook hands.

"Just last night. I'm Tom Lenox. Cara, how're ya doin'?"

"Better before I got here," I said. "Did the police come out?"

"Yeah, and a bunch of fire trucks, too. They seemed to think it was an electrical fire. Hey, Nat, I have your birds. They're okay. Wanna see 'em?"

Natalie nodded and went inside Tom's apartment, moving with the ease of familiarity. Happy that she was out of the way, I realized that I didn't want her in the hall contemplating the ruins of our home. Good God. What were we going to do? Nat started back at school in just a few days, and we had no home, no clothes except the contents of our suitcases, nothing, zip, zero.

I stumbled down the hall toward the gap which had formerly housed my front door. My beautiful pine door, which I'd finished myself. Pushing down the yellow tape, I tried to get in. I could see that in the entry, portions of the walls showed blackened streaks. The varnish on the pine had bubbled. The peculiar miasma made my stomach pitch.

Fletch grabbed my arm. "Where do you think you're going?"

"I want to check out the damage."

"No way." Tom had followed us down the hall. "Your floors aren't safe. They said the hallway from the stairs to our door's okay, though, and our place is all right, but I'm not taking a chance. We're staying with Ellie's mom in Brooklyn. I just came by to get some clothes."

I peered through one of the holes in the wall into my home, trying not to cry, but my throat and eyes stung with unshed tears. "We need to call the police," I said to Fletcher. "And my insurance company." I dragged at my hair. The despair deep in my stomach threatened to engulf me, but I refused to give in to the panic. "What are we going to do?"

Fletch put his arm around me. "Honey, I'm gonna make sure that no one ever harms you or Natalie, ever again." Though his touch felt warm and comforting, his hard amber eyes held an expression I'd never seen. Alpha wolf protecting his packmates, I thought, my tension easing. I hoped my faith wasn't misplaced.

His voice was curt. "Tom, please ask Natalie to collect her

birds. Cara's jet-lagged and tired. We need to go."

Tom nodded and withdrew.

"Why were you so short with Tom?" I asked. "He's a good friend."

His mouth flattened into an uncompromising line. "I don't rule out any suspects."

"Suspects? He said it was an electrical fire."

"Is that so? I don't understand why this man's place is basically untouched while yours is destroyed."

"You think Tom's responsible? You're kidding."

"No, I'm not. Does he know Maggie Andersen?"

My jaw clenched. "Yes, he does. He recommended her to me. But—"

"But what? The man looks like a hopped-up biker. Is he on meth?"

"No! Tom's a good father. Natalie plays with his daughter in his place all the time. Are you questioning my parenting abilities?"

"No, of course not." Fletch sighed and rubbed his hand over the back of his neck. "Honey, I'm sorry. I'm just tired. Let's collect Natalie and go, all right?"

"Okay. I guess we'll stay at a hotel until I can rent another place."

"Oh, no. I'm not letting you out of my sight."

"Really?"

He eyed me. "Yes, really. I protect my investments. Too many strange things have happened to you. I want you under my eye at all times."

I was a foul brew of rocking, roiling emotions, fighting nausea born of anger and fear as I lugged my tapestry garment bag and my satchel—all my worldly possessions—down the thickly carpeted hallway of Fletcher's Central Park West condo. I turned right at the first doorway into a bedroom, wondering if it was mine.

Immaculate as any luxury hotel room awaiting a guest, there were no obvious clues to the room's occupancy. Its sole distinguishing feature was the boxes set on every possible surface, including the windowsills and the nightstand. Jolted out of my funk, I dropped my bags and gawked, enchanted.

Elaborately carved wooden boxes ordinarily would have impressed me but, in this grand company, they didn't capture my eye before I was diverted to more flashy or unusual items, which included enameled, glass, even stone boxes. Indeed, the word "box" seemed inadequate to describe these objects, most of which would have borne the title "sculpture" comfortably.

Hearing a rustle, I turned. Fletcher lounged in the doorway.

"Is this my room?" I asked.

He came toward me, as gorgeous and predatory as the timber wolf whose name he shared. Now that I knew what he could do to me in the sack, he turned me on even more. "Sure, if you want."

I grasped his meaning just before he came in for a kiss. "Now wait a min—"

He evidently viewed my open mouth as an opportunity, because he plunged in without a shred of inhibition, as usual. He slid his arms around me, tucking his hands into the back pockets of my jeans. Pulling me close, he deepened the kiss while caressing my entire body with his.

When he finally let me go, I stared at him, silent. I didn't know what to say. His kisses always seemed to wipe my mind clean, like a sandblaster scouring graffiti off a wall.

"C'mere, Mom." Natalie darted into the room and grabbed my hand, dragging me out. "Our rooms are at the end of the hall. They're really neat. We have our own bedrooms and bathroom and everything." She hauled me into an elegant, ivory-carpeted bedroom, then turned on me, looking horrified. "What were you doing? That was Fletch's room. You can't sleep with him."

Guiltily aware that she had no idea what had transpired in Italy, I recovered the power of speech. "It was an innocent mistake."

"Yeah, right. It was obviously his bedroom. It even smelled like his cologne."

I eyed her with concern. "You notice a man's cologne? Sweetie, you're growing up too fast."

She drew up her slim little body. "I notice everything about the man my mother is becoming involved with."

"I'm not involved with him."

"Yeah, right. That's why you're all red. Let's get our bags and unpack."

"I don't know why we have to bother," I grumbled. "We won't be staying long."

"Why not?" Fletcher stood in the doorway with my bags.

I glared at him. "It just isn't a good idea."

"Yeah, why not, Mom?" Natalie asked. She stood next to Fletch, the two of them presenting a united front.

"It wouldn't be . . . it wouldn't be . . . it wouldn't be entirely proper."

Both stared at me as though I'd suggested wrestling a rattler for light entertainment. He started to chuckle, then laugh. "Not entirely proper? Oh, honey, that's too sweet." Still laughing, he left the room, shaking his head. I'd bet my company that he was thinking about our wild weekend in Florence.

"Wake up, Mom! We have no home."

"Just put away your stuff, all right? And don't use all the drawers in the bathroom!"

Darkness had fallen when I woke up. I realized that while I

slept someone, most likely Fletch, had washed my dirty clothes. Nice, because after I showered, I was able to put on clean clothes. Wearing jeans scented with caviar and lovemaking wouldn't have cut it.

I wandered into the kitchen, where Fletch fussed at an electric range. Natalie was giving fresh water to the lovebirds. She wore a cameo ring on the index finger of her right hand. "Did you thank Fletch for your gift?" I asked.

"Oh, yeah. Thanks, Fletch."

"Natalie!"

"I'm kidding. Of course I did."

"Don't sass your mama." He stirred a sizzling pan of vegetables.

She shot him a long, cool look.

I sighed. Our CPW sojourn would be hell if Natalie and Fletcher didn't make peace. Why hadn't he changed his approach to her now that he knew she had issues? I didn't have the energy to deal with them now. Despite the hours of sleep, I didn't feel rested. Too many dreams filled with fire and smoke had interrupted my snooze. "So what's for supper?"

"Vegetable stir-fry on Chinese noodles. We've eaten out so much lately that I wanted an evening at home."

This place wasn't home, but why argue? "Nat, did you nap a little?"

She nodded, her damp, curly hair waving over her shoulders. She wore clean shorts and a T-shirt reading "Virginia is for lovers."

Fletch must have caught sight of the direction of my gaze because he said, "Maybe I should take you to Darkrider Farm soon. Natalie, do you think your mom would like Virginia?"

"Yep." She poked a stick at Chelsea, who chirped before fluttering to the other side of the cage.

I shoved a hand through my hair. "Maybe we should go shopping after supper. I'm the wrong color."

"What?" He turned, staring.

"This red hair. It's all wrong." I bit my lip. "On top of that, I have only one pair of contacts, which is boring, and no clothes. Neither does Nat."

"I don't understand. Red hair was fine last week. What's wrong with it now?" he asked.

"I feel as though I'm wearing a stop light on my head. Doesn't suit my mood."

"If you say so. But I'll miss my little carrot top." He drained the noodles in a colander, adding splashes of sesame and chili oil. "But you can't go tonight. We're expecting the arson investigator to bring the report."

"Oh." Tension seized my shoulders.

"It's all right, *Cara mia.* We'll get to the bottom of this." He divided the noodles into three portions, dumping them into bowls decorated with blue carp. The veggies went over the noodles with sprinkles of sesame seeds and crumbled seaweed.

"Awfully strange fare for a meat and potatoes man," I said.

"Oh, I'm aware of your tastes, honey, as well as my cholesterol count."

My mind tilted and whirled, as though I was on a carnival ride. I had never envisioned myself living in the world of *Leave It to Beaver* with Fletcher playing Beaver's mom. Ann's lousy dossier hadn't revealed that corporate raider Fletcher Wolf knew one end of a wooden spoon from the other, let alone that he liked nori and sesame on his stir-fry. I'd expected better from hotshot AnnMarie Slye.

The arson investigator, a short, dapper black gentleman, arrived at nine o'clock. He introduced himself as Jonas Draper. I'd expected a firefighter in uniform, but Draper wore a suit and carried a briefcase.

"Thank you for coming out so late," I said as Fletch led the three of us into a small, wood-paneled study. I chose a straight-backed chair. I didn't want to sit on a sofa and risk Fletch snuggling with me.

"No problem." Draper sat on the leather-covered armchair Fletch indicated. "I work night shift. I was on duty when the call on your place came through at four in the morning yesterday, or rather, today."

"Four o'clock?" What the hell? I felt as though the devil had dragged me out of my comfortable world and thrown me into a particularly evil parallel universe. "Fletch, if we'd come home on time . . ." I couldn't finish the sentence. The implications were too ghastly.

"I know," he said. He turned to the investigator. "We've been told that it looked like an electrical fire."

Draper frowned as he removed papers from his briefcase. "Who said that?"

"One of Cara's neighbors."

Draper's brow cleared. "Yes, we told the neighbors that so as not to worry them. Actually, the fire appears to have been deliberately set."

My gut twisted, and I closed my eyes, feeling ill.

Fletch took over the conversation. "Mr. Draper, Ms. Fletcher and I just returned from Europe today, but we'd originally planned to come back yesterday. If we'd returned on schedule, Cara and her daughter would have been asleep in that home. If it was arson, you'll have to consider this case as an attempted murder."

"Oh, it was arson, all right. There are traces of accelerant in the townhouse, especially in the upper-story bedroom." Draper handed Fletch a stapled sheaf of papers. "Here's the preliminary report. It looks as though the perpetrator broke through the skylight, dumped gasoline through the hole, and tossed in a match. With all the varnished wood, the loft bedroom went up like a torch. The rest of the apartment sustained heavy structural and smoke damage."

"Excuse me." In a feeble attempt to keep my dignity, I dragged myself into the kitchen before ralphing half-digested stir-fry in the sink. After rinsing my mouth, I leaned my elbows on the tiled counter. My vision blurred. Raising my head, I heard the rumble of Fletcher's bass as he showed the investigator out, followed by a burst of canned laughter from the TV program Natalie watched in the living room.

Tears flooded my eyes as Fletch's arm wrapped around my shoulders. "Oh, honey. Don't cry. Please don't cry."

"S-someone tried to k-kill us."

"I know, baby, I know."

"Who? Why?"

He kissed the tears off my cheeks. "Someone who's in a lot of trouble, believe me."

"Adam, Maggie, Tom . . . and where was Damon?"

"Oh, baby, it wasn't Damon. He can be quick-tempered, but it wasn't Damon. Trust me, he didn't make a move while we were away that Sam didn't know about. Damon was more than happy to have Sam at his beck and call while we were gone."

"I d-don't understand. I don't understand any of this, anything that's happened." I buried my head in Fletch's shirt. God, he felt so good, so warm and comforting.

He hugged me fiercely. "I don't understand either, baby. I don't understand why your assistant, after an excellent track record in business for a decade, suddenly decides to embezzle from you. I don't understand why your workshop gets trashed and your house burned. I don't understand anything, but I swear to you that by the end of this, I sure as hell will, and whoever's responsible will pay."

He took a deep breath, and his grip tightened. "No one, but

no one is going to mess with you again. Now come on, let's go to sleep. We have a big day tomorrow."

Fletcher kept his word. I went to bed without him for the first time in nearly a week, but again, I couldn't rest. Stressed-out beyond belief, I wanted to fall asleep nestled in his arms, but I didn't want to be so weak. I didn't know how long he'd be around, so I figured I'd better take care of myself and Nat rather than depend upon him. Men could be flakes; Kenney had proven that.

Besides, there was still the Natalie factor. I had to set an example.

The digital clock by my bed read 1:08 when I crept out of bed to check on Nat. The air conditioning in the condo made my naked skin prickle and chill as I stole down the hall.

The door to her room was ajar. I peeked through the gap to see moonlight glinting off her hair, flung over the pillow like a wind-whipped flag.

Warm breath stirred the hairs at my temple.

"What are you doing here?" I whispered.

Taking my arm, Fletcher led me away from Natalie's door and to my bedroom. "Same as you. I couldn't sleep. Decided to check out who was rambling around the house at one A.M. The security here's good, but we can't be too careful." His watchful topaz eyes glimmered in the dim light.

"I can't sleep from worrying."

"Honey, there's no use fretting. We'll find out more in the morning. Now let's get some rest." He held out his arms.

"You're off-limits."

"I know. But what's more important, how we look to Natalie or our health? She's asleep. Tomorrow's a big day. Next week's bigger still. We have a show in two months." He walked me down the hall to my room.

"We?" I couldn't help smiling. The thought of the big bad Wolf putting on a fashion show tickled my funny bone.

"Yes," he said firmly, shutting the door. "We. You and me and Damon and whoever he finds to help us out."

I slipped between the sheets, snuggled into the pillow, and closed my eyes. The bed creaked when he lay down beside me, but he stayed outside the bedclothes. Probably doesn't need to get any hotter, I thought, and chuckled.

"What's funny?" Spooning me, Fletch cuddled.

"You."

His voice sounded mystified. "I'm glad I'm entertaining."

"You are. You are definitely the most interesting person I've ever met."

"Funny you should say that." He nuzzled my neck.

I purred with pleasure. "Why?"

"I feel the same way, honey. I just can't stay away from you. Never could."

"Then we're a matched set."

"We are. Like the top and bottom of a box."

"And you collect boxes, don't you?"

"Uh-hmm." He draped an arm around my waist, anchoring me close.

"So I'm part of your collection," I said, too tired to be miffed.

"A very prized part. Now go to sleep."

He stroked my hair, a soothing touch. Next thing I knew, sunlight poured through the curtains and the scent of Zanzibar coffee drifted past my nostrils.

I sat up, pulling the sheet around my breasts. Fletch was gone, but Natalie stood in the doorway, clad in her Raiders T-shirt, rubbing her eyes. Her hair, a wild, tangled cloud, surrounded her sleepy face.

"Oh, darling. We should have braided your hair before you went to bed."

"I was too tired."

"We'll pay for it today. Bring me your brush, and I'll get out the tangles."

Natalie disappeared, quickly replaced by Fletch, who carried a mug. He handed it to me. "Hello, sleepyhead."

I took the coffee, sniffing the steam which curled from the dark surface. "Yum, thank you." After sipping, I set down the cup on the bedside table as Natalie came into the room, hairbrush in hand. She ignored Fletcher as she plopped down on my bed, and I wondered how long he'd let that go by. I winked at him over her shoulder, then started to brush out my daughter's hair.

"Good morning, Natalie." Fletch's Virginia timbre carried more than a hint of amusement, as though he enjoyed his combat with her.

Who would break first? Natalie could be as stubborn as a stuck door, but Fletcher was both the original irresistible force and the immovable object. I decided to take a hint from his attitude and enjoy the process.

"Good morning, Mr. Wolf," Natalie recited in a singsong voice.

"Oh, you can call me Fletch. We're living together. We don't need any more mister and miz, do we?"

Nat's head jerked, and I accidentally pulled her hair. "Youch!"

"Sorry, honey, but you need to keep still." I met Fletch's eyes, which brimmed with laughter.

"And I'm wearing shorts," he said. "No way can someone in shorts with their knobby knees hanging out be a mister. Okay?"

"If you say so." She shrugged, again causing a yank. "Mo-om!"

I gave up. "If you're going to squirm, you can brush your own hair. Get the tangles out, and I'll braid it for you. And get dressed. We're going shopping today."

She headed out, brush in hand.

Fletch sat on my bed. "Now I can say good morning properly." He leaned over to kiss me.

I gave him a brief peck and a quick push. It was like trying to move a mountain off of my bed. "Scram. No hanky-panky with Natalie around."

He didn't budge an inch. "This isn't hanky. Or panky. Just a friendly good morning kiss." He scooted closer to tip up my chin with one finger. "We're still friends, aren't we?"

"Of course." My heart started to beat faster. How did he do that?

His lips nibbled mine. "So, good morning, sweetheart. I slept well. Did you?"

I picked up my coffee, then put it back down. A hot beverage wasn't necessary at this point, since I was already hot enough. Feverish, even. "Yeah, as soon as we lay down together, I fell right asleep."

"You just keep that in mind." Standing, he stretched, arms reaching for the ceiling. The muscles under his polo shirt bunched and flowed.

I gulped. With Fletch only one bedroom away, celibacy was going to be tougher than I thought.

Chapter Seventeen

"Hey, Fletch! Lookit my new bra!" Natalie danced into Fletcher's study, waving a tiny white training bra over her head as though it were a trophy and she an Amazon warrior returning triumphant from battle.

I followed to see Fletcher, who stood near the sliding glass doors to his balcony, back away. His eyes bulged, and his face flushed. He banged his shoulder on the metal doorpost as he tried to escape.

"Good afternoon, Fletch." I said in a demure tone which I hoped matched my new brunette 'do. "We indulged in some retail therapy at Bloomie's. Would you like to see the rest of our purchases?"

"Natalie, honey, I really don't need to see your underthings, okay?" He sounded tense.

Nat shot him a sly look from under her lashes. "But this is my first bra, Fletch. Mom says I'm becoming a woman."

His mouth opened and closed, sort of like a grouper. Not even the yellow suspenders with the little horseshoes had been so funny. I tried hard not to laugh, but he was just too cute. Pressing my lips together, I covered my mouth with one hand.

"That's wonderful, honey," he said, his voice forced. "Congratulations. So where would my two women like to have dinner tonight?"

I recovered myself. "We had Chinese last night."

"How 'bout deli?" he suggested.

"Or pizza," Natalie said enthusiastically. "Hillary and Chelsea like to peck at the leftover crusts."

"We'll have plenty of pizza on football nights," Fletch said. "Hey, should I get season tickets to the Eagles for you two? Damon and I always go."

I raised my brows. "Oh, please. The Eagles? We're Bills fans."

"The Bills? That figures. Upstate. But they won't win the Super Bowl any time soon."

"Yeah, their quarterback sucks," Natalie chirped.

Fletcher gaped.

This time I laughed out loud. Needle-sharp Nat was full of surprises, and Fletch had just been hit with two of them. Watching them interact could be an unexpected bonus of the fire, almost fun enough to hang around for, but I had already decided not to stay with him for long. I didn't have time to play house with Fletcher. Hopefully, my apartment would be rebuilt soon, and life could go back to normal.

I managed to avoid being alone with Fletch for a weekend of shopping madness, during which Natalie and I replaced our lost wardrobes, toiletries and other necessities. He'd been a perfect gentleman, lending us the limo and Sam, then taking us out to dinner Saturday night to the Russian Tea Room. Natalie, who wore a dress, heels, and her new bra, had handled her first "grown-up" evening out with poise and aplomb. Though I was really quite proud of her, I felt a little wistful. She was growing up fast, and I had missed so much of her childhood.

I found that shutting the door on Fletcher at night didn't shut off my dreams, which were all about him, but I didn't have to fantasize anymore. Hot, wet memories of his lovemaking filled my thoughts whether I was awake or asleep.

Sex with Fletcher had been beyond amazing. We hadn't just had sex, we'd made love, at least the first time. I'd never again look at a brocade sofa again without getting an erotic thrill up my spine.

The rest of the vacation had been pure, unabashed sex, getting it on, making whoopee, doing the horizontal bop, the old in-and-out. I'd taken what I wanted, and as with the best sex, my selfish taking had turned on both of us.

We'd done it every which way, and it was great, but what did that mean to Fletcher? I bit my lip. Nat and I now shared his life even more intimately. What if she became attached? How'd she feel if the relationship tanked?

Seated on the couch in Fletcher's condo, I reached for a slice of pizza topped with julienne vegetables. Its melted cheese stretched and snapped as I lifted it out of the box, which sat on the coffee table. Next to me, Fletch cracked open his second beer of the evening. In front of us, the Sunday night football game occupied the television screen.

Natalie came in, wearing her training bra, a see-through mesh top, and an attitude. So much for a mellow evening.

"I hope you're not planning on going out wearing that," I said as she plunked down on the couch.

She pushed out her lower lip. "I'm going bowling with the kids from computer camp. You said it was okay this morning."

"That's not the issue, and you know it."

"I want everyone to know I got a bra. That creep Donna's been acting like she's the only kid who's growing breasts."

"I must have been truly evil in a past life." Fletch mumbled.

I ignored him, eyed Nat and said, "No way."

"But you wore a top like this last year!"

"That was last year," I replied. "That style's been passé for at least eight months. Go and put something else on, pronto."

Fletcher stared, and I caught his eye with a grin. "Kids. You struggle for 'em, you do your best for 'em, and this is what you get. Think I should ground her?"

He gulped more beer. "Sorry. I didn't have a great example to follow, remember? I'm more like the father from hell."

"No, that was Kenney."

"Is Sam taking her to the bowling alley in the limo?"

Obviously Fletch couldn't handle my adolescent daughter any better than her father had, so he changed the subject. "Yeah. She's the envy of all her friends. I've got to say, we'll miss all this luxury when we go home."

"You're going to move back to the same place?" He set his bottle down with a snap.

"Why not? Lightning doesn't strike twice, you know."

"We're not talking about lightning," he said through gritted teeth. "We're talking about an insane arsonist with an obsession about you. You're not going back there, ever."

"What did you say to me?" I was thoroughly ticked.

"Did I mumble?"

"No, but I actually thought I heard you telling me what to do and where I can and can't live. Your authority doesn't extend that far."

"Oh, yes, it does. I'm not letting the most valuable asset of my corporation willfully place herself in danger."

Livid, I jumped to my feet. "I can't believe this. You're upset because an asset of your company is in danger? Pardon me for having the strange notion that I'm a person, not an asset, and that I run my own life." I stalked out of the room.

I slammed my bedroom door and sat on the bed, seething. I would've cried if I hadn't been so angry. Corporate asset, indeed!

I grinned suddenly. I had to hand it to Fletch. Not only did he end up with all the pizza and beer, plus the only TV in the condo, but he'd taken my mind off my problems. My gut wasn't twisted with fear. Maybe I ought to thank him.

Ha!

I charged out the door smack into Fletcher's chest and started talking at the same time he did. I rubbed my nose where it had whacked into his sternum. "You are really something else—"

"Cara, I'm sorry, but you're so damn stubborn—"

Fletch started to laugh, and so did I.

"Come on, let's eat dinner before everything gets cold. And I don't want to talk any more about you leaving, you hear?"

"I can't stay here forever."

"Let's debate that later. But Jonas Draper thinks returning to your old place while this guy is still at large would be a big mistake. So just stay put for a while. Please?"

"For now. So what's with her?" I nodded at Natalie's door.

"Oh, she wore another slutty shirt, and I wanted her to change it. We had words."

"Sometimes you just have to put your foot down. We shouldn't bend on the clothing issue. She'll be dating soon. I don't want her to look like Lust on Wheels."

Fletch slipped his arm around me. "Thank you for saying 'we.' "

"I did?" My face heated. "You know what I mean."

"I hope I do."

I didn't know what to say, so I just went back to the living room, with Fletcher following. A burst of crowd noise from the TV accompanied a completed pass. "It actually feels nice to worry about Natalie rather than thieves, vandals and stalkers."

"Feels nice? For whom? If she were my kid, I'd be terrified."

"Ha. The boys around here are the people who should be scared."

On Monday morning, I watched as Fletcher took out a jar of honey from his cupboard and put it on the kitchen table. "Want some honey on your toast, sweetheart?" His eyes teased.

I grinned, and tried not to turn into a puddle of warm honey myself. He knew it, that devil. I winked at him. "Why, thank you, Fletch, I do believe I'll have some honey this morning."

I took the jar, opened it, stuck in a spoon, then lifted it out. The thick syrup flowed off the spoon like molten gold, reminding me of the Italian sunshine that had streamed through the curtains of our room while we'd made love.

The honey thinned, and I twirled the spoon to cut off the thin yellow thread. Meeting Fletcher's laughing gaze, I lifted the spoon to my mouth.

I licked it. Yum.

His eyes widened.

I took my time, meticulously tonguing every bit of the luscious syrup off the bowl of the spoon.

I licked the back of the spoon, then swirled my tongue around it.

Fletch gulped, his Adam's apple bobbing. He slid one finger into the collar of his dress shirt, loosening it a fraction.

I slid my tongue along the long stem of the spoon, then put the entire round end of the spoon into my mouth.

"Excuse me." He dashed out of the room.

Natalie, busy at the toaster, turned. "What's his problem?" She spread peanut butter on her toast and brought it to the table.

"Beats me. How does that new uniform feel?"

She flexed her shoulders. "A little itchy, but it'll be okay after it's washed."

"You ready to go yet?" Fletcher came back looking considerably calmer.

I beamed at him. "But I haven't finished breakfast yet."

"Oh, I think you've had enough to eat. Come on." He herded us out.

It was Natalie's first day back to school, so we dropped her off early so she could find her way to her new classes. Then we went to the atelier to reopen the workshop. I hoped to get back into a routine. There was plenty of work to do, and I headed right into it despite Maggie's unexplained absence.

"How do you do that?" Fletch demanded as I draped a length of lemon-colored linen over a mannequin that afternoon.

I snipped here and there, then tugged on a couple of threads. I pinned it to another, similar strip of fabric, and it became a sleeveless jacket. I smiled smugly. "Beats me. How do you raid corporations?"

Before he could protest, I climbed onto a nearby table and clapped my hands for attention. "People, gather 'round!"

The cadre of designers crowded in, visibly curious.

"Here's the concept for the show." I gestured at the dummy. "Check this out. Instead of front and back sections of the jacket sewn at the shoulder, we have an un-constructed tabard joined with seams at the sides and back. The tucks here create a flowing drape over the breast."

"Wow," Santo said. "There's no horizontal lines at all."

I nodded. "Not one. The vertical seams make the wearer seem slimmer. And what does every woman want?"

"To look thin!" Everyone shouted at once.

"Right!" I bounced up and down in new high-top sneakers. These were bright pink. "The real beauty of this design for us is its simplicity. We have only seven weeks, people, so let's go! You'll find patterns for these jackets in your computers under the file name 'autumn 1.' "

Woo-hoos of approval, then a flattering patter of applause broke out before the designers headed back to their mannequins and sewing machines.

Fletch followed me up the metal stairs to the loft as I continued to talk about the new design, which I loved. "We'll put them over light blouses, drawstring pants with wide legs, loose, slim shifts. They'll be incredibly comfortable. Dressy, too, in the silks we bought in Italy. Oh, Fletch, I'm so excited!" I stopped at the top of the stairs and flung my arms around him.

He hugged back, picking me up and swinging me around the loft. "I can see that."

"I feel this way every time I get the concept for a line. I love it when all the ideas come together. It's a special moment."

He kissed me. "Congratulations, honey. I have to admit that I'm relieved. These last weeks have been pretty bad. I didn't know how long it would take for you to focus on work."

"I love my work. It's a part of me. No matter what else is happening, a little chunk of my mind is always busy designing—"

Sam appeared at the top of the stairs, and one look at his face shut me down. He twisted his cap in his hands. His normally immaculate black uniform looked creased and crumpled. His sandy hair stuck out and his blue eyes held more than a hint of worry. "I don't know how to tell you this," he said. "Natalie wasn't at her school when I went to pick her up. I don't know where she is."

Chapter Eighteen

My world spun, and black flecks crowded my vision as I swayed. Cramps seized me; I bent over at the waist, praying I wouldn't retch as bile flooded my throat. Fletch grabbed me and plopped me in the leather armchair. I huddled into its comforting clasp as he perched on one arm of the chair, keeping a warm hand on my shoulder.

I let myself slump. "Are you sure you were at the right exit? Nat changed classrooms this year, and might have left another way."

"I'm sure. I circled the school three times." Sam gulped. "I even got out to look for her. I'm sorry, but she's gone."

I groaned and buried my face in my hands. "Oh, my God, Nat! How could this have happened?"

"I don't know," Fletcher said. "Cara, do you have the phone number of the school? They shouldn't have let her leave with anyone but us."

Fear gripped me, but I tried to control my sobs. "You're right, of course. It's . . . the number's programmed into my cell phone. Fletch, could you call for me?" Despite my panic, I struggled out of the chair and went to the drafting table to find my phone. Shiny and red, it was blessedly easy to see.

I glanced at Sam as Fletcher punched buttons. I hadn't understood the strength of the link between Sam and Natalie, but it made sense. Sam had picked up my daughter from school or camp for weeks, ferried her to activities, shared snacks with her. I knew Sam was trustworthy, had checked him out thoroughly, but hadn't known they'd become buddies. Now Sam looked as though his own child had been kidnapped.

Kidnapped. My heart clenched. What more could happen? Whoever it was had harassed us, trashed the workshop, burned us out of our home, had now apparently abducted Natalie. My precious darling.

And I was helpless to save her. Helpless just as I'd been when those people had died. I hated helplessness, and judging by Fletcher's hand clenched around the phone, he didn't like it much either.

"I want to speak to the principal. Now," he said into the telephone. He rubbed my shoulders to no avail; my muscles were rock-hard.

"Put it on speaker. It's the silver button in the center." I pointed, and he pushed.

"Mrs. Whelan here." The principal came on.

"This is Fletcher Wolf. We weren't able to pick up our child, Natalie Fletcher-Madden, because she wasn't where she was supposed to be. Apparently someone unauthorized took her out of class or picked her up after school. What do you know about this?"

There was a pause. "Are you saying she's missing?"

"Yes, ma'am. The last anyone saw of her she was in school. Your school." His voice was calm, but I could see his jaw muscles clench.

"We had a short day today, and Natalie's last teacher would have been Mr. Robles, for art. He should still be here, cleaning up. Please hold."

"She seems to know her business," Fletcher said to me.

"Yeah, I checked out the school pretty thoroughly." I slouched back into the chair and wrapped my arms around myself, shoving away the nasty thought that the abduction could have been a professional job, making it even harder to track my child.

"Mr. Fletcher?" A male voice came on.

"This is Fletcher Wolf. I'm calling about Natalie."

"Yes. I'm sorry, I thought they'd tell you. Natalie was taken out of school by her grandmother. She was on Nat's emergency card, so we thought it was okay."

"Mom?" I was astounded. "If Mom had come, why wouldn't she phone? And what about Dad?"

"Are you sure?" Fletcher said into the phone.

"Sure, I'm sure. Natalie was excited as could be to see her grandma."

I relaxed, but only a little, and Fletch said, "Fine. I guess we don't have anything to worry about. Thank you." He clicked the phone off. "It sounds as though your mother's in town."

I stared at him. "That's not like Mom. Why didn't she call?"

"Because I didn't want to interrupt your work." My mom entered the loft, Natalie at her heels.

"Mom!" I jumped to my feet and shot over to hug both of them at once.

"We should have called. I'm sorry, but I didn't realize it would upset you so much. We thought we'd get here before you even noticed she was gone."

When my mom took a tissue from her purse and dabbed at my face, I realized I'd been crying. "I'm okay. I guess it was just a miscommunication. But with everything else—"

"I know. That's why I came down. Honey, what on earth's going on?"

I sighed. "Natalie, do you have homework?"

"Yep, sure do." Natalie hefted her book bag which, even at the end of the first day of school, looked as though it would burst.

"Now's a good time. Find a desk downstairs."

"If you're going to talk about me, I should be here."

"We talk about you all the time," Fletch said. "If you listened to every conversation, you'd never get anything done. Now scat."

She narrowed her eyes. "You owe me one, Fletch."

He narrowed his eyes back. "One what?"

"Maybe the Russian Tea Room," she said. "I liked that place."

"We'll discuss payback later. Go." He waved a hand toward the stairs.

Natalie went, and Fletcher grinned at Mom. "Your granddaughter will bankrupt me."

"You've created a monster," I said, trying to analyze my mother's mood. "She'll never eat plain pizza again."

Mom put down her suede hobo bag beside the teal leather chair and hesitantly lowered her jean-clad bottom into its aged seat. Despite her slenderness, the chair creaked, and she shifted to perch on the edge instead.

"Mom, would you like a cup of coffee?" I buzzed around the loft feeling like an anxious hostess at a boring cocktail party.

A faint smile flitted across my mother's face. "Yes, I'd like to try some of that famous Zanzibar blend, please."

Fletch raised an eyebrow at me. I felt my face heat. Now he knew I'd gossiped to my mother about him. Oops.

I poured coffee, then added sugar and cream to a battered ceramic mug, fixing it the way I knew she liked. "This cup is one of Natalie's best." I hoped I sounded perky, but my mother's unexpected visit bothered me. Leaving my dad to fend for himself and coming to Manhattan unannounced was totally out of character for her.

"I think I'll step downstairs and see if Natalie needs any help with her homework." Fletch must have noticed the tension, because he made a quick getaway.

"Honey, I can't hide that I'm very concerned." Mom sipped coffee, continuing to regard me over the mug's rim.

I sat behind Maggie's empty desk. "So am I. But I trust Fletcher to take care of us."

"That's what I'm worried about."

"I don't understand."

"Don't you think that everything's fallen into place for Fletcher Tool and Gear a little too neatly?"

My stomach twisted. "But I thought you supported the joint venture with Fletcher's company."

"At the time, I thought it was best. But now . . ." Mom faltered. "I might have been wrong. Look at what's happened! Fletcher Wolf runs your entire life. You have no home, and Nat says you're living with him. He's accused your closest assistant of theft. Where is Maggie, anyway?"

"I don't know. She was due back today with everyone else, but she didn't show up. At this point, I don't care. I can do my work without her, and I'm not looking forward to a confrontation with her about the irregularities in the books. That's Fletcher's problem."

"This is exactly what I mean. Everything you have, he controls, and you can't walk away."

"I don't want to walk away. Why should I?"

"What happened to your desire to be independent?"

I didn't know what to say. His kisses were so sweet that I'd forgotten my lifelong dream. Had I thrown everything away to have Fletcher Wolf? Rising from Maggie's desk, I began to pace back and forth across my loft.

"Ever since you were a teenager, you wanted only one thing—to run your own couture house," Mom continued. "When you won that scholarship to Parsons, I remember you telling me that your clothes would make the cover of *Vogue* in ten years. You did it in six. What's happened to the ambitious, independent daughter we raised?"

I breathed deeply, trying to collect my thoughts. Maybe Mom

was right. Maybe Fletcher controlled too much, too soon. "But Dad says we live in an interdependent world."

"That's not what I'm talking about. It's like you're a different person. A frightened, defensive person."

"I didn't realize that I'd changed so much." With a start, I remembered that I'd asked Fletch to phone Natalie's school. Good God. I'd even abdicated responsibility for Natalie to him. That was wrong, plain wrong.

"My job as a parent is to teach you to stand on your own two feet. I don't like to see my daughter go backward, not forward, in life."

But I needed his help, didn't I? And I'd told him that I wouldn't leave his home . . . yet. I didn't want to go back on my word. "But this is a special situation. I'm being stalked. This place was trashed. Nat and I were burned out of our home. But I'm sure that Fletcher wasn't responsible, if that's what you're hinting at. He was sitting right beside me on a plane when it happened."

"He's got hundreds of employees."

"I can't accept that Fletch ordered vandalism and arson."

"Who's to say that a rogue employee didn't do all of this?"

"But why? Cara Fletcher Couture is part of Fletcher's company. There's no profit in an arson of my home. All it does is cut into future earnings if I can't produce a fall show."

Mom paused, then said, "That's a very pretty ring you're wearing. It's like Natalie's. She told me that Fletch gave it to her."

I squirmed. "Yeah, mine too. He thought it would be nice for us to have matching rings."

"You're wearing yours on the ring finger of your left hand. Honey, are you sleeping with him?"

This was new. Mom hadn't asked about my personal life for at least ten years, possibly because I hadn't had much of one until Fletcher Wolf came along. I evaded. "No, I'm not sleeping with him, um, now. But I have to admit it's tough to stay out of his bed. He's very—well, he's beyond attractive. He's romantic and compelling and very, very seductive."

She smiled. "It's easy to see that he's interested in you."

"Which is why I don't think he's responsible for any of the bad stuff. That's not Fletcher's style. Fletch is a deal-maker. He works by persuasion and, in my case, outright bribery."

Mom's smile broadened. "Can't argue with five million dollars. But what about an employee? Someone could have decided you were bad news. What's the corporate structure of Fletcher Tool and Gear?"

"I don't know much about it. I think that Fletcher's family owns a controlling interest. It's a corporation that issues shares and brings in unrelated people when necessary. Fletcher and his brother Damon, along with one other fellow, actually run the firm."

"Who is this other person?"

"A man named Emill, who's responsible for day-to-day production and operations."

"Have you met him?"

"No, but Fletcher mentions him once in a while. I've heard him talking on the phone to his secretary about Charles Emill."

Mom rubbed her chin. "Didn't you say you hired an investigator?"

"Yeah, a woman named Shila Chong. Ann recommended her. But she hasn't done much since I entered into the joint venture with Fletcher Tool and Gear."

"Strictly speaking, your personal troubles aren't Fletcher's responsibility. I think you should call this Ms. Chong up and get her onto this Emill person, as well as the arson. And what about Trent Whiting? Wasn't he at your last show without an invitation?"

"Yeah, he was." I began to pace again.

"I don't trust him."

"Me either. I'll have him checked out."

"I also think that I should take Natalie back home with me."

"What?" Stopping short, I glared at her. She couldn't have hurt me more if she'd slapped me in the face. "Are you serious? Don't you remember what a disaster January was?"

Closing her eyes, Mom winced. "Of course. How could I forget? But it's for her safety."

I pressed my lips together. "What did Nat say about this?"

"We didn't discuss it. But I never reveal her confidences." Having calmed herself, Mom opened her eyes and smiled at me.

"I bet she said that she's happy here."

"Yes, but she's a child. This is a decision to be made by the adults who love her."

I touched my mother's hand, finding her fingers cold, as usual. "I know that you're concerned, but I can't agree. She's adjusted to life here. She got good grades in June—"

"Excuse me, ladies, but I wanted to review some materials I left up here." Fletcher had appeared at the top of the stairs.

Mom regarded him with guarded blue eyes and asked, "How's the homework going?"

He seemed unperturbed by her scrutiny. "Natalie's fine. She'll have a challenge this year in math, but it's nothing that she can't handle. Mrs. Fletcher, I know you must feel very concerned about everything that's gone on, but I want to assure you that Cara and I can take care of Natalie." He knelt in front of my mom's chair and took her hand in his. "Believe me, we'll keep her safe and happy."

Boy, was he ever pouring it on! I wondered if Mom would fall for it. I knew that Fletch's major motivation was to keep the two of us in his condo. Mom was right about one thing: Fletcher had a mania for control, especially if he sensed a threat. But since the man could sell ice to Eskimos, I bet that not even my mother would be immune to his persuasion.

Mom glanced at him, and her eyes twinkled as she withdrew her hand. "I'm sure you're more than capable." She rose. "Cara, will you walk me to my car?"

As we descended the stairs, I said, "I'm glad you came down. Will you spend the night?"

"No, your father needs me at home." She passed Natalie at a desk, caressed her hair, then bent and kissed her on the cheek. "Come see us soon, honey."

"I love you, Grandma." Natalie put her arms around my mom's neck and hugged her.

"Me too. Bye, sweetheart." Mom straightened, then walked with me out the door of the atelier.

"This is a long day of driving for you," I said.

"It's all right. I feel better just seeing that Natalie's well and happy." She stepped over Tony Ramirez, slumped in the gutter covered with newspapers. He looked up at me and grinned, revealing his excellent bridgework, thoroughly at odds with his appearance and his stench.

"Hi, Mr. Ramirez," I said. "Have you met my mother?"

"Hi, Ms. Fletcher, Mrs. Fletcher." Ramirez leaped to his feet.

Mom looked startled. "Er, hello."

"Mr. Ramirez is Fletcher's security chief. As you can see, he blends in with the neighborhood." I gestured at Ramirez's paper bag, which no doubt concealed a bottle.

"I'm happy to see that everything's under control." She tried to smile at Ramirez, but I guessed that the man's reek challenged her acting ability.

"I don't know if 'under control' is the term I'd use." I continued walking. "Let's say that we're doing everything we can."

Mom dropped her voice. "Yes, as long as you have your investigator working for you. Natalie's school seems to be well run, so I really can't argue with your decisions." She took out her key chain and pressed a button. Her van's alarm system chittered, and she opened the driver's door.

I circled the vehicle. "The locals are falling down on the job. Looks like you still have all your hubcaps and tires."

"That's why I didn't stay very long." Mom hugged me. " 'Bye, now. Take care."

I allowed myself to lean into her warm embrace. "You've given me a lot to think about."

She smiled. "That's part of my job. Love you."

"You too, Mom. Love you." I released my mother and watched her drive away.

I climbed the stairs, reentered the loft, and hopped back onto my stool to resume work.

"What's this I heard about January?" Fletcher asked from behind his desk. He tapped the eraser end of a pencil against his teeth.

I blew out a breath in exasperation. I had a lot to do before November. Couldn't he leave me in peace? "Do I have to talk about it?"

"Why not?"

"January was an utter disaster for everyone, that's why. How do you know about January?"

"Forgive me, but I overheard you and your mother talking as I came up the stairs. What happened in January that was so terrible?"

"Kenney brought Nat to New York in January, and my parents sold me on the idea that she'd adjust better to life on the east coast in Ithaca, because both Berkeley and Ithaca are college towns. They were totally wrong."

"Your parents are older . . . was she bored?"

I hated talking about this and decided to get the info out fast. I worried about how Fletcher would take this 4-1-1, but he'd asked, so . . . "Beyond bored. She felt abandoned by both parents, sank into a depression, and tried to off herself using some of my dad's painkillers. Luckily, she threw up instead."

He whistled through his teeth, but didn't show any other reaction.

I brushed hair out of my eyes and smiled at Fletch, though I was on the verge of tears. "That was when I put my foot down and brought her to Manhattan with me early in February, where she started at a new school, new semester. And that's the story of January, and of how Natalie came to live here."

"I think you're doing a terrific job. Considering everything, she seems well-adjusted to me."

A shout came from below. "My ears are burning!"

I laughed with Fletcher, who stuck his head over the railing of the loft to speak to Natalie. "May I assume you're finished with math?"

"No. May I assume you're finished with your work, Mr. Wolf?" she asked.

"Er, no." He sat back down at his desk.

"What are you doing, Fletch?" I asked.

"These are some of Maggie Andersen's phony computer records. I'm comparing them to the information from Conti and your other suppliers. Basically, I'm trying to recreate the transactions. If I know how much she stole and when she took it, maybe we'll be able to trace it and get some back. At least I'll know what to look for."

"I wonder where she is."

He shrugged. "Probably on her way to Rio or Djakarta. I bet she decided that her game was over as soon as we went to Italy. She must have figured out that Signor Fabrizio would blow the whistle on her and her cheating. She's long gone."

"Was Damon able to contact her when we were away?"

"No."

"I guess the thing to do is hire another assistant and put the November show together. I'm glad I had that brainstorm about the jackets. They'll be easy to make. We don't have much time, so I hope that everything gets back to normal."

Later that day, tears drenched my eyes. I dropped the police report onto Detective Briggs's battered metal desk and buried my face in my hands. Normalcy wasn't just around the corner. Less than a year ago, life had been perfect. My business was solvent, I had my daughter back, and a modern-day Jack the Ripper hadn't killed Maggie.

Chapter Nineteen

I pulled the shreds of myself together and managed to ask, "Who could have done this?"

"Suicide is a possibility," Briggs said. His voice held more than a note of doubt; it was more like a full-bodied chorus. "Her wrists were slashed, and there was a note confessing to the fire, the embezzlement, everything. She says also that the vandalism took place to cover up the destruction of financial documents, so all that's left are the doctored computer records."

"You did say, Cara, that she was dating a well-known model. If the relationship went sour, maybe that pushed her over the edge," Fletcher said.

"What's this man's name?" Briggs held his pen poised.

"Adam Covarrubia, C-o-v-a-r-r-u-b-i-a. I don't know his address, but you should be able to contact him through his agent." I rubbed my cheeks with a damp tissue. "Good God. Maggie dead. I can't believe it."

"Believe it," Briggs said. "That apartment wasn't a pretty sight. There was blood all over the place."

Fletcher tapped his teeth with the eraser end of a pencil. "When did this happen?"

"We won't know until forensics comes back with a report, but we suspect sometime over the weekend. We discovered the body early this morning when we went in to serve a search warrant for her financial records."

I closed my eyes. My stomach twisted. While we'd eaten a

sumptuous dinner or shopped at Bloomingdale's, Maggie had fought for her life—and lost.

"You suspect homicide?" Fletcher asked.

"I'm afraid so. The note is being analyzed by a psychologist, but our homicide division chief thinks that there are too many defensive wounds on her arms to rule out murder."

I shuddered, curling up in the hard, plain chair as tightly as I could. Though Fletcher's hand warmed my nape, I couldn't stop shaking.

"Detective, I need to get Cara home. This is too much for her. Send me the reports, will you?" Fletch whipped out a business card.

Detective Briggs accompanied them to the door. "Keep safe and alert. Does your building have security?"

"Yes, and we've installed a new system at Cara Fletcher Couture. I'll keep her safe."

"I believe Cara's the focus of the attacks." Briggs had lowered his voice, but I could still hear him murmur to Fletch, "There's no reason for him to stop now."

Back in the limo, Fletch asked, "Honey, how are we gonna tell Natalie about Maggie?"

That issue had also been on my mind. "And when. Someone's sure to mention it at school tomorrow if it hits the news."

"That's not too likely. Crime is a fact of life these days. I doubt the kids will talk about it." He scooted closer to wrap his arm around my shoulders.

"I guess we can take that chance. But we should sure discuss it with her in case she happens to catch a glimpse of the story on TV or the Internet." I again dropped my head into my hands.

"So she'll go to bed worrying about it? I think we should keep the TV and the computer off, let her get a good night's sleep and talk about it with her in the morning."

"Maybe. We could get her up early to discuss it. Fortunately, Natalie and Maggie weren't close. She'll be worried, but not particularly sad." I squeezed his hand as the limo halted at the atelier, and Nat got in.

As soon as we arrived at the condo, Fletcher helped me hustle Nat through dinner and into bed. The day had been stressful by any standard. Natalie's first day at school, Mom's visit, followed by the news of Maggie's death . . . I grimaced. How would we tell Natalie about Maggie? I didn't have a clue, and hoped an answer would come to me magically in a dream.

Fletch slipped into my room at about midnight. I knew because I was lying awake, worrying. He took off his robe and boxers, tossing them at the foot of the bed next to my new chenille robe before he slipped into bed beside me. I turned to him, and he took me in his arms.

Guilt struck. "We shouldn't be doing this," I murmured. "Nat—"

"She's asleep. I just checked on her." He kissed me, and I faintly tasted toothpaste overlaying his natural flavor.

He spooned with me, cuddling one hand around my breast, and I fell deeper into the easy comfort of having him close.

I awakened to the sound of Natalie shouting. "This is all your fault!"

"What happened to Maggie is not my fault!"

I blinked. Dawn's thin light was filtering into my room. I listened more closely, and could hear background noise . . . like a newscast. Damn. Had Natalie heard about Maggie's death on the morning news?

"Everything bad started when you sued my mom!"

"What? They're completely unrelated! Nat, if you'd sit down and listen—"

Stomping and a slammed door cut off Fletch's attempt at

reasoned discussion.

I hauled my butt out of bed, dragged on a robe, and found him on the sofa with a cup of coffee. The newscaster droned on about the weather, to my relief. "What happened?" I asked him.

"She saw the newspaper, asked about Maggie, and I felt I had to tell her."

Speechless, I could only glare.

"I couldn't lie, honey."

I sighed. "You're right. She freaked out? I'm surprised. Like I said, they weren't close."

"She says Maggie's death is my fault."

"I heard. She says everything bad started when you sued us."

He slumped into the sofa, looking truly dejected, and I went over to him and patted his knee. "She's wrong, you know. Natalie's had a fractured life. She overreacts, or she's mouthy, or she retreats and doesn't communicate at all. Don't worry about this. I'll talk to her, and we'll get her to her therapist tomorrow. She'll be all right."

"Honey, I'm sorry. I didn't want you to have to fix anything." I'd rarely seen Fletch look so miserable. "What if she, you know, tries again?"

I pressed my lips together. I knew what he meant, and said lightly, "Well, I guess we'd better keep her away from knives, sleeping pills and open windows."

He shot me a startled glance. I said, "Upsets happen when you're a parent. Don't be concerned about it. I'll talk with her."

I went to Nat's room, aware that this conversation would tax my newfound parenting abilities.

Her mouth drooped. Her frizzy hair had come loose from its nighttime braid and surrounded her face like a fuzzy, reddish halo.

"Mom, are you mad at me?" Her eyes were puffy and bright with tears. "I yelled at Fletcher."

My heart broke wide open, and I hugged her. "Oh, sweetheart, of course not. And he's not mad either. He understands, really he does."

Turning her head into my chest, Natalie began to cry helplessly, great gasping sobs that racked her thin body. I stroked her hair, then eased her back onto her bed to cuddle with her.

"I'm scared," she choked out.

"Oh, honey, don't worry. This building's security is excellent. No one's going to hurt us here. Plus, Fletch has someone looking out for us all the time, so we'll be okay. The police are on the lookout for whoever hurt Maggie, and I bet they'll catch him soon." I forced hearty assurance into my voice as I wiped away her tears.

She heaved a deep sigh. Rising, she reached for her uniform shirt with leaden hands.

After we piled into the limo, we swung by the workshop, where Fletch introduced Natalie to Tony Ramirez. Sam dropped Fletch and me off, then left with Nat for her school.

"That was a good idea," I told Fletch as we mounted the spiral stairs to the loft.

He shifted the bag containing his fresh coffee beans and cream from one arm to the other while he tightened his grip on his briefcase, bulging with Maggie's financial records. "Yes, she looked relieved. I think that we should get her a pager or a cell phone, just in case."

"Good idea. Most other kids have them, and—Ella, sweetie!" I hugged my favorite model who, to my surprise, was standing in the loft with none other than Damon Wolf. Today, Ella's blonde, curly hair was teased high in an eighties-style Texas bouffant. Her hourglass body was clad in a gorgeous yellow print Versace.

"Yo, Fletch, Cara." Damon swung out of the teal leather chair.

"Hey, Big D. What brings you here?" Fletch set down his bag.

"This gal." Damon jerked his head in Ella's direction. "Cara, meet your new personal assistant."

"What?" I went rigid with shock. "Oh, noooo!"

Damon cast me a dagger-sharp glance. "What's wrong with Ella? She attended a very respectable secretarial school and has a degree in administration."

"She can't do both!" This was too much. I just wanted to lay my head down and cry.

"Do both—what?" asked Damon the dimwit.

"One of the major responsibilities of my assistant is to handle the logistics of the runway shows," I tried to explain. "She can't do both, Damon. Ella's the best plus-sized model in the world. In the world. She's been in every one of my shows." Would he understand? I doubted it.

Ella hugged me again. "I'm sorry, Cara, but it's time for me to move on," she said in her distinctive west Texas twang.

"Oh, please. You're fabulous. Look at you in that Versace." I gestured.

"Listen to me. I'm at a crossroads in my life. I can't display myself anymore." Ella put one hand on each of my shoulders, forcing me to stare into her eyes. The effect was disconcerting; she'd never done anything like this before. "I didn't say modeling's done with me. I'm done with modeling. The contract with my talent agency is at the end of its term, and I didn't renew."

I gulped air, blinked, and realized that there was much more going on inside Ella than met the eye. Or, at least, my eyes. She was an adult and I had to accept her choice. "If that's so, I'm delighted to have you. But you have to decide you want to be here. Did you hear about Maggie?"

Ella went over to Fletcher's desk to retrieve a big, square handbag and withdrew a folded newspaper. "Everyone's heard about Maggie."

I looked at the banner headline and garish photo, splashed with dull red. "Does your building have security?" I tried, without success, to control my tremors.

"I'll take care of her." Damon put his arm around Ella's shoulders.

Interesting, I thought, then collected myself. "Okay, so let's get to work. Target date is November tenth."

"Cara," Fletch interjected. "You too, Damon. I need a favor."

"What can I do for you?" I asked, thinking, What now?

"We have our annual stockholders' meeting coming up in Wilmington on November second. I've been thinking that it would be great PR for the stockholders if you'd put on the show there as well."

"Oh, great." I collapsed into the leather armchair that Damon had vacated. "You want to put the show on twice. That's not quite double the work and the expense, but it's still a chunk of time and money. Models are pretty expensive people, huh, Ella?"

"Sure are," Ella said. "And Cara's very selective."

"We don't have to show more than a few outfits," Fletcher said.

"Okay. That's no big deal. You probably want to highlight Fletcher's Gear, right?" My mind worked furiously. "We can bring in, say, ten models and show the sportswear and a couple of gowns. That's reasonable." I glanced at Ella. "So, Ella, here's your first assignment. You're responsible for all the logistics of two runway shows in November."

Ella's bluebonnet eyes widened.

"You sure you want this job?" I asked.

Chapter Twenty

"I can't believe Ella went for it." I poked a chopstick at a water chestnut in Fletcher's serving of sweet-and-sour shrimp. It skidded across the plate.

"Think she's competent?"

"I don't see why not. She knows the business and she's always struck me as a sharp mama."

"Good. We need sharp." He added rice from a covered bowl to his lunch. He seemed weirdly concerned about the proportions of food, sauce, and rice.

"Of course, I thought that Maggie was honest and intelligent, too." I spread plum sauce on a doughy pancake, then topped it with mu-shu style tofu.

"Quit beating yourself up over that," he mumbled around a bite of shrimp. "Mistakes happen in every business. What happened to her isn't your fault. She was a good risk."

"Until Adam Covarrubia got his hands on her. Have you heard anything about him?"

"His agent told the police that the Covarrubia twins are working in Paris and Milan for this season."

I picked up the folded pancake. "Fine. Let's hope they stay there so I can relax and do my job. Even with Ella on board, there's a lot to do before November second."

Fletcher's cell phone rang with a businesslike chime, nothing frivolous like music. After putting his chopsticks on a china holder, he answered. I ignored the conversation while munching on mu shu. Sauce dripped over my fingers, and I licked it off, conscious of his scrutiny.

He closed his phone. “Damon and Ella are on their way over.”

I rubbed a napkin over my hand. “Okay. Do we need to discuss any other personnel issues before they come?”

“Yes. How much do you want to pay her?” After putting the phone away, he picked up his chopsticks.

“Ella? She knows the business but can’t provide the range of services Maggie did.”

“Good. I don’t expect her to embezzle funds.” He crunched a snow pea.

“Ha-ha. Let’s offer her two-thirds of what we paid Maggie, full benefits, and see if she takes it. Fair?”

“Fair enough.”

We fell silent when Damon and Ella approached. Damon, clad casually in a T-shirt and jeans, held Ella’s elbow in a firm, possessive grip.

“Good afternoon, all.” Damon’s voice was amiable.

Ella sat on the red vinyl banquette next to me, wearing her usual sunny smile. It matched her corolla of teased golden hair and her yellow dress. She bubbled with excitement. “I have the greatest idea for the Fletcher Tool and Gear runway show.” Her accent seemed even more pronounced, due to her enthusiasm, perhaps. “How would the two of you gentlemen like to be models for a day?”

I dropped my napkin.

Fletcher’s busy chopsticks stilled. He leaned back in his seat, no doubt remembering some of the more creative outfits in the April show—perhaps the silver Mylar tux, or the feathered capes. Fletch would never put on a costume and prance down a runway, but I’d pay money to see it. If Ella could do it, I’d give her a bonus. “Well, Ella,” he said, “you certainly have a way of getting attention.”

"Yeah, what do you mean?" I asked.

Ella batted thick lashes. "I think you'll agree that the Wolf family has some fine-lookin' members.

"Members, hmm?" Fletcher winked at me.

I know I turned red. I felt the burn.

"Let's put the Board of Directors in the Delaware show," Ella continued. "The shareholders will love it."

I picked up my teacup. "It'll be more work, fitting the clothes onto non-professionals."

"We may have a problem getting the stockholders to accept this joint venture," Damon said. "A lot of them have owned Fletcher Gear stock from time immemorial, and it'll be a stretch for them to swallow a foray into designer clothing. Anything we can do to help should be done."

"As long as you want to do it, Ella, I have no problem with the idea. It's no crazier than other stunts I've pulled for the runway shows."

Fletcher looked cornered, while Damon and Ella wore the hopeful expressions of kids at the door on Halloween night, confident and certain of a treat. "I guess so," Fletch said, sounding dubious. "As long as I don't have to wear anything, umm, odd."

"What, exactly, do you mean?" I asked coldly.

"Your last show was influenced by the space program and Renaissance jesters. I won't dress up like Robin Hood or Neil Armstrong."

I raised my brows. "And you, Damon? Will you put on parti-colored tights and a tunic to make Ella happy?"

Damon tossed down his menu. "How 'bout a T-shirt and jeans?"

I sighed. "That's what you're wearing right now. I guess I'll design a couple of new suits for the corporate crowd. How boring."

The morning of Maggie's funeral dawned sunny and bright, one of those vivid October days which deny the threat of winter. Fletch kept my hand warm in his as we walked from the limo into one of the small stone churches that dotted Manhattan's neighborhoods. Maggie had lived in this area, worshiped here in this sanctuary, I guessed while gazing at a stained-glass window, blazing with color.

The crowd of mourners surprised me. I'd pictured Maggie the workaholic as lonely and friendless. According to the small program passed out at the door, she'd been an active churchgoer, even sang in the choir.

I could hear the gossip swirling; the murmurings and mutterings of the throng warned me that these people blamed me for Maggie's sad end. Apparently Maggie had changed after she'd come to work for Cara Fletcher Couture, ditching her old friends for new ones and neglecting church. Fortunately, no one knew who I was, and I had dressed soberly for this event. No parti-colored tights and certainly no parti-colored hair. Instead, a navy suit, with brown hair and tortoise-shell glasses.

I tried to keep my head down while scanning the crowd of mourners, trying to spot suspicious characters. Maybe there was truth to the detective movie myths that criminals couldn't stay away from the scene of the crime or the funeral of the victim. But if any knife murderers lurked in the congregation, they blended in with the group.

The service, conducted by a balding minister speaking in somber tones, was blessedly quick. Neither Fletch nor I wanted to attend the burial, so we lingered only to ensure that the floral tribute we'd sent had arrived. I had ordered a starburst of white gladioli and yellow chrysanthemums to represent the purity and glory of the soul. "No matter what she became, Maggie was still a child of God," I'd told Fletch.

Shortly after the service concluded, I touched his arm. "I'm going to find a women's room, and then I'd like to get out of here."

When I entered the restroom, I was surprised to see Shila Chong staring in the mirror and touching up her lipstick. She turned to me with a slight smile. "Great minds think alike."

I raised my brows. "Glad to see you're still on the job." I took my makeup case out of my satchel and used it.

"This new event puts the Wolf brothers out of the running for Creep of the Year, but just in case, I checked them out. No issues."

As I left I said, "Well, it's good to know that there's no problem with them."

"No problem with who?" Fletch asked.

Damn and double damn. I knew I looked like a kid caught with her hand in the cookie jar. "Oh, uh, this is Shila Chong," I babbled.

"Ms. Chong." Fletch transferred his coat to his left arm so he could shake her hand. "I'm Fletcher Wolf."

"Pleased to meet you." Shila, fearless as usual, looked him straight in the eye as she shook his hand. From her expression, she seemed to examine and photograph him for catalogue and storage inside her very quick mind.

He smiled. "How are you acquainted with Ms. Fletcher?"

I, unlike Shila, wasn't ice-cube cool. Instead, I twitched nervously.

"Oh, we occasionally do business." Shila said in a casual tone of voice.

"What part of the couture industry are you in?" he asked.

"Information retrieval. I work for a company that gathers, uh, data."

"How useful. May I have your card?"

For the first time, Shila looked edgy. I knew why. Her card said clearly that she was a PI. But she carried it off, saying, "I'm afraid that I don't have one on me right now, Mr. Wolf. But you can contact me through Ms. Fletcher."

"I'll be sure to do that. I often find a need for information."

"Nice meeting you." Still wearing a slight smile, she left, no doubt heaving a sigh of relief. I know I did.

"Who was she?" Fletch asked me.

"I told you. Shila Chong."

"Both of you were acting as though you had something to hide."

I tried to look mysterious and alluring. "You have a vivid imagination, Fletcher Wolf."

"Actually, I don't. Most people regard me as stolid and unimaginative."

"Most people don't know you. I do." I took his arm. "Let's get some lunch. I'm tired of churches and funerals. All they do is remind me of death, and I bet you feel the same way."

"You're right. I think about my father a lot on my good days, and this is fast turning into a bad one." He glanced at me as we left the church. "But you've got a secret, and I'm going to find out what it is, *Cara mia.*"

"For goodness's sake! If you must know, Shila Chong is an investigator. I had asked her to look into some personal matters regarding the stalker, okay?"

"I put Ramirez on that."

Sam opened the limo door, and Fletcher helped me in.

"Two heads are better than one, aren't they?" I tucked my satchel at my feet as he slid inside the car.

"I suppose so. Did she find anything out?"

"Nope. So we're back where we were before: the Covarrubias."

The limo started away from the curb.

"Were they here today?"

"Oh, no. Believe me, you would have noticed them."

"I remember meeting him. Adam. Skinny guy in black leather?"

"That's the one. I thought he used to have a crush on me." I shuddered. "But Maggie turned out to be his type."

He took my hand. "Don't worry, baby. The Covarrubias are in Europe, and I'm here. I'll keep you safe."

A week later, Fletch and I returned from lunch to find the loft inhabited by a southern steel magnolia. Veronica Carter Wolf sat in the big chair behind Fletcher's desk, looking as though she'd been born to run corporations.

Suspicion flared before I tried to squelch the unfair emotion. However, Veronica's appearance in the loft couldn't be just happenstance. I had learned that little to do with any member of the Wolf pack was mere coincidence.

"Good to see you, Mama." Fletcher leaped to kiss his mother's cheek. "Coffee?"

Veronica inclined her head. "Calm down, Fletcher. I'm not here to see you."

Ouch, I thought. Subtlety's not this woman's strong point.

However, he didn't look upset. "So what can we do for you?"

"I'm here for my fitting," Veronica said.

"A fitting?" I couldn't have been more surprised if the Pope had walked into the atelier to purchase a muscle-T.

"For the fall show, of course." Veronica removed her cloche hat and smiled at me. "Ella didn't tell you?"

I shook my head, and Fletcher looked as puzzled as I felt.

"My second son and that assistant of yours cooked up a plan to use the Board of Directors to model your designs at the meeting."

"Yes, I was aware of that, Mrs. Wolf. I've been working on appropriate clothes for Fletch and Damon."

"Well now, honey, you can do your magic for me, too. I'm the co-chairperson of the board." Veronica fluttered her lashes. "I've always wondered how it would feel to walk down that runway."

"I'm not sure I can dress you better than you are already, Mrs. Wolf. What a gorgeous ensemble." Veronica wore a classic ensemble: red Chanel suit, matching purse, even gloves. The woman didn't need clothes, that was for sure.

Nope, the matriarch of the Wolf clan was here to see what was going on. She had to know by now that Natalie and I were staying with Fletch in his condo. I eyed Veronica, seeing old school money and old school morals.

However, did I really have anything to hide? Fletch had behaved like a perfect gentleman for a week now, leaving me alone in my bed after a chaste good night kiss outside the bedroom door. For reasons known only to himself, he'd withdrawn. But I wasn't going to ask, since I'd said we couldn't mess around in Manhattan.

I didn't really want to know. Time shot by and the November shows drew closer. After working fifteen-hour days, I fell into bed exhausted, snatching every precious minute of sleep I could grab.

"What suits and dresses are you showing this season, dear?" Veronica intruded upon my thoughts.

I hurried over to my portfolio of drawings for the show and hoped that one of the designs would meet with approval. I hadn't felt so worried about my work since before I'd graduated from design school.

Fletcher crowded in to add his two cents, as usual. I didn't bother complaining; I could no more get rid of him than a barnyard dog could eliminate fleas.

"I've seen this dress. It's beautiful," Fletcher said to Veronica as I showed her a drawing of a silver sequined gown with marabou trim at the neckline and hem.

Frowning, Veronica squinted at the sketch. "That's a little daring for me, dear."

Next, I tried a pantsuit. The conservative outfit, in cranberry silk, had a poet-style blouse tucked into slim trousers.

Veronica winced gracefully.

"Now, Mama."

"It's all right, Fletch." I made an effort to sound amused, sure that Veronica didn't understand the difference between a salesgirl and a designer. But I told myself that I wasn't temperamental and wouldn't take the rejections personally. I tried not to grind my teeth.

The next dress was a knee-length cocktail frock in the fluttery silk georgette that I adored, and had used for the canary yellow gown that the vandal had destroyed. This number was bias-cut, green with silver embroidered trim.

"Yes," Veronica announced with the absolute certainty of God creating the universe. "This is the one."

Fletcher looked as relieved as I felt, as though he personally had to ensure Veronica's satisfaction.

"Let's take some measurements." I whipped out a tape measure.

"Fletch, could you step out? I don't want my son to know my bust size."

He obeyed, grabbing his briefcase before he clattered down the metal stairs.

"Just as well," I said. "You do have to take your jacket off, and if you have shoulder pads in your blouse, that has to come off also."

Veronica slipped off her jacket, folding it precisely before laying it over the back of Fletcher's chair.

"Ah. Just as I thought." The blouse Veronica wore beneath the jacket sported eighties-style linebacker shoulder pads. "Can't measure with that on."

After Veronica removed her shirt, I laid the tape measure across her back, checking the width of her shoulders. Then the length of the back, around the bust and waist, waist to knee. "I can make this knee length, like the drawing, or take it down to the ankle. Which would you prefer?"

"Floor-length, I think. I can wear it to the Hunt Club Christmas ball."

I scribbled numbers directly onto the drawing, then knelt to measure down to the instep. "Are these similar to the shoes you'll wear?"

"I don't rightly know. I hadn't thought about shoes. At my age, I generally wear low heels."

"I'll send you a fabric swatch. You can match the silk or wear silver sandals. There, all done." I stood, then twisted to stretch.

Veronica's lips twitched. Her small, ironic smile reminded me of Fletcher. "Relieved?"

"What?"

"Never try to lie, dear. You have a most transparent face." She patted my cheek, shocking the hell out of me. "Don't worry. You have nothing to fear from me. Natalie's a well-brought-up child, a credit to you."

"Thank you." I was proud of Natalie, but could I really take the credit? Could Kenney? In a way, Natalie was her own creation.

"You just bring that son of mine to heel. I'm not getting any younger, and all my friends have grandchildren. I'm starting to feel left out. So hurry up, you hear?" Veronica picked up her blouse and thrust her arms into the sleeves as I went downstairs.

My brain spun like a dervish. I guess the Wolf Mama approved, but Veronica had jumped to conclusions that I hadn't yet reached. And heaven only knew what Fletch wanted. He sure wasn't saying.

But who cared?

I did, dammit.

What could Veronica be thinking? And why? The situation between Fletch and Natalie was still in flux, and then there was that thirty-page prenup. I'd deal with that later, if at all. Now, I had to get the Wolf Mama out of the door.

Veronica was following me downstairs, and I tried to rid myself of the sensation a fawn must have while being trailed by a hungry predator.

Nat was seated at a desk next to Fletch. I asked, "Nat, what are you doing here? It's only two o'clock."

"They're having a teacher training day, so we left after lunch. Hi, Veronica." Natalie twisted in her chair to hug Fletcher's mother around the waist.

"Hello there, honeychile." Veronica stroked Natalie's braid.

"Looks as though you get along well with Natalie, Mrs. Wolf."

"Oh, she's easy as pie, your daughter. As I said, Natalie does you proud."

I glanced at Fletcher to see how this pronouncement affected him.

There was that arching brow again, along with the ironic little smile that seemed to be a Wolf family characteristic. Fletcher caught me staring. His eyes flickered with amusement before he turned to Veronica. "It's been very nice seeing you, Mama, but Cara and I need to get back to work." He bent to kiss her cheek. "Sam will take you to the airport. When's your flight out?"

"So, did she talk to you about her friends' grandkids?" Back in the loft after Veronica left, Fletch propped his hip on the edge of his desk, watching me.

I squirmed. "Uh, yeah."

"Don't pay any attention to her, honey."

Yeah, right. "I guess your mother wonders why none of her three grown sons has married or borne children."

"Childbearing is a little out of my league."

Out of his league? "What are you talking about?" I sat behind the drafting table.

"I'm saying, it's up to you."

"Oh, no!"

"Is that what you think of having a child? 'Oh, no'?"

"I remember giving birth," I said grimly, unpleasant memories racing through my mind. "Never again."

"Didn't you use anesthetics?"

"No."

"So it's completely out of the question?"

I looked at him and saw confusion, rare indeed on Fletcher's face. I hesitated. This could be a relationship-changing conversation, and nothing to joke about. "Not completely, but it doesn't appear to be likely. I have a show to put on, remember? And then I'll need to find a sperm donor." I grinned at him, wondering how he'd take the comment.

He leaned over my drafting table, his mouth just a couple of inches away. "Any time, baby." He nibbled on my mouth.

Whoa. I drew back in shock. This was too much, too soon.

He noticed, of course. "Just tell me something. Are you happier with me, or without me?" He fiddled with my hair.

I knew what he wanted me to say, and resented it. "I'm happy either way."

"Is that so?" He stepped back.

"Well, yeah. Frankly, Fletch, Nat and I did fine before you came along."

"Is that right?"

"Sure it is. What do you expect me to say? I wasn't Rapunzel in the tower before I met you. I was happy and productive."

"Happy and productive? You were stalked and your office was vandalized before I started working with you."

"One thing has nothing to do with another."

He straightened. "Have it your way, Cara." His voice was cool, and a little smug.

That wasn't good.

What was he planning?

Chapter Twenty-One

The next day, I awakened with the insistent feeling that something was wrong. October light, dimmed by autumn clouds, filtered through the curtains, but I couldn't sense the normal sounds and aromas of morning. What was going on?

I got up and went to investigate. The kitchen was empty and quiet, unlike most weekdays, when Fletch, an early riser, would brew coffee and make toast. I switched on a light and found a note in the middle of the table.

Cara mia,

Left early with Sam to put out a few fires in Delaware—back later in the week.

Fletch

Just "Fletch." Not, "Love, Fletch," or "Warmly, Fletch," or even, "I'll miss you, Fletch." No goodbye kiss and no warning.

I searched for coffee, juice, and breakfast while trying not to get annoyed. I should have seen this coming, I thought, as I measured coffee and poured water, then poked the button to get the machine going.

"G'morning." Natalie came over for a sleepy hug and kiss. "Where's the Wolfman?"

"He went to Delaware." I handed Natalie a glass of orange juice.

She sipped. "How long is he gonna be gone?"

"A few days, I guess."

"It'll be like old times, huh? Just you and me." She sounded wistful.

Did she prefer the old days when we'd been alone? If yes, it wasn't good for the fate of romance.

Before I could ask Natalie about her feelings, she said, "Did Sam drive him?"

"Yeah."

Natalie found the wheat bread. "Want toast?"

"Please." I poured coffee into a mug with the Fletcher Tool and Gear logo.

Natalie dropped two slices of bread in the toaster. "So who's gonna take me to school?"

"We'll get a taxi, like we used to. Hey, I wonder if I have any cash." I'd quit carrying much money since I'd returned from Europe. Fletcher always seemed to take care of everything.

Mug in hand, I went to the living room to search the satchel. Oops. I had only a ten-dollar bill and some change, not nearly enough for the day. I hurried back to the kitchen. "Nat, we have to zip along. It's already seven-fifteen and we have to find an ATM before we get a taxi."

Natalie stuffed toast into her mouth as she scuttled down the hall to her room. I followed, leaving my toast. I figured I'd nibble on it after we caught a cab.

Forty-five minutes later, we stood on a wind-whipped corner of Sixty-first, vainly waving at taxis, all of which seemed to have fares. With no time to get ready, my hair hung limp and I wore tortoise-shell glasses instead of contacts.

Natalie, in her school uniform, looked a little better, but I hadn't had time to braid her hair. She'd protested when I'd tried to put it in pigtails—too little-girl, she whined—so Nat's wild hair, confined at her neck by a single scrunchie, was destined to become a frizzy, tangled cloud by ten o'clock.

Finally a taxi detached from the flow of traffic to pick us up. After a ten-minute ride, I slapped a twenty into Nat's hand as the taxi pulled up to her school. "Make it last, honey. See you at three."

My designers and seamstresses were already hard at work when I arrived at five minutes after nine. Only Ella and I worked in the loft that day, so it seemed peculiarly empty and dull. Already mid-October, the bulk of my design responsibilities were over, so I worked on picking models and helping everyone else.

Dinner without Fletch was also quiet, the kitchen again taking on an air of mystery. I didn't know where anything was, so I ordered pizza. Natalie didn't stop whining and complaining. She'd had a hard time getting a cab after school. Her hair was horrible and she wanted to shave her head. Her math instructor was a stupid witch who couldn't teach her way out of a wet paper bag.

The grumbling went on and on until I wanted to scream. After settling Nat at Fletcher's desk to do homework, I took a long bath by candlelight.

I sat in the warm water, trying not to grumble to myself about Fletcher's many sins. But after leaving without any advance warning, he hadn't phoned all day long. He was rude and inconsiderate. The situation had grossly inconvenienced me, and he'd said he'd take care of everything. Where was he, anyway? How could he just up and leave without a word? Was he angry? He'd seemed to be fine, even cheerful when we'd last shared our modest good-night kiss.

Actually, it had been a pretty hot kiss.

I brooded some more, then realized:

Life with Fletch was smooth and easy.

Life without Fletch sucked.

Everything, from breakfast to dinner and all the moments in

between, had been more difficult. How had I managed before? Dammit, why had I become so dependent upon him?

I bet that had been his plot all along. He'd schemed to get me to agree to this joint venture and then taken over my life.

Mom had been right.

I remembered yesterday's conversation. He'd left, no doubt to drive home the point that I needed him.

I swore to myself that he wouldn't win. No way was I going to become a weak-willed little princess dependent upon her prince.

The next day I was prepared. At seven o'clock, I phoned a cab company so a taxi awaited us outside precisely at seven-forty-five. "Your cab should meet you at three," I told Nat as we approached her school. "Do you need more cash today?"

With Natalie at school, I headed to the atelier for a nice, uninterrupted day at work. However, the phone rang at ten o'clock, just when I'd become pleasantly absorbed in the task at hand.

Ella took the call. "Cara, it's Fletcher."

I looked up from the silk drawstring pants I'd pinned around the fitting model. Damn. Why should my heart stutter as though it needed a pacemaker just because Fletch was on the phone? "I'll be a couple of minutes," I said to the model, who smiled and settled down to wait. The slender, pretty brunette was one of an elite cadre of perfect bodies whose main job was just that: to be perfect. I doubted that the poor woman had ever eaten a doughnut or a candy bar.

Ella handed me a portable, and Fletcher's deep bass rumbled in my ear. "Cara?"

"Yes, it's me. What's up?" I hoped my businesslike tone would hide my annoyance.

"I called to see how you're doing."

"Oh, Nat and I are hanging in there."

"Miss me, honey?"

Oh, God. What could I say? Of course, I missed him. Without Fletch, both condo and loft seemed too big. I missed our good-night kiss and cuddle. Natalie was cranky and difficult. But should I show weakness?

"Umm . . . the condo feels nice and roomy."

"Is that so?"

"Yeah. And we only had to order one pizza last night for supper, since the carnivore was out of town."

"Is that right?" Fletch drawled out his vowels, a sign of—what?

"I slept really well. The pictures on my wall aren't vibrating from the snores coming from the bedroom next door."

Silence.

"Natalie misses Sam."

"I guess we'd better hurry back," Fletcher said, voice heavy with sarcasm. "It'll never do for Natalie to be unhappy."

He sounded pissed. Still . . . "Natalie doesn't like change in her life," I said. "I try to keep things stable for her. By the way, when *are* you coming back? I, umm, need to fit your suit."

"Didn't you take measurements?"

"Yeah, but this is going to be a custom-made suit. Fit you better than fur on a cat."

"I'll be back in a couple of days. See you later, Cara."

The phone clicked off. I stared at the handset, dumbfounded. Fletch hadn't given me a chance to say goodbye. He'd hung up on me.

On the other hand, I'd deserved it. I wondered if I should bother thinking of a way to redeem myself.

Heck, no. Veronica had asked me to bring her son to heel. That might be fun. The fastest way I knew to do that, given Fletcher's predatory nature, was to pretend indifference. But I didn't like to play silly games with men. I never had before.

Never had needed to, really. And here I was playing the oldest of entrapment games: hard to get. Hopefully it wouldn't backfire.

I returned to the model, who asked, "What's so funny?"

Then I realized I'd been chuckling.

In the workshop's loft three days later, I found myself in a position I thought unwise under the circumstances: kneeling in front of Fletcher. However, I was armed with a pincushion on my wrist. Despite my weapons, I could feel smug satisfaction emanating from my would-be lover. I tried to ignore the sexually charged situation, professionally tugging at his cuff before running a hand up the inseam of his trousers to check the smoothness of the fit.

"Hey, cut that out!" I poked the rising ridge in the crotch of his pants.

"Your mouth is just three inches from me," Fletch said through gritted teeth. "I'm only human."

"You're tenting the fabric. It spoils the line of the trouser."

"Don't act as though it's my fault."

"Can't Mr. Happy be . . . less happy?" I pinned the waistline for a closer fit.

"Ow!" Fletcher jerked. "I think you've solved the problem of the, er, tenting. Can't you be a little more careful? I don't like those pins near my vital parts."

"I've never stuck a professional model. Hold still." I finished adjusting the waist, then pinned the inseam. Slipping behind him, I could see his firm ass beautifully framed by the fine wool of the trousers. I couldn't resist, and passed an admiring hand over his buttocks. "Perfect."

He turned his head to raise a brow. "Is that right?"

I felt myself heat. "The fit, I mean."

"Modest, aren't we?"

"It's a nicely cut pair of pants, if I do say so myself. And the fabric is beautiful." I stroked him again, then smacked him lightly. "Okay, that's all for now."

He spun around and hauled me up, stretching me tight against his length and kissed me. This kiss was demanding and frustrated, accompanied by a thrusting tongue and a nice squeeze on my butt. I couldn't help a moan . . . I was pretty frustrated myself.

Dammit, he stopped. Manipulative jerk.

"You're playing with fire, sweetheart. Make sure you don't get burned."

I pulled away, lips tingling and mind blank with desire.

"If you're done, I guess I'll change out of these pants." Pinning me with his gaze, he unbuttoned the waistband. He wiggled his hips a little as he unzipped.

I'd jump his bones right there and then if I didn't get out of that loft. I leaped down the stairs, hearing his mocking laughter chase me out of the studio.

Chapter Twenty-Two

Spotlights glinted on the silver streaking Fletcher's hair as he stood before the assembled shareholders of Fletcher Tool and Gear. Attired in his new Fletcher's Gear suit, he looked great. Seated with other speakers in the front row of the vast auditorium in his corporate headquarters, I gave myself a mental pat on the back for a job well done, then turned my attention back to his speech. He'd droned endlessly about profit and loss, dividend and growth, but now he seemed to be getting to a subject near and dear to my heart: Cara Fletcher Couture.

"A new millennium has brought new challenges and new opportunities. In response, we will expand out of our traditional niche into other, time-tested areas. Thus, we have engaged in a joint venture with Cara Fletcher Couture, a young but strong contender in the upscale ready-to-wear and designer clothing markets. Its founder, Cara Linda Fletcher, hails from upstate New York. A graduate of prestigious Parsons School of Design, she received the Azzedine Alaia Gold Thimble Award upon her graduation."

I squirmed as Fletch continued to heap praise on me.

"Immensely talented, Cara Fletcher founded her own company five years ago. This firm rapidly expanded to a gross income of twenty million dollars in those few, short years.

"Decorating the body is one of the oldest human instincts. This tendency crosses cultural barriers and will forever be a source of profit."

I grinned as I remembered what I'd told Fletch at that first disastrous dinner. He smiled back at me from the podium's height, and I pressed my lips together to keep from laughing out loud at our private, shared joke.

"This acquisition ensures that our products will appeal to a wider consumer mix."

Acquisition—ha, I thought. He'd better change his tune if he wants a happy, helpful corporate asset.

"In honor of this joint venture, and in recognition of this significant expansion, the majority shareholders and your Board of Directors have voted to rename this corporation 'The Fletcher Group.' Now, I introduce to you our joint venturer, Cara Linda Fletcher."

The thunderous applause made the response I'd received at my runway shows pale into insignificance. Surprised and delighted, I joined Fletch at the podium. After he adjusted the microphone for me, he gave my fanny a discreet pat before he let me take center stage alone.

Thank God the harsh lights would wash my face clean of color, so no one in the packed house would see me blush. The last two weeks had been a test of my will in so many different ways. Faced with a task which would daunt the most dedicated workaholics, my staff and I had worked night and day to finish on time for the two shows scheduled in November.

Fletch had worked as hard as anyone else—maybe harder. At the same time, he never stopped flirting. He'd stare at me, gaze laden with intent, at the most unexpected times. He'd occasionally step over to my drafting table or mannequin to look at my work, which seemed to fascinate him. He continued to touch me constantly, while he helped me in or out of the limo or when he escorted me into the workshop in the morning or into a restaurant for lunch . . . and at every other conceivable time.

I'd gotten spoiled and had come to expect the small

courtesies and attentions he lavished. On those days when he left Manhattan for Wilmington, the condo and the atelier seemed too empty. Just as he'd planned, the wretch.

He was the most distracting man I'd ever met. This fall show was a minor miracle. How had I managed to work at all?

His physical presence was an unbearable temptation, morning, noon and night—especially at night, when I longed to be held and loved. But he'd respected my privacy, never invading my bedroom. Fletcher's surface docility reminded me of a timber wolf masquerading as a compliant collie. All the while, he watched and waited. For what?

I tore my mind away from Fletcher-the-lover and acknowledged Fletcher, the CFO "Thank you for your warm introduction. Cara Fletcher Couture is proud to engage in a joint venture with The Fletcher Group. Many of you have seen our winter line of clothing in stores, but this afternoon we are pleased to preview a few selections from the forthcoming spring line, including the popular Fletcher's Gear sportswear. Lights, please!"

The overhead lamps in the hall dimmed, while a runway lined with lights leaped into vivid illumination.

"And our first model is your CFO, Fletcher Wolf, attired in a tailored navy gabardine suit. The jacket is double breasted and double vented. The trousers feature front pleating for comfort."

I glanced behind me to the giant video screens, which contained multiple images: Fletcher from three angles as well as me. The Fletcher Group spared no expense to make its annual meeting a success.

"Next, your Vice President of Marketing, Damon Wolf, shows Fletcher Gear's safari-style suit with a silk-linen blend shirt with a subtle jacquard weave."

Ella's idea to use the Wolf brothers as models was a hit with the shareholders, who seemed to eat up the spectacle of their corporate officers showing off couture clothing. The crowd clapped louder and louder.

"Here's the family matriarch, the co-chair of your Board of Directors, Veronica Carter Wolf."

A roar of acclaim greeted Fletcher's mother, who modeled the leaf-green, bias-cut silk gown she'd selected.

"Everyone's heart went out to Mom after Dad died," Fletcher explained as he ushered me into his quiet office later in the evening.

"I can see that the shareholders think a lot of her." I dropped my satchel on one end of the leather sofa, sighed with relief, and massaged my shoulder where the strap had bitten into me, thinking that I really ought to clean out that bag some day. But I'd been so busy lately that I'd had to shove such mundane tasks to the back burner.

"They think a lot of you. You and your clothes were the stars of the show, honey."

I shook my head. "No way. They liked me, but they revere you."

"Maybe. For these folks, the bottom line is just that—the bottom line. I make money for them. If I'd lost the company they wouldn't vote for me to be dogcatcher. Hey, let's toast our success."

"With what?"

"Come with me to the casbah, my princess."

The casbah turned out to be a kitchen down the hall from Fletcher's office. Opening a refrigerator, he removed a bottle of Dom Pérignon. "Glasses are in the cupboard to your right."

"Any munchies?" I took two flutes from their place, then found some paper napkins nearby.

"I'll take you to dinner later, but sure, we could use some appetizers. Aha. Here's some cheese, and I know that Miranda keeps saltines in her desk. With her morning sickness, they're the only food she says she can keep down."

I trailed him back to the cushy sofa, where he popped the champagne and filled the two flutes. "To our joint venture, *Carissima mia.*"

"To us." I sipped. "And thank you, Fletch."

"For what?" He put his arm along the back of the couch behind my head and ruffled my hair.

I gulped, searching for the right words. Why should expressing gratitude feel so difficult? Maybe because I wanted to say much, much more to him, but didn't dare without knowing what he really wanted. How deep did his desire run?

"You could have destroyed me and you chose not to," I said.

He laughed. "Baby, hurting you was never my intention—at least, not for long. Oh, I'll admit that I was madder than a hornet's nest when I saw that TV commercial. But I realized very soon after we met that wrecking your company would have been stupid. You're an extraordinary woman. Don't thank me. Everything I've done has been out of self-interest, I assure you." He lifted his glass. "To you, my beautiful Cara. Have I told you how lovely you look tonight?"

"Are you flirting with me?" I tried not to preen.

He sipped and smiled, his eyes glimmering over the rim of his glass. "Of course. I'll never stop. By the way, that dress is gorgeous. I'm glad Esme could reconstruct it." Fletcher ran one finger down the v-neckline of the embroidered yellow silk.

My skin rippled in response to his nearness, his touch, and I drew in a steadying breath. "She worked eighteen hours every day to finish on time."

"It was a big hit. With those spotlights on you and your red hair, you shone like the sun walking down that runway." His voice took on a tender note. "They adored you."

Yeah, but what about you? I wanted to ask. Lacking the guts, I kept my mouth shut. Fraidy cat, I thought.

"I'm surprised you changed your hair color," he went on. "You've stayed with brown hair and glasses for a long time."

"I went red for the show. The canary yellow is so overwhelming that I had to balance the color. Otherwise, the dress would wear me, not vice versa. What's in here?" I reached for a wooden box that sat on the table.

"It's a humidor. Keeps cigars fresh." Setting down his glass, Fletch flipped open the lid and took out a cigar. He ran it through his fingers, then sniffed appreciatively.

I rolled my eyes and avoided saying *ick.* I took my Swiss Army knife out of the satchel and used it to spread cheese onto a cracker, and offered it to Fletch.

"Thank you." He washed the munchie down with more champagne, then used some sort of small tool to clip the end of the cigar. "Do you have matches in there?"

"Yep." I pawed through the mess, removing a variety of items before locating matches. "Here."

I ate more cheese and crackers while Fletcher lit, puffed and smoked. I didn't understand the point of ruining great champagne with a stinky cigar, but each to his own.

"Nice office. Was your desk near that wall before you moved it to New York?" I pointed to the left, where a plastic chair mat partially covered the forest-green carpeting.

"Yes. I haven't found a replacement that I like. Haven't had time to look."

"Where do you work when you're here?"

"I use Damon's office, or the sofa. I'm not here all that often. More champagne?" He met my eyes and smiled.

Good God. That heartthrob smile again, the one that never failed to turn me on. I'd been so busy lately that dealing with my feelings about Fletcher hadn't been difficult. But now . . . Were my toes actually curling?

Fletcher refilled my glass. After he put the bottle back onto the table, he leaned into the sofa while scooting closer. Nestled into the curve of his arm, I became acutely aware of his warmth. I recalled how my breasts would swell when he'd cupped them in his big hands. Now, my nipples hardened and tingled at the memories.

Should I or shouldn't I?

Why not? I loved making love with Fletcher. He'd been a generous lover, enjoying my pleasure as much as his own. He'd given completely, never holding anything back. Neither had I. But, on the other hand, should we start something up again? Natalie—

"Sweet Lord Almighty! What happened?" Fletcher stood in the sudden darkness.

"Must be a blackout. See, there're no lights, even outside." I heard a thump.

Fletcher swore. He must have walked into the coffee table. Moments later, I heard his voice from near the window. "You're right, not a light anywhere for blocks. Kinda spooky."

Damn, I thought. "Please, Fletch. I've just managed to convince myself that everything bad in my life is over." I'd kept in touch with my investigator, but Shila Chong hadn't come up with anything at all. If there had been a stalker, he'd disappeared.

I heard Fletcher's footsteps approach before his hands massaged my shoulders over the back of the couch. "This blackout's no big deal. We'll just wait it out. Hell, I have everything I want right here. Food, drink and you."

"What do you mean, we'll just wait it out?"

"If this is a complete power outage, we're stuck in this building, probably alone. This place is the mecca of high tech. Most of the doors require electronic card-keys. If the power's out, we can't get into the stairwells and the elevators sure won't work.

We're stuck up here in the penthouse."

Anxiety crept along my nerves. "What are we going to do?" My voice had gone high pitched with panic. I hadn't taken any tranqs for weeks—no need to. But now I scrabbled in my satchel for my pills.

"Nothing to do, honey. Just gotta wait 'til they get the lights back on."

"That's nuts. What happens during a fire?"

"The sprinklers are heat-activated. A sensor melts, and the water comes down."

"You don't understand. I have a child. I have to know what's going on with Natalie." Why didn't he get it? Any relationship had no future unless Fletch got the message about Natalie.

"Honey, she's in Manhattan with her friend Jennifer, isn't she? She's three states away. They probably don't have a problem there." I heard rustling as he sidled around the sofa and sat next to me.

Forget the tranqs. Where was the damn phone? I continued to search for the cellular, trying to find it by touch alone. "I can't see anything. Where are those matches?"

"Here." He lit one.

"Ooh, I'm glad I didn't get around to cleaning out this bag. Look at this." I pulled out a couple of votive candles.

"What are they? These matches don't give much light."

"Candles."

"Cara Fletcher, you're some kinda crazy genius, you know that?"

I grinned. "Where should we put them?"

"I have coasters somewhere, or we can use ashtrays. Give me a candle." He put a lit match to each wick, then set one votive at each end of the coffee table. "Perfect."

The candles illuminated the couch area with a mellow glow. The darkened windows reflected a romantic scene: champagne, crystal, and appetizers, lit by the votives' glimmer. The shifting light bounced off several of Fletcher's box collection, scattered around the room. The dark wooden ones receded into obscurity, while a glittering sphere set on a shelf leapt into prominence.

I ignored the seductive setting while I found my cell phone and searched through its programmed addresses for the phone number of Natalie's friend. I punched the buttons furiously, plagued by some unnamed fear that gnawed at my insides. Too many bizarre events had taken place in the past six months for me to accept this new incident as innocent. At the very least, I was vulnerable and didn't like it.

However, I had no trouble getting through to Merrilee Givens, who assured me that Natalie and Jennifer were occupied with homework. There was no blackout in New York City, and everything was fine.

"Do you want to talk to her?" Merrilee asked.

"I don't like to interrupt homework, but yeah, I would."

"I'll get her settled back down again. She's a good kid, no trouble at all. She can stay over any time."

I could hear Merrilee's footsteps thump as she carried the phone to Natalie.

"Oh, hi, Ma."

Ma? When had she started calling me Ma? But so what? "Hey, honey."

"You sound weird. What's going on?"

"A blackout. I just wanted to make sure you're all right."

"Oh, I'm fine. Let me talk to Fletch."

"Huh?" I turned to him. "She says she wants to talk to you."

He smiled at me. Overwhelmed by work, I'd apparently missed something in the development of the relationship between Fletcher and Natalie.

He took the phone. "Hey, half-baked."

A pause, and then he said, "She's okay. A tad frazzled around the edges."

She'd asked about me. I was pleased. He eyed me, still smiling. "No problem. Bye." He clicked off the phone and put it down on the couch. He raised his brows and said, "Still a child of few words."

"Yeah, she is, at least on the phone. Why'd she want to talk to you?"

He shrugged. "According to Nat, I have my uses."

"It's a relief to know that she's fitted you into her life. One problem solved."

He slipped his arm around me. "I didn't realize you'd worried about the two of us so much." He nuzzled my hair.

"I had."

"Does this mean we can sleep together again?" He tickled the skin at my waist.

I giggled but said, "Nope. Well, maybe. Not just yet. Hey, I wonder how widespread this blackout is."

"Let's find out." Taking the phone, Fletch pushed 9-1-1. He frowned. "Busy." He tried again. "Still busy."

"Everyone's probably trying the same thing. See if you can get hold of Damon or Veronica."

"My mother's supposed to be at our Wilmington house. I don't know if the phone lines will be working. I'll try Damon." He pressed buttons.

"Hello, it's me," he said into the phone. "Where are you?"

"I need to get you a better cell phone," Fletcher told me, then said, his voice pitched loud, "I thought you were taking Ella to that bistro on Delaware."

"We're stuck in my office." He held the phone away from his ear. I could hear Damon laughing before Fletcher said, "Yeah, you got it, Big D. We're trapped."

His gaze slid over to me. "Tough, huh? But we'll find a way to stay warm." He winked at me, and I smiled back while he ended the call.

"Mama's okay," he said, clicking the phone off.

I reached for the phone. "Let me try 9-1-1 again. Oh, hello."

"What is the nature of your emergency?" The dispatcher sounded harried in comparison to the many times I'd called for help in New York City during the last six months.

"There's a blackout, and we're stuck in a building where all the doors and elevators are electronically controlled. We can't get out."

"Are you injured?"

"No, but we're trapped."

"I'm sorry, ma'am, but there's nothing we can do. Paramedics and relief workers are taking care of those who were injured when the power went out all over downtown."

"I can understand that." I fought for calm. "We're okay, so I guess we'll wait in line until you can get to us."

"The electricity will probably come on before anyone will be available to get into your building. So just sit tight."

"What happened?"

"Someone crashed a car into a big transformer. It blacked out a number of city blocks."

"Okay, thanks." I clicked off. "I guess we're stuck."

Fletcher had moved away to stare out of one of the windows that was outside the candles' glow. I could see the tip of his cigar flare as he inhaled. "So, relax and have some champagne. Any cheese left?"

"You never fail to surprise me." I found myself laughing.

"What now?"

"You're so calm."

"There's nothing to be upset about. Come over here and look at the stars."

I slipped over to the window without hitting any furniture, then leaned back against his chest. He stubbed out his cigar in an ashtray that sat on the windowsill next to a china box.

His hands spanned my waist, reminding me of the way our bodies, so different, fitted together so perfectly, as did our lives. Closing my eyes, I relaxed into his warmth.

He'd filled every gap in my life. I never would have guessed that this tall, striking man, so unlike me in every way, was my missing link, the lost part to my puzzle. Card number fifty-two in the deck of my life. Good God, was he my better half? Was he my Mr. Big? What a thought!

And Natalie seemed to have accepted him. Why else would she have demanded to speak with him?

His breath feathered my hair, sending my jumbled thoughts straight into space as he kissed my temple. Nothing mattered but the moment as he slid his hands up to caress my breasts through the thin silk dress. His lips made their way to my ear, nibbling on the lobe. My knees went weak as he nuzzled my neck.

My zipper buzzed when he lowered it, and a wash of cool air flowed over my back, naked except for a thin bra strap. The silk dress pooled at my hips, then fell to the carpeted floor. I stepped out of it carefully.

Fletcher drew in his breath. "You wicked, wanton woman. What are you wearing?" His hands stroked my thigh through silk lingerie, heating my blood. "What are these called?"

"Tap pants."

"Satin and lace. Over . . . what?" Fingers slipped underneath the lace edge of the tap pants. "Not much at all. Garters and . . . God, Cara. Stockings, and nothing else underneath. And those spike heels are so sexy. Lady, you're a dream come true." He rubbed the textured lace against my inner thigh, then cupped my mound.

My nerves went taut with need. Reaching back with one arm, I managed to pull his hips closer to my backside. His hard-on rose against my furrow, hot through the fabric that separated us. I moaned as he moved back and forth against me.

I turned, reaching for his belt buckle. "Take off your clothes."

Even in the soft candlelight, I could see his eyes widen and his jaw drop. "Yes, ma'am." He shrugged out of his jacket and draped it over the back of the sofa. He loosened his tie, pulling it out of its Windsor knot. "Let's try the couch. We have a good history with couches, don't we?"

I grinned. "We sure do." I unbuttoned his shirt and pulled it open, caressing his chest as he bent to kiss me. His tongue flirted and teased, taking me higher, making me want him more than ever before.

Sex in Florence had been mega-hot with the excitement of a new lover. Now that I knew how good we were together, I wanted him all the more. The weeks without him in my bed had sharpened my desire, increased my need to an unbearable pitch.

I bent one knee, raising my leg to wrap it around his hip, but pulled back when I heard a strange, metallic tapping. "What's that?"

"Sounds like it's coming from the walls. But that's not possible." Lifting one of the candles for light, Fletcher prowled the room.

"What about that duct?" I pointed to the wall above the plastic mat. The wall, partially covered by shelving, held part of his box collection and a number of books. Above the shelves, an elaborate grille covered a large, square duct. A bizarre and frightening combination of taps and rustling came out of the dark gap.

"The one above the desk area?" He frowned.

"That's the only possible place anyone could be, unless you've got mice in the walls. Sometimes they get in and chew the wiring."

He shook his head. "This building isn't old enough to have an infestation like that. Let's check the duct." He placed the candle he held on a shelf, then dragged the coffee table over to the wall beneath the duct to climb up for a better look, using the second votive for light. "I can't see anything through this grille."

"Let's take it off."

"How?"

"There's a screwdriver on my Swiss Army knife."

"I'll never laugh at all the stuff you carry around again."

I handed him the knife. "You never did."

"Not so you could hear."

"What's that supposed to mean?"

His mouth twitched as he fitted the screwdriver against the first of eight screws holding the screen to the duct's opening. The office had cooled since the power went off, and I rubbed my bare arms.

He grunted. "I bet they used an electric screwdriver to tighten these screws. Let's hope it isn't soldered. I'll never get the grille off if it's soldered."

Metal grated as the first screw reluctantly came loose. "Got the first one. Hey, can you get me a drink?"

"Sure, if you think champagne is thirst-quenching." I topped off his glass and brought it to him.

"Thank you." After sipping, he put the flute on a nearby shelf, then continued to work on the second screw.

I watched, but my edginess made me bounce up and down, twitchy beyond belief, trying to ignore the tendril of fear snaking up my spine. I sensed someone was there, someone who was up to no good, maybe the same nasty little someone who'd been responsible for all my trouble and pain of the last six months. With all the exits electronically locked, this could be my chance to catch the creep.

As Fletcher removed the fourth and fifth screws, I visualized my hands squeezing the neck of an assailant whose features remained shadowy. My eyes narrowed. I wanted to shake him the way a cat kills a cornered mouse.

I didn't want to put Adam Covarrubia's famous face on the front of that mysterious head. I didn't think he was smart enough to plan the series of evil pranks. Besides, wasn't he just slime rather than evil? And though the clues pointed to Adam, the latest information placed him in Milan, working their fashion week shows.

"This is the last one. Honey, get ready to catch the grille." Fletcher pushed the grating against the opening, holding it so he could get the last screw out. "Here it comes."

Climbing up on the table beside him, I reached for the bottom of the screen. "Got it."

"Okay." He gripped the grille at the top. "Together, now."

We lowered the heavy grid, and then I hopped off the coffee table to guide it to the floor. "Boy, that's dirty." I looked around for something to wipe my hands on, and found the napkins that remained from our snack.

"That's not a place the janitors can get to." He peered into the duct. "I can't see much, but I think there's a light where there shouldn't be one. Yes, definitely something there. It could be an emergency light of some kind, but I can't get in to check. I'm too big."

"I bet I can do it."

"Absolutely not."

"Don't be silly, of course I can get in there. Move over and I'll show you."

"That's not my point." His voice rose. "It isn't safe."

"You would if you could."

"So what?"

"So why is it safe for you but not for me?"

"It wouldn't be safe for me either, but it's an appropriate risk for me to assume."

I set my hands on my hips and did my best to skewer him with a really mean glare. "Then if we're equals, it's an appropriate risk for me."

"Absolutely not. I won't allow it."

"You can't pull rank on this one, partner. This has nothing to do with work."

"It's not safe."

"You're being patronizing and over-protective. It's not safe because I'm female, right?"

"It's not safe because you're a small woman. If you were bigger, I'd consider it."

"You're still talking as though it's your decision."

He folded his arms across his chest, looking infuriatingly smug. "My building, my decision."

"In a pig's eye. Off." I climbed onto the coffee table and gave him a firm push, forcing him back. Then I reached for the edge of the duct and hitched myself toward the dark gap. Wedging an elbow in, I hauled up the rest of my body.

"Cara, get out of that duct."

"Shut up and give me a candle. I can't see a thing in here."

He reached for my hips, tugging me halfway out. I flailed wildly with my legs, trying to shake him off. I heard a thud and an "oof!"

Well, hell. I'd kicked him in the head with my spiked heel.

I heard Fletcher crash to the ground.

Damn, damn, damn. I'd knocked him out. Overwhelmed by guilt, I leaned my forehead against the chill metal of the duct. He'd done nothing but try to protect me and I'd frickin' assaulted him.

I slid back out of the duct to check on him. *Thank God, he's breathing.* I couldn't find any swelling where I'd whacked his head, so he wasn't hurt too badly.

I hesitated, then went for it. Grabbing Fletcher's jacket from the sofa, I took a candle. Pushing it ahead of me, I climbed back into the duct.

"Adam, here I come."

Chapter Twenty-Three

I gained a new appreciation for electricity as I crept through the narrow, shadowy duct. Pushing the lit votive on its ashtray in front of me without setting my hair on fire or broiling my own flesh was a unique challenge, since the duct sloped upward before it leveled out. Even worse, the candle prevented me from seeing any other lights, such as the ones we'd spied from the office. I also wondered if the vandal could see I was coming. Well, so be it. Let him be afraid for once. Let him be the pursued rather than the pursuer. Besides, the only other option was blowing out the candle, which would leave me in darkness. Not an acceptable choice.

Metal banged while ghostly laughter echoed through the duct. I froze, stiff with fear. The hair at my nape prickled. I'd heard that sinister giggle before. Where? When? My mind flipped through the possibilities like a cardsharp shuffling, but I drew a blank.

Moving forward, I came to a junction in the ductwork, so I could see in four directions. The left tunnel would be a dead end, for that went toward the side of the building. I looked to the right and saw a dark shape a few yards away. Another burst of the evil laughter made my heart wrench. After a few moments, though, I noticed that the shape didn't move.

Nor did I. Moments passed as I hesitated, frozen by dread.

Silence. Stillness. I figured that it would be safe to investigate, and inched forward.

The nasty chortle echoed down the duct as the answer came to me, sickeningly and suddenly like a fender-bender during rush hour. I'd heard that irritating laugh accompanied by clashing metal before—in the locker room of my athletic club. This creep was the same yahoo who'd stolen my wallet and nearly gotten me arrested!

My teeth clenched. Nothing would stop me now. I'd get this jerk who'd made my life a misery.

As I crawled into the right-hand tunnel, I heard scraping and clattering in the direction I headed, but the noises seemed to be receding. Damn. He was leaving! I tried to speed up, but squirming faster through the metal shaft wasn't easy. The narrow duct became colder and colder every moment. I hadn't put on my dress for this adventure, not wanting to spoil Esme's beautiful embroidery or the delicate silk. Plus, I figured that the fluttery layers would get in my way. So I was squirming through the chilly metal duct wearing only lingerie and heels, with Fletcher's jacket for protection against the chill. The cameo ring he'd given me clicked softly against the metal shaft.

"Remember what the man said, Cara," I muttered to myself. "Live a little. Have a new experience."

The bundle turned out to be a black leather jacket and a zippered bag. *Maybe there's an ID inside.* I opened it with shaky fingers, then dropped it immediately without touching the contents: a syringe and a small baggie with a white powdery substance. "Adam," I breathed.

I headed back to show Fletch my discoveries. When I reached the office, I peered down and saw him pacing back and forth, scowling and rubbing his head where I'd mistakenly kicked him.

"I'm back! Help me down, would you?" I extended a hand to him, holding the candle.

He took it, placing it on a shelf next to its mate, then grabbed me beneath the armpits and hauled me out of the duct.

Red-faced, he shook me as though he were a terrier and I a rat. "Don't you ever pull a crazy stunt like that again, do you hear me!"

"Fletch, jeez, calm down. Everything's okay."

"I am not okay." He articulated every word precisely, as though I were an idiot who needed everything explained carefully and slowly. "First you knocked me out. Then I had to wait here while you got yourself killed. Do not ever do anything like this again. Ever. Ever."

My eyes filled. "Oh, honey, I'm so sorry. I didn't mean to hurt you." I buried my face in his chest, wetting his shirtfront.

"I know you didn't." He sounded exasperated rather than infuriated, a distinct improvement. "You have got to think before you act. Your opinion is only one of two here."

Raising my head, I glared at him. "This is my battle. This creep has been torturing me, not you, for the last six months."

"How do you know it's the same person?"

"I'm sure. I found a black leather jacket and drugs in the duct. There's someone there, all right, and I bet it's Adam Covarrubia."

Fletcher visibly tensed. "Did you find any weapons?"

"No, but he could easily have a knife." I shivered despite his warm embrace.

"You're freezing, baby. Put your dress back on." He led me back to the sofa.

While I dressed, he plotted. "We need to cover up that hole," he said. "It's the only way in or out of this suite. If we secure it, he can't get to us."

"Should we put the grille back on?"

"That would be a start, but if he has a gun, he can blow right through it. Let me think."

A solid object streaming foul grey smoke bounced into the

room from the duct's opening. I screamed.

"Sweet Lord Almighty!" He leaped off the sofa and grabbed the object. "Shit, it's hot!" He juggled it from hand to hand.

"Throw it back! Throw it back!" I shrieked.

He tossed it back toward the duct. He missed. It hit the wall and bounced to the carpet.

Grabbing it again, he threw it overhand into the duct as far as he could, and he had a good right arm. I bent over at the waist, coughing and choking, tears streaming from my eyes. I became light-headed and dizzy, terrified I'd pass out and never wake up again.

"Get to the other side of the room!" Grabbing a leather cushion from the sofa, he crammed it into the duct's opening. "This should trap the fumes. He'll get smoked like jerky."

"I can't stop coughing!" Still bent over double, I staggered to the far side of the room where I hoped the smoke was thinner.

"Get down." He pushed on my back. "The fresher air will be near the floor."

I dropped to the carpet, rolling over and coughing, while he reeled. He picked up the coffee table and rammed one end of it through the nearest window. Glass smashed and tinkled. A gust of chilly air exploded into the room, scattering the noxious cloud.

"Good God, Fletch. What have you done?"

Turning, he raised a brow. "I thought we could use some fresh air."

"Look at this place. We've trashed your office."

"You do what you have to, honey. The gas could be toxic. I wouldn't put it past that rat to throw a poisonous stink bomb in here."

"You're right. Didn't he knife Maggie to death?" I tried to stand up, and he rushed to support me. Everything felt bad, but I said, "I'm okay. Just a little dizzy. Oh hell!" I clutched my belly. "I think I'm gonna be sick. The smell—"

Fletch ran to try the door of his washroom while I stuffed my knuckles into my mouth and swallowed repeatedly. My infamous touchy stomach had decided to take issue with the stench left by the stink bomb that Adam had thrown, and I struggled not to toss my cookies, no matter what. I wouldn't shame myself again.

Meanwhile, Fletch jerked on the locked bathroom door. Cursing, he took a step back and let fly with one of his elegant Italian loafers. The door crashed open.

"The executive washroom, my dear." He bowed and gestured.

I dashed in.

He followed with a candle, remarking, "These votives are burning down, but they'll do for now. We'll have to find more soon." Leaving the candle on the counter, he closed the door when he left.

I appreciated that little gesture, which showed that he respected my need for privacy during a moment of weakness. What had been in that horrible smoke? My stomach tipped and twisted. My mouth was desert-dry except for sticky, thick bile. My contacts itched abominably. I'd bet my eyes were red as stoplights.

Cupping my hands, I drank some water from the tap before looking up to check the lenses. Lettering in blood-red lipstick marred the mirror.

DIE DIE DIE

Screams erupted from the depths of me. The world went dark as the black spots in front of my vision coalesced. I scrabbled for the doorknob frantically as though the crimson words were a fateful curse condemning me to an immediate and terrible death. I couldn't stop the shrieks which burst from me like fire sirens at a four-alarm blaze.

"Cara, Cara, Cara." Suddenly, thankfully, Fletch was there,

enfolding me in his arms as he sought to calm me down.

Oh, thank God for him. He'll keep me safe. I clung to the open halves of Fletcher's shirt, still damp from my guilty tears. "Look!"

His gaze followed my pointing finger. "What the hell is going on! That settles it. I'm calling 9-1-1, Damon, Griff, everybody. Honey, we're gonna get out of here right now."

He dragged me from the washroom, hunting for the cell phone I'd left on the sofa. Keeping me tight at his side, he started punching buttons. "Damn, 9-1-1 is busy. Figures. You know, what I don't understand is how he got into that bathroom."

"Let's check the grate in there." I stood and went back to the washroom on quivery legs while he remained on the couch, still trying to use the phone to get through to someone.

I didn't have a chance to check out the grille in the washroom before a hand came over my mouth and cold steel pressed against my temple.

"Move, scream, and you die," a voice hissed.

I went absolutely stiff with fear. Someone pushed me out of the washroom into the office.

Fletch looked up. His entire body tensed, as though he gathered himself to spring at my attacker. I wanted to scream, *Don't, Fletch!*

"What do you want?" His voice was a low growl.

"Oh, I have what I want."

The muzzle of the gun rubbed up and down my head. Ice encased my soul, and I closed my eyes.

I opened them to meet Fletcher's gaze. He'd never looked so feral, so wild. I knew with absolute certainty that this man could kill, would kill, if given the opportunity. He waited only for the right moment. But if he leaped, wolflike, surely he'd die. Even the fiercest predator was no match for a bullet.

I couldn't live with myself if he died because of me.

He stood.

"Don't!" I screamed.

The gun jerked away from my temple toward him, and I took the chance, possibly the only one I'd have. Jamming my spike heel down onto where I hoped the attacker's instep would be, I used both hands to wrench the gun upward, pointing the barrel toward the ceiling.

With an inarticulate roar, Fletch hurtled himself at the dark, shadowy figure, who yanked away from me, lowered the gun and shot him.

Chapter Twenty-Four

I shrieked. Both the gunman and Fletch staggered back. Blood stained the shoulder of Fletcher's white shirt. The report of the weapon echoed in the room.

The gun spun out of the attacker's grasp. He'd lost his balance, and I realized that the caliber of the revolver must have been too much for him to handle with only one hand.

I kicked his crotch, then his stomach, then punched him in the face. He crashed to the floor, and I stomped on his head. Thank heaven for my aerobics class, where I punched, stomped and kicked for an hour three times every week. My killer moves had become reflex actions.

I grabbed the nearest object off one of the shelves. It felt heavy and bumpy in my hand. One of Fletcher's boxes?

I whacked the creep on the head once, twice, three times. Once for myself, once for Natalie, and once for Fletch. *Fletch!*

"Oh, God, Fletch!" I ran to him. He'd fallen back onto the couch, clutching his shoulder. I dropped the box.

He made a strangled cry. "My egg! My egg!"

"What?"

"My Fabergé egg. You used a diamond-encrusted, solid gold Fabergé egg to brain the creep." Standing, he fumbled unsuccessfully for the box.

"A Fabergé egg? You own a Fabergé egg?" I stared at him, amazed. If he was worried about one of his stupid boxes, that had to mean he wasn't seriously hurt. "Oh, Fletch! You're all right!" I flung my arms around him, hearing the solid thump of his heart beneath my ear, adoring his blessed male scent and the warm aliveness of his flesh. I framed his face in both hands, peppering it with light kisses.

He kissed back, deepening the contact between our lips until I gasped for breath. He cuddled me close with his unhurt arm and nuzzled the top of my head. "I don't know about all right, sweetheart, but I doubt this is too bad." Tugging away from me, he took off his shirt with a wince. He dabbed at the wound with a shirttail, grimacing. "How does it look?"

I found one of the flickering votives and moved it closer. "You're right. It's not too bad. It seems as though the bullet didn't really go in, just scraped over the top part of your shoulder."

"Good." He slid his arms back into the shirt's sleeves, then picked up the egg and held it up to the dim light of the votive. "Find some more candles, would you, honey? We need to see what we're doing. Do you have any duct tape in that bag?"

He carefully replaced the egg on its shelf and poked the gunman with his foot. He peered down. "Good Lord, this can't be Adam Covarrubia. This is a woman!"

I gasped. "Oh, my God. Andrea!"

"The twin?"

"Yeah. She always seemed so lame and stupid to me. I never suspected that she'd be involved."

"Why not? Ella Langer told me that they're the Siamese twins of modeling. Where she is, he is, and vice versa."

"So where's Adam?" I stared at Fletch, my mind churning. "I don't like this line of reasoning."

"Neither do I, but someone had to damage the transformer after she got into the building." He thought for a moment, his brow wrinkling, then seemed to come to a decision. "Let's deal with one problem at a time, shall we? Where's that tape?"

I dumped the contents of the satchel onto the carpet. "Here's masking tape and some more candles." I lit two more votives.

"That'll do." He bound Andrea's wrists and forearms together at her waist, then taped her ankles. "Check her for weapons, will you?"

I stooped over Andrea's limp form to pat her down. "Oh, my God." I pulled a knife out of Andrea's back pocket, flicking the tab so the lethal-looking switchblade snapped open. "Do you think this knife killed Maggie?"

"Could be. Put it down, it's evidence." Fletcher picked up the phone. "Good. I finally got through to 9-1-1."

He gave directions and information to the dispatcher as I watched Andrea's eyes blink open.

The model looked up at me with a baleful glare. "Bitch."

"Excuse me? Hey, I'm the victim here. What did you think you were doing?"

"You screwed with my brother. Mess with him and you mess with me." Andrea squirmed, trying to pry her hands free.

"I believe in family loyalty, but that's taking it a little too far." Fletcher came to my side. "Don't bother trying to get loose. I taped you up real tight. You're not going anywhere until the police take you to the precinct."

She spat at him.

He raised a brow. "Looks like I'll have to get these pants sterilized. In the meantime, why don't you clue us in? How did Cara shortchange Adam?"

"Why should I tell you anything?"

"I'm running Cara Fletcher Couture now. If there's been a wrong, I'll right it."

Andrea hesitated, then said, "She didn't think that Adam had the right look for Fletcher's Gear."

"So what?" I asked. "He's still a top model, and so are you. He gets plenty of work."

She shot me a bitter glance. "Not nearly as much as before, and that was the beginning of the end. Then you chose Benton for the print and TV advertising. You made that little snot. Adam and I lost a lot of business."

"You're blaming me? Everyone knows you two have a drug problem."

"We party. We don't have a problem."

"Partiers don't carry their rigs wherever they go," I said. "I found a syringe and drugs in the duct. Who were you partying with there?"

"Bitch. I'll do what I want."

"Did that include killing Maggie Andersen?" Fletcher asked.

She hesitated, a crafty look stealing over her features. "Yeah, I killed Maggie. She was getting cold feet and wanted out."

"Wanted out of what?" I wanted to know the extent of the embezzlement, if possible. Fletch hadn't spent hours poring over computer printouts for nothing. "Where did the money go?"

"That's for me to know and for you to never find out."

I managed to stop myself from kicking her again, but it was tough. Instead, I decided to push her buttons. "You're lying. Adam killed Maggie. You don't have the guts for it."

"You leave my brother out of this!" she screamed. She thrashed against her bonds, grunting with effort.

When she'd tired herself out, I said, "We already know that Maggie stole thousands from my company. She wanted to stop?"

"When you went to Europe, she knew you'd be onto her and she wanted to take what was left of the money and run. She asked Adam to ditch me and leave the country with her. Naturally, he told me."

"What do you mean, what was left?" Fletcher asked. "I've been over the records. Maggie stole nearly half a million dollars."

I gasped. "You didn't tell me that."

"You had a show to put on. I intended to discuss it with you in a couple of weeks, after all the excitement died down." He poked Andrea with a toe. "Where's the money?"

She looked up and laughed, then made a snorting sound. "Let's just say there are a lot of grateful little druggies in Manhattan."

"They partied," I said to him. "They stole half a million dollars of borrowed money and put it up their noses or in their arms."

"Meth?" Fletch asked Andrea.

"Yeah." She closed her eyes. "We sailed the crystal ship on a lot of fine voyages." A mocking note entered her Jersey-accented voice. "We had our best inspirations while we were tweakin'. We could stay up all night, calling you on your phone, charging stuff to your credit cards, breaking into your house and your shop. Thank you, Cara."

I gritted my teeth and ground my heel into the carpet rather than stomp once more on Andrea's head. "How did you get to Maggie? I checked her out thoroughly before she was hired. She was clean as a whistle."

"Maggie was a pushover. She hadn't gotten any in a decade. Do you think Adam really wanted her? Hah. That's a laugh. He used to joke about Maggie all the time, how he hated to touch her scrawny old body, but he'd hang around her to get to you. That was how he knew everything you did. Maggie told him everything we needed to know, usually in bed after he'd gotten her high. Adam could get anyone he wanted. Except you, you bitch."

"He resented that as well?"

"He was obsessed with you. The great Cara Fletcher. He used to make jokes about the *late,* great Cara Fletcher."

I collapsed onto the couch. My heart felt as though it was

squeezed by a giant, merciless hand. I couldn't breathe, couldn't think.

"And we got close, until you came along." Andrea scowled at Fletcher. "We knew it was over when she moved in with you."

"But you caused that when you burned Cara out of her house. Why'd you do that?" he asked.

"Maggie thought when you two went to Italy, you'd see the original records and figure out what she'd done. She wanted to leave, but we thought we could cover up the entire scheme by killing Cara. It was her debt and with her dead, everything would be a mess. It could be months or even years before any problems would be discovered. We'd get away scot-free."

"The Siamese twins of modeling," Fletcher said thoughtfully. "The two of you cooked up a plot to embezzle funds from Cara Fletcher Couture, enticed Maggie into it, then decided to burn Cara alive. I bet they both killed Maggie," he said to me. "Torture and murder. Is there a death penalty in New York, Andrea? You'd better hope not."

"It'll be worth it. We really got to you, you bitch. I wish I'd seen your face after we took apart your workshop. Maggie said it was classic."

The world whirled and rocked as though the sofa beneath me had turned to tidal waves. I slumped. "Maggie knew. She deserves an award for the acting job she did."

"Of course she knew. She had to destroy the records to cover up the thefts," Fletcher said. "So she had to vandalize the entire workshop. If she'd destroyed only the records it would have drawn too much attention to them."

I said, "You caused this blackout, too, I bet. Did one of your tweaker buddies crash a car into a transformer?"

"Bite me."

Fletcher grinned a death's head smile. "No, thank you. But

I'm sure someone big and bad in prison will take care of all your needs."

Epilogue

I stood beside Fletcher on the curb outside The Fletcher Group's headquarters in the chill dawn, watching the local police take Andrea Covarrubia to jail.

One of the detectives who had responded to Fletcher's 9-1-1 call bustled over to tell us that an extradition order for Adam Covarrubia would be obtained later in the day, and that Interpol would arrange for Adam to be taken into custody in Milan, Italy.

"So, it's all over," I said to Fletch.

His arm tightened around me, and I looked up at him. It had been nearly twenty-four hours since we'd left Manhattan for Wilmington. The craggy lines of his face, dark with stubble, seemed softened by fatigue.

The night, long and stressful, had changed both of us. I hadn't been certain, but now I knew. If Fletcher had died, life would have turned gray and empty, and I would have gone mad from guilt.

"It's not over. There's one more thing to be done." He took my hands in his. "Honey, when I saw you with that gun pointed at your head . . ." He closed his eyes and swallowed convulsively. "I knew then that if I let you go without a fight, life would be worth nothing to me. But we did it together, Cara! We couldn't have done it separately, but together, we won. Will you please quit talking about leaving my home and . . . and marry me? I can't live without you. I don't even want to try."

I slid my arms around him underneath his jacket, glorying in the warmth of his love, and rubbed my face against his chest. "Yes, I'll marry you. Not because of how much you need me, but because of how much I love you." I stopped as a thought—a nasty thought—intruded. "But . . . but what about your prenup?"

His brow creased. "What?"

"Don't you have a prenuptial contract? I heard it was thirty pages long."

He laughed. "Honey, you shouldn't listen to gossip. Where did you hear that story?"

I blushed as I told him what I'd overheard in the women's lounge.

"Oh, baby." He laughed so hard that tears leaked from the corners of his eyes. He rubbed them away with the backs of his hands. "I guess I deserved to have that come back to haunt me."

"What are you talking about?"

"I used to date some questionable women."

I lifted a brow.

He put an arm around me. "Long before I met you, honey. Sometimes I suspected that the women I dated were more interested in my money than me. I'd tell these gals that I had this long prenup, and they'd disappear. I didn't realize you'd heard about it."

"So it doesn't exist?"

"No. I want a marriage built on love and loyalty. I trust you completely." He smiled. The shadows in his eyes lifted, like sun breaking through dark clouds. "I love you, my darling. And I always will."

ABOUT THE AUTHOR

Best-selling, award-winning author **Sue Swift** has visited over a dozen countries and lived in some of them. She has written over a dozen books, and some have been translated into over a dozen languages. She writes in numerous genres including nonfiction, romance, mystery, paranormal, historical, contemporary comedy, and erotica, which are published using a pseudonym.

A former trial attorney who's earned a second-degree black belt in kenpo karate, her current hobbies are yoga and world travel. Not surprisingly she is often confused by her incessant multi-tasking.

Her travel blog and website are at http://susanoverseas.weebly.com and http://www.sue-swift.com.